Never let a demon see y...

Zachariah Williams isn't just the darkest, most gothically gorgeous member of my new academy monster hunting squad...he's broken in a way I deeply understand. The son of a small-town preacher with a big-time skillset, he's faced down monsters his whole life, a natural-born demon hunter whose deep empathy and shattered soul makes me crave his glance, his smile, and, okay...his hands all over me.

Trouble is, he's also got one killer of a family secret: right after he falls in love, Hell on earth breaks out. The only way to stop it? Sacrifice whoever's captured his heart.

Talk about a second-date buzzkill.

Of course, I haven't been fighting monsters practically since the cradle to back down now. Zach and the entire Wellington Academy monster hunter squad are becoming my stand-in family, and that means more to me than I ever expected.

And if someone's gotta take out a bunch of fire-breathing demons without getting hot under the collar, I'm still the right girl for the job.

THE HUNTER'S CURSE

MONSTER HUNTER ACADEMY, BOOK 2

D.D. CHANCE

ZACH

She should never have come here.

I lifted my hands to test the cool morning air. Today's demonstration was supposed to be something simple, easy. I'd done this demon sunrise ceremony nearly a half dozen times now, though the ones in the late spring were always better than the ones in the fall. Demons weren't always afraid of the sunshine. They liked showing off.

They weren't the only ones. I'd be lying if I didn't admit to the rush I got from watching the faces of students move from skepticism to belief to awe. Not so much of a rush that I craved my own group of followers like my dad, but enough that I enjoyed impressing people.

Especially certain people—like a brand-new monster hunter I had no business looking at twice, even if she was now technically part of our team. Hell, especially because of that. I should stay far away from Nina Cross, keep her safe. Protected. Never mind the fact that she was Tyler's girl—a guy who'd been nothing but awesome to me since I showed up on campus, a fish out of water flopping around on the banks of Boston Harbor.

But I couldn't help myself. Nina was more like me than any of the guys were—reckless to the point of being stupid. Fierce. Angry. Proud. She was a fighter through and through, and she'd earned her scars. I knew what that was like.

She also wanted to find her family, and even though she should be careful what she wished for, I wanted to help her. More than that, I wanted to look deep into her eyes, connect with her. Truly *know* her. And though she was warded against me, I couldn't stop thinking about pushing into her mind more. Harder. In ways I shouldn't even be considering.

The moment Tyler, Liam, Grim, and I had all worked together to bring Nina into our monster hunting collective, it got a million times worse. Something seemed to crack wide open inside me, dark and forbidden. She was the girl I couldn't have. The girl I couldn't stop wanting. The girl I'd sacrifice to save my own fucked-up life, if I believed everything I'd been told.

I blew out a harsh breath. She shouldn't have come here.

Never mind my problems; we had a job to do. To hear Commander Frost talk, we were on the brink of a full-on monster outbreak, the first in generations for Wellington Academy. Nina wasn't just a hunter, she was a harbinger... and that meant monsters would be following hard on her heels.

I could handle that. Darkness shouldn't be feared or even respected, necessarily, but it did need to be understood. Right before it was blasted back into the bowels of hell. I'd always been good at that, though I tried to keep it quiet. I was here at Wellington to get smarter, stronger. To change the script for my family once and for all. So most of the time, I flew under the radar, playing it cool. These once-a-semester demonstrations for Demonology 101 were the only time I tried to tempt the demons out of the shadows.

The demons didn't always play along, of course, but part of me really wanted them to put on a show this time. Which was stupid. I needed to stay focused.

All I wanted to do was focus on her.

A light moan reached my ears, followed by a low, haunting laugh, as if someone was watching me from the decrepit old chapel that served as the stage for this sunrise ceremony. Bellamy Chapel had always bugged me, though it had long been abandoned, its doors hammered shut and sealed off from idle eyes. Now the old chapel served little purpose other than to look spooky on the edge of a monster hunter academy. But that moan, oddly, heartened me. The demons were going to show up today. I could already feel them.

Like I could feel *her*, despite the bracelet she wore to keep me from getting too close. That first moment we'd met, I'd touched Nina's mind, and my heart had nearly exploded. Liam had given her the bracelet to shield her, and she was clearly Tyler's girl, so I'd tamped down my emotions, hard. After all that, I'd thought maybe she'd stay free of me, maybe I could keep her safe. But then, we'd made the Run. She'd joined the collective. And I knew I was screwed.

The scornful laugh rolled over the cemetery, making my skin crawl. There was something there. The soft sneer was unmistakable, taunting me from the shadows. *Your time with her will come, boy. Enjoy it. Because then she's going to die.*

I rolled my eyes. Demons had been my family's stock-in-trade for generations. But I was done with them and the curse they'd laid upon us.

Fuck you, I thought back just as succinctly.

Fuck me, too. Because what I felt for Nina Cross wasn't safe, and it sure as hell wasn't smart. It was far more dangerous—for everyone.

"*Mine,*" I whispered.

She should never have come here.

1

No demons before coffee.

If that wasn't an official monster hunting rule, it should be.

I scowled at the darkened windows of the Crazy Cup, the glow from my phone screen confirming it was only 4:38 a.m. For some ridiculous reason, that was too early for coffee shops to open. I should just have made coffee in my apartment, but I was running low on supplies, again. And I had to be at the campus by 5:00 a.m.

"Slackers," I muttered, shoving my phone back into my hoodie pocket and turning toward the academy. Fortunately, it wasn't a long walk, and the morning was already warming up. The breeze rustling through the trees served up hints of the gorgeous May day to come that made so many people fall in love with Boston.

People like my mom, who'd been my entire inspiration for this road trip from North Carolina, this quest to find the family I'd never known I had. It had sounded like a made-for-Hallmark-Channel adventure—come to the big city! Find the family of your beloved late mother! Become a trust-fund princess—or at least find a new cousin or two. I'd even entertained the hope that Boston would prove to be an idyllic summer vacation haven, far quieter than my monster-crawling hometown of Asheville, NC.

Nope.

First had come a Technicolor wave of fearsome supernatural attackers, drawn to me like frat boys to beer pong and jumping out from practically every corner of my new, trendy Back Bay neighborhood. Then I'd found an actual school—a whole academy—dedicated to *training* monster hunters, along with a ridiculously hot group of college-age hunters who'd convinced me to join their ranks. I'd met, kissed, and damned near fallen in love with the head of said monster hunter collective, a guy so hot, he made butterflies form daisy chains in my stomach whenever he was near. He was an entitled asshat, sure...but he was *my* entitled asshat, the first boyfriend I'd allowed myself since my very unfortunate junior prom and the even more unfortunate bugbear incident behind the school. Poor Joey Porter would never be the same.

But Tyler Perkins was a hunter, and so were his three best friends. Who were also, coincidentally, the three best friends I'd started *lusting after out of nowhere.* Because *that* was *totally normal.*

I sighed at my own ridiculousness, cutting down a street that would take me toward the far end of campus, not its main entrance. This morning's class location was some chapel on the west side of Wellington Academy, a place I hadn't visited yet in my scant week as a freshly minted monster hunting student. But it'd be a far *better* class experience if I could score some...

I slowed, squinting down the row of restaurants. Most of them remained as dark as the Crazy Cup had been, but one still had a red, flickering OPEN sign glimmering in a high window. The White Crane. It was a bar, not a coffee shop, but...bars had coffee, right? Especially bars still open at four in the morning, something I didn't even think was allowed in Boston.

My need for anything resembling caffeine carried me forward. I pushed open the tavern's door and stepped into a gloom only slightly more illuminated than the predawn streets outside. I scanned the tables—all empty—but there were a few questionable types hunched over their drinks at the bar, and a bartender with wild, gray-streaked hair leaning against the far counter, eyeing me as I approached. The other patrons paid me no attention.

"Coffee?" she smirked, turning to a bubbling pot by the line of beer taps. I didn't care if she was judging me. I plopped right down on a stool as soon as the aroma of strong, dark coffee hit me. My mouth watered so hard, I didn't even protest when the woman added a splash of deep amber liquid to the mug.

"House rule. Gotta have something in it for me to serve you at this hour," she said, and I blinked at her gravelly voice. Up close, she seemed younger than she had from a distance, her pale, heart-shaped face partially obscured by her heavy fall of hair, an ebony mane shot through with stripes of icy gray. Her eyes were also gray, and if she wore any makeup, I couldn't tell in the low lights.

"Thanks," I managed. I picked up the coffee, inhaling a rich scent enhanced by the sharper tang of alcohol. "I didn't realize you guys would be open this late. Or early, I guess."

"We set our own hours." The bartender shrugged. She peered at me, her head tilting. "How do you like the academy so far?"

Surprise skittered through me. I'd only been in the

7

White Crane once, and I didn't recognize this woman, but I'd been here with Tyler and hadn't really paid much attention to anyone but him. I took a long draft of coffee, sighing with real appreciation as the twin fires of heat and whiskey hit the back of my throat.

"It's good," I said. "I've got a five a.m. class this morning, but otherwise, it's good."

The bartender lifted brows that suddenly seemed more winged than they had been a few seconds ago. I tried to focus on them, but she turned again, so instead my gaze lingered on the crow's feet tracing her temple, the deeper lines bracketing her mouth. She'd been tending bar a long time, I suspected. Maybe she even ran the place.

"Five a.m.," she echoed. "Demon sunrise ceremony? It's about time for that this semester."

I tipped my mug to her. "Yep. Professor Newton."

"Uh-huh." She picked up a cloth and pint glass, turning back to regard me as she leaned again against the far counter, absently polishing the glass. "You should be a little more careful, you know. With your questions. Boston may be a big town, but this neighborhood, not so much."

I blinked at her, smothering my surprise at her comment with another slug of coffee. My pulse quickened, though, and I couldn't help straightening. This woman was a bartender. Bartenders *heard* things. They knew things too.

"What questions would those be?" I asked, and she snorted.

"I don't know any Janet Cross, so don't get your hopes up. But I know you're looking for her people, and that means I'm not the only one. In a place like this, the right questions have a way of reaching the wrong ears. You should watch yourself."

"But—"

8

A bell at the front of the bar sounded, and the woman glanced over, the light catching her in such a way that she seemed far older—her face lined, her jaw soft. I dropped my gaze to my coffee again as she offered a familiar greeting to the newcomer, and finished off my mug. She said she didn't know my mom, so I shouldn't care too much about what she did know, but still...

I looked up to find her regarding me again as the newest arrival ambled over to his buddies at the end of the bar. She seemed to be waiting for something, but I didn't feel like spoon-feeding anyone this early in the morning.

"Any other advice before I go?" I finally asked, standing up from the stool. I reached into my pocket for my wallet.

She waved me off. "Drink's on the house. You'll need it where you're going. But yeah, now that you mention it..." She leaned closer, and I felt a whisper of energy move through me, rocking me back on my heels. Was this woman supernatural? Or merely super creepy?

"Yeah," she said. "Stay close to your guys. They need you more than they think they do, especially given what's coming."

I opened my mouth to say something flip, but closed it just as fast. *Monsters.* She meant monsters, of course, who followed me around like stink on moldy cheese. Since I'd hooked up with the monster hunters of Wellington Academy, our team had already successfully shut down the area's first legit in-public monster attack in generations, and the guys were absolutely convinced that episode was only the first of many. Probably not surprising that the ever-so-slightly woo-woo bartender at the edge of a monster hunting academy shared their belief.

"Noted," I said.

The woman nodded, her smirk back in place as she

9

turned away to her newest guest. But I felt her gaze slide back to me as I made my way out of the White Crane. Were other people out there waiting for this monster outbreak to happen, too? Hoping for it? And who among them would care about me looking for my mom?

I checked my phone again, picking up the pace as I angled toward Wellington Academy and scrolling through my email until I found the one from Professor Newton. In it, the demonology prof briefly outlined the extra-credit sunrise ceremony for his students, clearly as a reminder for them, though I'd learned about it for the first time just yesterday.

I peered at the annotated map he'd included, trying to orient myself. Bellamy Chapel was at the far edge of campus, past the dotted line I assumed was the outer wall of Wellington Academy. It wasn't the only section of the school that lay outside the reinforced footprint of the institution, but if we were dealing with demons, shouldn't it be in the most secure environment possible? And shouldn't that be *inside* the section of campus with updated security, and not the moldering ancient wall that was...porous at best?

Dew gathering on my running shoes, I tramped across the campus, my neoprene tights and running jacket the best gear I could manage for such an early morning outing. The professor had instructed us to dress for easy movement, like we were going to be practicing Tai Chi or something, so if everybody else was dressed in their academy best, too bad. He got what he got.

I found the far wall a few minutes later, heartened by the fact that I wasn't the only student heading in that direction. The campus, for the most part, remained quiet. But here students were gathering in groups of two and three, as well as a few solo stragglers. I hadn't attended a demonology class yet, but I didn't recognize anyone from my other classes, either. I imagined the study of demonology took all kinds, and I wondered briefly if any other monster hunter minors would be here. So far, I'd only met the guys—Tyler, Zach, Liam, and the appropriately named Grim—and they were all juniors, which put us at more or less the same age. Despite the bias against the minor, I knew there were a few younger monster hunters at Wellington...no sophomores, I was pretty sure, but maybe two or three freshmen.

I peered at the mix of students around me and wondered. There was the expected combination of bright and perky as well as slow and shuffling, while I fell somewhere in between, even bolstered by my laced coffee. I really *was* a morning person more often than not, but I hadn't been sleeping well these past few nights since the guys and I had completed our first unofficial task as monster hunters. Tyler had been great at keeping tabs on me since then, but I hadn't really seen much of the other guys, and I felt out of sorts.

Mine.

The word flashed through my mind so clearly, I whipped around, expecting to see someone standing right behind me—but there was no one there but a group of bleary-eyed students, hunched and shambling in the direction of Bellamy Chapel.

I sighed, regretting that I hadn't scored a second coffee for the road from the White Crane, never mind that I was already seriously on edge.

A soft, chittering laugh seemed to roll across the murky graveyard, fading away just as quickly, and I rolled my eyes at my twisted-up nerves.

Time to face my demons.

2

Our little group of pilgrims turned the corner, and a new building came into view, hunched over in full creepy splendor. Bellamy Chapel was a small stone structure crawling with vines, its narrow-paned windows bleak and cold, and the tiny Christian cross topping its steepled roof barely visible in the murk. The building looked like it hadn't been used in the last hundred years, at least for anything other than—apparently—demonology sunrise ceremonies.

There was a microscopic cemetery off to one side, and in the gloom, I could see that a tall, wrought iron fence surrounded the space. That made me feel marginally better, but I wasn't sure if those feelings were warranted. Iron was a good protection against the average run-of-the-mill monsters I'd encountered, but I'd never dealt with a demon before. Did they have different rules? They almost had to, right?

The murk lightened as we approached, and I bit my lip as a thread of worry snaked through me. I'd worked in a graveyard throughout my high school years, but ours had been…tidier, I guess was the word I was searching for. In the fields surrounding the old Southern church, the grave markers that had tumbled over and congealed into the turf seemed almost genteel in their disarray. Here, the tombstones seemed squashed and overburdened, like they were carrying the weight of the world on their shoulders. They were also disconcertingly close to the path we were on. The other students seemed to notice as well, and we all merged a bit more together, forming a close group as we slowed outside the front door of the abandoned chapel.

"Around to the back," someone shouted, the sharp sound making more than a few of us jump. I looked up to see a student in a bright red jacket gesturing us on. "Come on, he's about to begin."

A murmur of interest rumbled through the students around me, curiosity finally overcoming fear. We obligingly moved around the chapel to the back, where a wide field ringed with trees opened up. Here there were more graves, these much more neatly arranged in careful rows and seeming newer than the jumbled stones in front. I wondered when they'd stopped burying people on campus grounds… and why they'd ever started in the first place. Granted, it was a monster hunter academy. Exactly how difficult had those first few years of classes been?

All those thoughts flew out of my brain when I reached the growing collection of students gathered around someone who was *not* Professor Newton. It was Zachariah Williams, my monster hunting collective teammate, looking so unexpectedly gorgeous that I barely avoided whimpering as heat swept through my body, warding off the last of the cemetery's chill.

Whoa.

Tall and athletic without being muscle-bound, as fair as

an angel, with deep black hair and haunting eyes so blue they appeared purple, Zach *seemed* to be the most easygoing member of our little team ninety-nine percent of the time... but there was something about him that made me think the one percent I hadn't yet seen would scare the hell out of me.

I knew virtually nothing about him other than the fact that he was the son of a preacher and had scored some impressive experience with demon hunting at his father's church. I'd vaguely pictured shouted ceremonies at tent revivals, with a younger version of the dark-eyed Zach doing a laying-on of hands or holding a crucifix or whatever you needed to convince the faithful they were healed.

But even with all that in mind, why was he here as a stand-in for Professor Newton? He hadn't been mentioned in the email. I would have noticed that. And I definitely would have brushed my hair.

Zach seemed to sense my presence. He looked up, our gazes meeting across the open space. It was too far away for us to really see each other, but there was no denying the spark of awareness that blossomed through me, warming me in a way that the coffee hadn't even begun to. I felt myself blushing, glad for the fog that seemed to get thicker as we approached. I glanced up, but the sun was taking its time rising. Sort of defeated the purpose of a sunrise ceremony if you couldn't see the actual sun. Maybe it was waiting for us to assemble? That didn't make me feel much better.

"Getting close, guys," Zach said, loud enough for the stragglers to hear. "Obviously, I'm not your usual instructor, but Professor Newton has come to rely on me for this particular lecture. I've done it every semester for the past three years, even when I was a freshman, so don't worry, you're in good hands."

"Are we actually going to raise a demon?" The question came quickly and was undeniably nervous. We all shuffled a little, chuckling with whatever false bravado we could muster.

"Could be," Zach allowed. "It happened the first spring semester I was here, but not last spring. This year, though? I'm not sure which way things will roll."

Another voice popped up. "But *shouldn't* you know?" This from a tall redhead, her freshly scrubbed and lightly made-up face prettier than any one person should be before sunrise. She looked at Zach as if she was coming home, and I scowled at her, then refocused on him. All the guys in the collective were fit, healthy, and attractive. But Tyler had sort of dazzled me from the beginning, and I'd never really studied Zach objectively. Now that it was completely inappropriate, I took the opportunity of him explaining how demon summoning worked to ogle the poor guy.

The poor guy was *hot*. That was all really you could say about it. His hair was a dark mop of jet-black waves, his skin etched in porcelain, and of course...those eyes. This morning, he was clad only in running pants and a light tan T-shirt that stretched over a frame appreciably more defined than I'd given it credit for. My mouth began watering, and I focused on Zach's biceps as he lifted an arm to gesture back toward the church. Belatedly, I realized I should probably be paying attention to what he was saying.

"—consecrated ground," he finished. Not exactly illuminating, but the students around me seemed to have gotten more from his explanation, a few of them nodding wisely. I needed to focus.

"The transition between night to day, and day to night, is when demons are most likely to be seen, unless they've got you trapped in a building." Zach smiled, and my heart gave a little tug. "I wouldn't recommend that. But when you're outside, the gloaming time is their favorite. The light plays tricks on the eyes, and demons love nothing more than to deceive."

A question lifted from the back of the group. "You're talking Christian demons, right? Manifestations of Judeo-Christian mythology, set to turn humans away from the one true God."

"Typically, yes, though the definition of the one true God varies from faith to faith. Christians don't corner the market on that concept, and demons don't care all that much about what God you follow. They're only interested in uncoupling you from whatever faith you do possess, then preying on your unprotected soul."

I couldn't help myself, I made a face. Zach apparently was watching me. "Does that surprise you?"

He asked the question in a cool, academic voice, but once again, a thrill of awareness scattered through me. It was as if the group of students fell away, leaving only the two of us there, and heat flared in my belly.

"I've never fought..." I cut myself off in time to not look like a freak and amended my wording. "I mean, I've never really *thought* about confronting a demon, I guess. I always just assumed it was a Christian thing."

"In the United States, at least in the South and along the east coast, you'd be right. But different parts of the country have different factions of demons. There are dark spirits in almost every belief system, from those brought over from Europe and Asia to the indigenous cultures throughout Central and South America." He smiled, gesturing around, and it took me a second to stop looking at the curve of his mouth and zero in on his words.

"In this particular sacred space, we're looking at your

more typical demons. Most of you have done that reading already, so I won't bore you with it." He let his gaze settle back on me, electric with possibility. "For new members to the class, we can talk afterward, if you'd like."

The overture was so unexpected that I pursed my lips together, fighting a nervous giggle. I nodded, then attempted to appear completely disinterested. Fortunately, I didn't have to fake it for long. A soft, querulous moan sounded in the trees around us, stopping my fluttery heart cold in my chest.

"I'll be damned," Zach drawled, before giving us a slight wink. "It looks like we have company. Brace yourselves."

The trees exploded.

3

I hadn't fought demons before, but I knew what was happening here was bullshit.

The entire class screamed and collapsed into each other, several of them dropping to their knees, as lights scattered and screams burst forth from every corner of the graveyard. The Halloween scare fest cut out just as quickly and Zach raised his hand, grinning as students still spun this way and that, trying to find the source of the noise, the lights, or any evidence of the demon attack that had descended on us so rapidly.

"Sorry." Zach laughed so good-naturedly, it was tough to want to beat the crap out of him for the practical joke. Tough, but not undoable, judging from the mutinous expressions of some of the students. "Sorry," he said again. "But I did that for a reason. By my count, more than half of you immediately clasped your hands in prayer and dropped to your knees. Yet only five of you admitted to practicing your faith regularly on the pre-fieldwork questionnaire you all submitted to Professor Newton."

One of the students finally found his voice. "That was fake? You tricked us?"

"Not tricked you, tested you," Zach corrected. "And those kinds of tests are where the true strength of a demon lies. Now get up before you get wet from all that dew."

Grumbling, the students all stood while Zach continued. "Make no mistake, having an active faith life can help you ward off an attack...so long as it's actually *active*. But again, you're safe here today. When the sun rises in a few minutes, you may see signs of demons passing. Like I said, last year we had only the barest blip, which is why I created this little show for you. What you just experienced was much more like what we encountered the first spring I was here, as a freshman."

"Why was there a difference?" asked one of the students. "Like, why did they show up the first year and ignore you the second?"

"I've given that a lot of thought," Zach said. "It really comes down to a few things. First, I'm stronger. The first year, I didn't know a lot about protecting myself. Between my first and second years, I had to level up in a hurry, and I did. By the time I hit this ceremony sophomore year, I was more prepared and the demons might have sensed that. These are thinking beings, not mindless creatures. They have a sense of strategy and a keen desire for self-preservation. They could have decided I posed a threat."

He lifted one shoulder self-deprecatingly, and several of the students chuckled. Zach worked hard to give the impression that he wasn't a threat, I suspected. Was that because of the campus animosity toward the monster hunter program? It certainly had drawn enough enemies. Or was it something deeper?

"Another option could simply have been who and what I was," Zach continued.

"But you were a monster hunter minor both times," another student pointed out.

"True. Before I came to Wellington, however, I was also the son of a preacher in a small Southern church, one known for exorcisms." He said this without fanfare, but every single one of the students perked up, including me. "It's not like I dispelled demons on my own or anything, but they were familiar with me. They could even have been hunting me, thinking I'd be easy prey. Maybe after the first year, they gave that up."

Zach looked up toward the eastern horizon, and I realized the fog had lifted enough to make it reasonable to assume that the sun might actually make an appearance. Standing in this particular church cemetery, that seemed like a minor miracle.

"The fog is a good sign, ordinarily," he said, but his words were quieter now, focused.

"What should we do?" the redhead asked, sounding credibly concerned. I noticed that she was now standing closer to Zach. When had that happened? "I mean...if they do show up?"

Zach didn't answer right away, and a shadow passed over the sun. In fact, he didn't say anything for such a long time that the students around me moved uneasily, whispering and nudging each other, their soft murmurs filling my ears. Tension warped through me, and one of the students laughed nervously.

"You did *not* just say that." She giggled, shifting away from the boy next to her, but her words were a little strained. Another student huffed a startled gasp. And then a third, as murmurs spread through the group.

I tore my gaze away from Zach long enough to glance around, and froze. This was all wrong. There were twice as many students in our small group as there had been a second ago. I squinted, trying to make sense of the change, and the female student nearest the redhead lifted her hand and drifted it along the redhead's glossy hair. The sun pierced the clouds, and I could see right through the new girl's fingers. Then she leaned forward, as if to whisper in the redhead's ear.

"—out!" Zach's voice finally reached me, but it seemed to be coming from across the city, not a mere few tombstones away. I was already moving, reaching down for my iron dagger. I came back up, and the first thing I saw was the redheaded student, grinning at me ghoulishly. Her face was stretched too wide, as if she'd swallowed a gopher, her mouth a ghastly maw that opened to reveal a set of yellow feral eyes lurking inside her. Wait—was this the student from class, an apparition, or something even worse? What was happening here?

She launched herself at me the same moment that something sounded over near Zach, a loud crack as if two mighty hands smacked together. The creature inside the student jolted, its eyes going wide, and then it spewed out of her mouth toward me. It wasn't alone. Wraiths of varying size and thickness flowed through the air, hissing and dissolving into the ground, the shadows, the walls of the church itself. I turned to see Zach standing in the center of our group, while I now stood several feet away.

How had I gotten here? Had I somehow lost time? Was that even possible?

"Behold," Zach said. And I realized he wasn't alone. Caught in his grasp was one of the demons, a writhing creature about as big as a cat, but with long, skinny arms and legs that ended in hooked claws. It snarled and squirmed, straining back from Zach, its tail lashing violently.

"Your time has come to pay the price," the creature screeched. "Your sacrifice is due."

"*Silentium*," Zach ordered, and the demon's snarls turned into a screech, as if the words hurt it physically.

Around this center, the students gaped and stared. Zach spoke more in Latin or maybe Greek, some sort of incantation or prayer, and the demon responded with what sounded like epithets in a language that wasn't English yet sounded vaguely familiar. Zach switched to the same language, and somehow I recognized it as Akkadian, for all that I knew only a few words, having just had my first class a few days earlier.

Nevertheless, I'd already memorized the word for binding and for obey, and Zach used both of these as the creature twisted and jerked. And then, just as it seemed it might burst out of Zach's hands, it withered. Shrank down in front of our eyes, then dissolved into smoke.

The students burst into applause.

"That wasn't fake, right?" the skeptical kid asked, his face rapt with excitement. "Those were actual demons this time?"

"Those were actual demons," Zach agreed. "Older ones, though, not the typical lot. That's why they didn't respond to the orders that I gave them in Latin."

"Why would they respond to orders at all?" another student asked.

Not a bad question. Zach had an answer for it. "All demons are constructs of God. Whether *you* believe in the one true God or not, *they* do. As a result, anything spoken to them in the name of that God with enough authority can constrain them. It's the authority part that's the hard thing. As mortals, we're not used to playing God, for all that we may want to be. Demons know that as well. They work to undermine our sense of authority, our belief in ourselves. It's one of their best tricks."

He spoke with absolute knowledge, but something in his tone struck me with unexpected force. Did Zach doubt his own ability with demons? Surely, he wouldn't have made this attempt if so. Right?

"But I'm still confused," another student protested. "We are on church grounds here. I thought that was supposed to be safe from demons. I thought that was kind of the whole point of church grounds."

Zach nodded. "A lot of people think that, and depending on the demon, they're usually right. But also, it depends on the church. What you've got here" —he gestured around —"is a church that hasn't maintained its consecration. It's been abandoned, boarded up, and allowed to go to rot. That makes it no longer safe on a basic level, and more of a magnet for demons."

"So this had nothing to do with the sunrise?" said one of the other students, a thoughtful-looking kid with a mop of dark hair falling over his glasses. "You lured us here, knowing the demons would come for us? What were we, bait or something?"

"You were *not* bait," Zach said sternly, shaking his head. "If that were the case, we would have assembled experts in a secret operation well after school was let out. But the truth of the matter is, demons don't respect any place that humans have lost respect for. That's why they typically don't cross onto sacred ground, because mortals have imbued that ground with a higher purpose. As you can see, nobody has cared for this spot in some time. It's picturesque, but little more. I could've easily had this ceremony in a bar. Demons come or they don't. But congratulations, with your help and by maintaining the circle, we've made the world a little lighter today."

I blinked, and Zach said, "Look down."

4

I looked down, but I still didn't see anything out of the ordinary, not at first. Only when Zach pressed aside the grass did I notice the thin line of white crystals that gathered on one of the tombstones before disappearing into the grass again.

"Salt?" I asked. "But there's a ton of dew here. It's already dissolving. How could that help?"

"It couldn't help trap the demons, you're right," Zach said. "But it allowed the space where you all were standing to be reconsecrated, at least for a few minutes. The demons didn't feel that until they were right up on us. You were never in any danger."

That seemed to make everyone happier, and Zach spoke on for a few minutes, explaining that the demons had been dispatched forever and would not bother them again. This last he gave almost as a benediction, and I could glimpse the prayerful boy he must once have been, tapped to help his father banish demons from a frightened flock.

The students dispersed after that, no longer walking individually, but gathered together in groups of four and five. A separate, smaller cluster remained behind, peppering Zach with questions, and it took another ten minutes before he was able to send them on their way.

By then, we had all started walking back toward the main campus, and I breathed a sigh of relief when we entered the reinforced stone walls of Wellington Academy again. I didn't want to admit it, but that entire sesh had scared the crap out of me.

Zach seemed to notice. He turned to me after he sent the last pair of students off, his gaze heavy with concern.

"Are you okay?" he asked, and I nodded quickly.

"I am, I just...I mean, that was kind of creepy, right? The demons standing among the students, looking like they were part of the class? And some of them straight-up going inside the students until you called them back out? Were you expecting that?"

He grimaced and scanned the central quad, apparently convincing himself we were alone. "Truth?" he asked. "Not even remotely. That little demonstration was way off the charts. Even during my first year here, I didn't attract that kind of attention. And those guys were not messing around." He glanced around again and lifted the hem of his shirt. I blinked. A deep, bright red furrow now marred his abs, joining other long-since-faded marks.

"Whoa! When did that happen?"

"When the first one hit," he said. "Stupid of me, but I wasn't prepared. It caught me off guard and got a swipe in before I was able to neutralize it."

"Does it hurt?" I asked and winced. "Sorry, dumb question. Of course it hurts."

He laughed a little grimly. "Not as much as you might think," he admitted. "It looks bad, but it's all in the eye of the beholder."

"Well, my eye is beholding it, and it looks pretty awful to me."

"Ah, but remember, a demon's greatest magic lies in illusion. You were expecting to see something bad when I lifted up my shirt, not just get treated to my super-sexy, rock-hard abs."

I snorted, ignoring the fluttery bump of my heart against my rib cage. Zach did have super-sexy, rock-hard abs. And the kind of scars I knew all too well. "Fair enough. And—your neck too. They got you there."

"Really?" Zach's brows went up as he lifted his hands to run his fingers over his neck, wincing at the abrasions. "So they did. Normally, I notice when something's trying to choke me to death, but that's the problem with demon attacks—humans are wired to forget the trauma as quickly as they possibly can. Good thing nobody but you could see so much. I mean, they witnessed the demons, yes. But not the damage the demons left behind. They'd have been way more freaked, and we need that like a hole in the head. The monster hunting minor has enough bad press."

"Yeah—though it *was* kind of cool, what you did, fighting the demons and sending them away. So maybe...?"

"Cool is in the eye of the beholder too," Zach countered, grinning. My heart jittered again as we shared a glance, ignoring my attempts to shush it. We were bonding like normal people. Like friends. That's it. I needed to get ahold of myself. "All it takes is one student flipping out about how I led them into danger, and it'd be lights out. So—I'm careful. Most of the time, they only see what they want to see. Sort of like with ordinary monsters."

I nodded, my fingers drifting to the bracelet that was wrapped snugly around my wrist...the one that kept Zach from reading my mind. "Yeah." It was true enough. Most people never realized monsters were right on top of them until it was too late. And they never saw me fighting anything supernatural. The only guys who ever had were monster hunters themselves.

"I'd say a good half of those students talked a good game, but they were pretty stressed when they showed up for class this morning. Now, hopefully, they're impressed."

I lifted my eyes. "Well, I'm impressed, and you're not even reading my mind."

He nodded, but a definite edge entered his eyes as he watched me, making my breath catch. "Just think of how much more impressed you could be if I had an unfair advantage. Wanna test it out?"

"I..." I swallowed as, too quickly, the answer formed. Yes, I did want to test it out. I wanted to slip this bracelet off my wrist and see what it would feel like to have Zach touch my mind, know my thoughts. I wanted him to push into my mind while he skimmed his hand over my skin and—

Down, girl.

"I—think that would be pretty interesting, eventually," I finished lamely, not missing the strange flash of fire in Zach's eyes. Had he known? Had he sensed what I was thinking, despite the mind-warding bracelet? "But you're not the only demon hunter at Wellington, right? I mean, that class was full, and none of those students are in the monster hunter minor."

Zach's features smoothed out, and he gave me a quick, conspiratorial wink.

"Despite the general disdain for monster hunting, there's a full-on demonology major here, as it turns out. Little known fact, though: true demon hunting is an inherited job skill, not a learned one. More than that, not every kid born to every demon hunter gets the mind-melding talent—the Williams family is just particularly lucky. I didn't even know I was doing it when I was a kid, until my dad figured it out. That would've been right around the time my mom cheerfully announced that I could eat my favorite sugared cereal for breakfast *and* lunch. I thought it was the greatest thing ever. The honorable Reverend Matthew Williams, not so much."

I winced. "Did he come down on you hard?"

"Not as hard as he could have, though arguably a little harder than maybe he should have for a six-year-old boy who had no idea what he'd just done," Zach said, with a wry smile that spoke volumes. "But that's my dad. His world is heavy on the black and white, not all that great with shades of gray. It had to be, given what he did for a living. He yelled at me, and, though I can't really believe it now, I yelled *back*, protesting my innocence of doing anything on purpose till my voice went hoarse. I got sick after that and thought God was mad at me, which made Dad feel pretty bad, I think. He was super nice for like, weeks."

"Aw, man." I laughed, not sure whom I felt worse for. "Parenting must suck sometimes."

"Yeah—and to be fair, the ability to push minds is only a tiny talent for us, but it's there, even if it's much less prominent than our ability to *read* minds. Dad needed to both make sure I stayed safe, and to protect other people from my budding abilities and questionable impulse control—especially my mom and my little brother. He also needed to try and guide me the best he could. Not everyone handles the experience of being a demon hunter well, inherited skill or not. His own dad had sort of fallen apart on the job—his wife died suddenly, and he sort of cracked. He gave Dad to a local preacher to raise. So Dad was adopted by the preacher, but it's not like he didn't know my grandfather. My grandfather just couldn't raise him anymore. Not after what happened to my grandmother."

"You're kidding me. Your grandfather gave up your dad for adoption?" I protested, my eyes wide. "That...isn't that terrible?"

He shrugged. "No more terrible than growing up with a broken-down demon hunter drifter who didn't know how to care for you. Family's what you make of it sometimes."

"Yeah..." I considered that, remembering my mom's carefully worded letter to her own family, added to over so many years...but never sent. "I guess."

"In my dad's case, it turned out to be for the best. The preacher and his wife took Dad in, he grew up absolutely loving the work with the congregation, and eventually, he found a wife of his own. I showed up after that, with my little brother following a few years later. Fortunately, Jeremy avoided being a freak. He's a senior now at the local high school, not an ounce of weirdness to him. But once Dad realized I had the gift of demon hunting and mind reading as well, and could handle it, he put me to work."

"As a six-year-old?" I asked almost playfully, expecting him to say no. To my surprise, Zach shrugged.

"You'd be amazed at how quickly people relax when an exorcist shows up with a little kid in tow. It made everyone unwind and believe that it was all going to be okay. Which was part of the game. The more riled up you get in the midst of a demon possession, the more power you cede to the bastards. They'll take every advantage that you're willing to give up. Unfortunately, most people have no idea how easy they make it on the very creatures they're so desperately afraid of."

"I bet you were a lot of fun at birthday parties," I said

30

drily, and he laughed. I liked making Zach laugh, I decided. I got the feeling he didn't laugh all that often.

"Guys!"

I looked up to see Tyler and Liam heading toward us, my heart catching as I focused on Tyler. Tall and even more well-muscled than he'd been when I'd first met him several days ago, he was now a pinup model for Big Man on Campus: dark brown hair tumbling over his brow, whiskey-colored eyes that made you feel like you were his entire world, an easy smile that bordered on smug most of the time—and when it didn't border, it was right smack in the middle of it. Tyler was confident, strong, and smart as hell, with an added dollop of spell-casting prowess that made him a natural leader for our little monster hunting collective. Even better—he was mine...and I was his.

And that was all that mattered, dammit.

I set my jaw, determined not to pay *any* more attention to Zach, or to Tyler's best friend, Liam, who walked beside him, with his darkly tanned face and river-stone hazel eyes, his messy fall of brown hair that made him look like he'd just pulled an all-nighter studying. Liam was hot in a way that made me shiver—smart hot. A-guy-who-knew-stuff hot. A-guy-willing-to-try-anything hot. A—

Will you stop! I ordered myself, glancing away from Liam's face to his hands. Which was when I realized that Liam and Tyler were holding enormous cups of—*oh thank God.* Coffee.

Liam reached us first, high-fiving Zach as Tyler stopped to pull me into his arms for a kiss. I went willingly. Never mind the weird fluttery feeling I got with Liam and Zach right there—especially Zach. With our impromptu demon fight still fresh in my mind, I felt his energy more than Liam's—and that energy had a dark, possessive resonance

I'd never felt with Tyler, even when he was being overbearingly rude. Which was a lot of the time, especially when we first met.

Then Tyler's mouth came down on mine, and I couldn't think of anything else. The connection we had was so intense that it took my breath away. Kissing him should've felt like coming home, except for I didn't have much of a home to go back to anymore.

We broke apart, and he grinned down at me. "You taste like sulfur," he said.

I shot him a horrified glance. "Are you serious?"

"Sulfur?" Zach asked at the same time. By now, we'd turned toward the monster hunter quad, the guys setting off at an easy pace. "Well, that's kind of cool. I don't know if I've ever experienced that. I wonder if it's because you're part of the collective now—we're, like, more connected now?"

"Really," Liam echoed, with a tone of voice that made me think he was going to add this little tidbit to some journal he was keeping about all my rogue monster hunting quirks. I fought the flush—what kind of information would he record, exactly? Did I really want to know?

Zach's speculation sparked a lively round of discussion that took us through the rest of campus and under the stone wall that separated the main section of Wellington Academy from the monster quad. This morning more than ever, I was happy to see the collection of tidy brick buildings and open fields. While technically still part of the campus, the monster quad was surrounded only by the original stone walls of the academy, not the reinforced barriers that protected the core of the school. It had become as segregated as the monster hunter minor itself, pushed to the side for more popular majors, never mind that it was the school's original prime directive. Much like with Tyler's kiss, however, the moment I stepped onto these hallowed grounds, I felt like I was coming home.

When we neared Lowell Library though, Zach's steps faltered. A man was waiting in front of the building, looking like any one of my professors, right down to the somber suit and scowl. Also like many of the professors, he was glaring at us.

"Son of a bitch," Zach muttered as I took in the tall, fair, dark-haired man. "It's my dad."

5

The door to the library opened as we approached, and Commander Frost stepped out. While technically a guy named Dean Robbins was in charge of the monster hunter minor at the academy, Frost was the minor's unofficial leader, not to mention a badass monster hunter in his own right. Today, Frost was going full-on Paul Bunyan, all lumberjack muscles, plaid shirt, and heavy jeans, three-day beard, and world-weary frown. He wasn't sporting suspenders, thank heavens, but all he needed was a big axe over one shoulder and I'd start looking for a blue ox.

Frost scanned our group, then beyond us, paying no immediate attention to Zach's father. "Grim?"

Tyler shrugged. "Classes. We all just sort of met up, not on purpose. I..." Tyler frowned, looking around. "I don't even know why we're here, come to think of it. Did you need us? I didn't get any ping to my phone."

"Dammit, Dad..." Zach muttered again, this time under his breath.

"Language," the reverend chided heavily, making Zach roll his eyes. Meanwhile, an amused expression flitted across Frost's face, then he turned to Zach's father, who apparently wasn't a stranger to him.

"Good to see you, Matthew. Come inside."

Zach's dad took his time, his disapproving gaze lingering on Zach, who didn't rise to the bait. I didn't have a lot of experience with parental disapproval, but a wave of indignation swept up through me at the stare. Tyler squeezed my hand, and I stayed quiet.

"Zachariah," Reverend Williams finally said, nodding. His voice was strangely light, almost warm, in direct contrast with his expression. "You've fought recently."

Zach spread his hands. "Demonstration only. Something for school. Over at Bellamy Chapel."

"The chapel?" his father asked sharply. "You mean the grounds."

"Sure, yeah," Zach agreed. "The graveyard. We did a sunrise ceremony, nothing major."

His father narrowed his eyes at him. "And...were you hurt?"

"Not at all."

I kept my face carefully neutral, and Reverend Williams nodded. "I'll want to hear more about that, then. The number of the horde you attracted, anything unique about them. It's important."

"Of course," Zach said, his words equally as easy, almost friendly, though not exactly warm. Not like I'd talked to my mom, back when we were still able to talk. How would I have talked to my father if I'd known him? More authentically than this, I was pretty sure. It made my heart hurt a little for Zach, and I'd barely met the man who raised him. Maybe passing on demon hunter genes took more out of you than I expected.

The preacher's gaze shifted to the rest of us. "You're all

classmates?" he asked, skipping over me to focus on Tyler and Liam. I didn't mind that so much. It gave me time to study the dark-haired, dark-eyed man more as Zach made hasty introductions.

Matthew Williams was taller and thinner than his son, but wiry looking in his simple suit. His clothes were well made but not fancy, and I imagined his hands were callused and his skin tanned beneath the shirt. He looked like any small-town preacher should, I thought, but I knew better than to discount him. If he was anything like Zach, he could read minds, and I didn't have a special bracelet to ward him off. Was the one I had against Zach's intrusion enough to cover both Williamses?

I hoped so.

"We should get inside," Tyler said as the preacher finally focused on me. The oddest riffle of awareness skittered over me, gone almost as quickly as it arrived, as Tyler gestured Reverend Williams ahead, his fingers still firmly interlocked with mine. I thought about that. Was Tyler protecting me in some way? Reverend Williams certainly seemed to take note of our connection, and his gaze was both assessing and congenial. I couldn't decide how I felt about him.

Zach's father turned and preceded us into the cool confines of Lowell Library, but I tugged Tyler back for a second. "Can you feel that?" I whispered when he glanced back at me. "The touch of Zach's dad's mind or whatever?"

"I mean, a little, sure," Tyler said, shrugging. "But Liam made sure our wards covered all the Williams boys. You're solid."

He turned forward, and I frowned. I wasn't so sure about that, but I didn't want to contradict Tyler—I mean, he had to know what he was dealing with, since he knew Zach, right?

We entered the library behind the others. Commander Frost waited for us in the main foyer, apparently oblivious to the weird overtones, undertones, and side tones of the preacher's arrival. Instead, he was all grins.

"I didn't think you'd ever step foot on campus again," Frost said, and Reverend Williams finally broke into a smile.

"You shouldn't believe the brash words of the young," he said, sending our group a wry glance. Once again, I found myself wanting to like this guy, and I didn't know if I was being coerced to do so or not.

"Wait, you went to school at Wellington?" Zach asked, clearly surprised. "You never told me that."

"I did, for a time," Reverend Williams acknowledged, and Frost snorted.

"By a time, he means less than a year. He had the same full-ride scholarship we all had, but he stayed only long enough to whip through every single demonology class the school offered, then split. Father LaRocca is still pissed."

"Father LaRocca, of all people, should know better," Reverend Williams said mildly. "I had a very specific reason for attending Wellington. Once that reason was met, there was nothing for me here. I wasn't trying to learn how to fight every monster in the world, just the kind that could be a threat to my adoptive father's community."

"But you sent me here," Zach protested. "Without any stipulation to stick to demon hunting or to leave early. And *you* didn't tell me you knew Dad from way back," he continued, turning to Frost. "You just made it seem like you met him during my application process, that the school had caught wind of my work at the church and contacted me because of that. How could you not have mentioned that Dad went to *school* here?"

"Because I asked him not to." Reverend Williams regarded his son again. "I didn't want my experience at Wellington to have any bearing on yours. I asked for discretion, and the academy granted it. As they should have."

Frost nodded. "Your father holds a special place in the hearts of those few people who remember him. Not to mention a viable path out of a now-despised minor and into a more respectable calling. For a while, he was the poster child for monster hunting rehabilitation."

Liam huffed a laugh as Zach frowned. "Well, I didn't leave the minor."

"You didn't," his dad agreed. "Nor did you return to tend to the church over summer breaks. If that had been your calling, you would have. So why do you think you remained at Wellington?"

Zach shrugged, but for the first time, he seemed a little uncomfortable. "There was more to learn," he said. "I found friends. Other interesting classes to take."

"Other interesting monsters to fight," Reverend Williams agreed, and now I could discern the slightest hint of judgment. "You have fought demons, and successfully. You were born to it, as I was. But you didn't want to stay with that exclusively. That's where we differ."

"That, among other things," Zach agreed.

Their ping-ponging conversation seemed pleasant and easygoing enough on the surface, but I could feel the glugging of swamp monsters beneath. Unlike a lot of young twenty-somethings with a parent he clearly respected, Zach wasn't backing down from his father. And his father, though clearly not entirely thrilled with Zach, wasn't going all lord and master on him either. There was something weird going on here, but it wasn't a lack of respect. Which made it... what? Too *much* respect? Was that even possible?

Either way, there were layers upon layers of push and pull here, a mental and psychological gamesmanship that exhausted me, and I'd only experienced it for a few minutes. Were they even aware they were doing it?

"Rest assured, I wouldn't be here now, disrupting your schooling, unless I had no other choice," Reverend Williams said, turning back to Frost as we moved into the main library room, with its towering stacks of books on polished shelves, gleaming marble floors, and enticing, shadowy study alcoves. In the week or so I'd been on campus, I'd never once seen anyone in the library other than the guys and Frost, but the place always seemed poised to fling open its doors and welcome droves of students. "We've been having some problems at my church that we shouldn't be."

Liam checked his stride, brightening. "A monster outbreak?"

Reverend Williams glanced toward him, his lips flattening into a grim smile. "For most folk, that wouldn't be cause for celebration."

Liam, however, was undeterred. "For those of us who can *help*, though, it's a chance to do so. No fireman ever hopes for a fire, but he's got the tools to fix it if it happens, and he's ready to use them when needed."

"Come this way," Frost interrupted, and we trooped after him. When we entered the small antechamber I'd come to think of as the library's war room, however, it wasn't empty. Frost reacted first.

"Goddamn—ah, hmmm," he amended, shooting a glance toward Zach's father. "Grim. What are you doing here?"

He wasn't destined to get a direct response. With his thick, white-blond hair lashed into a braid that fell past his shoulders, his granite-jawed face stern and unforgiving,

Grim Lockton, the fifth member of our collective, stood with his burly arms folded, focusing his pale golden eyes on a map on the wall screen. I blinked at it too. For once, it wasn't a close-in map of our area of Back Bay, Boston, home to Wellington Academy. This map had been expanded to cover the entire eastern coastline, from Maine to Florida, the Carolinas to the Mississippi River.

"These are bullshit," Grim rumbled, and I saw the other feature of the map. Green glowing dots up and down the coastline, focusing in a cluster in Massachusetts, northern Georgia, and eastern Tennessee. "They're not real."

"What's the significance of this?" Reverend Williams asked, striding forward. He jabbed a finger at the border between South Carolina and Georgia. "Because this is where I'm located, and if this is a map of outbreaks, we should be on it."

"Dad?" Zach asked, a new note of concern underscoring the word. "What's going on? Are the demons back?"

"You could say that." His father glanced at him. "What happened this morning—you've done that sort of summons before, yes? Did you experience any aberrations? A pattern shift?"

"Well—I guess a little, yeah," Zach said, lifting his hand to rub the back of his neck. He shot me a glance. "I mean, there were more demons than usual, and they dicked around a little more with the students, but in the end, they had no power within the sacred circle. They returned to the shadows."

"And they didn't address you in any way?"

Zach scowled. "Why?"

His father rolled his eyes. "Just answer the question directly, Zachariah. For once in your life."

I fought the grin. Maybe Zach and his dad did have a normal father-son relationship after all.

"I—I don't know..." Zach said. "I thought they had, but the words made no sense, and then they left me and of course, everything fades so fast. I could've imagined it."

"You didn't imagine it," I blurted before I could rein myself in. Everyone turned to me, even Zach. "It said your time had come, or something like that. To make your sacrifice. Then you shouted at it in Latin or maybe Greek and Akkadian, binding spells, I think, and it went poof."

"You've already picked up Akkadian?" Tyler asked, while Zach frowned at me. My eyes were on his father, though. He'd gone sheet white for a moment, then his face went carefully neutral again. There was something Reverend Williams knew that he didn't want to spill—at least not to all of us.

"Okay, well, there you go," Zach said, returning his focus to his dad. "What's it mean?"

"It means the horde is playing games with my family, and I don't like it." The other guys were all watching the preacher too, except for Liam, who I realized was edging toward a stack of books Frost had left on the table behind where the preacher was standing. I slanted a glance toward where he was heading...

Then I saw it. The second tome down, a thick text with a moldering, heavily seamed spine, emblazoned with a word I now knew, courtesy of my unusual affinity for learning Akkadian.

Apocrypha.

The word shimmered in front of my eyes, seeming to leap off the book. The Apocrypha. That was the text Frost had used to learn about the peculiar ramifications of me joining the monster hunter collective—a female pairing up with four male hunters. It was also the text that had completely freaked him out, revealing hints about my connection with the guys that went *way* outside the bounds of ordinary team building.

I needed to get that book.

Reverend Williams spoke again, sharply enough to pull my attention to him. "Why didn't you contact me about these attacks?" he asked Frost.

"Well, for starters, I didn't know anything was happening to you, and second, Grim is right. These attacks aren't real." The commander gestured to the screen. "Our system is going haywire. We went from getting absolutely no information about monsters anywhere to a slew of false alarms. I'm relying on networks that haven't been activated for a hundred years, and the infrastructure is profoundly broken. So maybe *you* should tell *us* what's going on."

As he spoke, Frost moved over to the table and dropped into a chair, pulling a laptop close. Reverend Williams sighed heavily, then started speaking.

"Understand, my church covers a wide range of mostly rural communities, some of which don't have a tremendous connection to the outside world, by choice more often than not. These people aren't recluses. They're simply more comfortable living off the grid. They work in the cities if they have to, but they don't stay there for any length of time if they can avoid it. More often than not, we go to them."

"Like tent revivals?" I asked, and Reverend Williams slid his warm gaze toward me. Could he seriously read my mind? If so, I needed a reinforced bracelet, I didn't care what Tyler thought.

"Exactly like that. We prefer that approach at my home parish. In fact, we plant a new church every weekend. We sometimes gather in larger buildings, lodges and the like, but if those aren't available, we have shelter to spare. Whoever wants to hear the word of the Lord can do so without having to leave their communities and farms. But we're based in a small town right on the border. Have been for generations. And sometimes people seek us out there."

"A lot of times," Zach put in. "Dad's sermons draw believers from a three-state area."

Reverend Williams nodded. "We welcome them all. But lately, it's the healing sessions that have drawn more attention. What we're being asked to heal...is disturbing."

"What do you mean, disturbing?" Zach asked before any of the rest of us could. "That's not a word you use. Ever."

"Not with the afflicted, no," Reverend Williams agreed. "But things are different now. The deceivers walk among us, as always, but their tactics have changed."

Frost leaned forward. "Explain."

Reverend Williams sighed. "Zach knows this, and I'm sure some of the rest of you have at least a passing understanding of what's involved, depending on your coursework. There are several levels of demon possession, from the occupation of spaces—such as rooms, homes, crypts, buildings, and the like—to eventual infiltration of humans and the gradual breakdown of the soul within. But despite what Hollywood would have you believe, most demons don't seek to create some sort of physical record of their attack, for the simple reason that they don't want individuals to seek or draw support from anyone else. Isolation is a demon's greatest strategy. But these demons aren't being discreet. They're driving their victims to my doors almost as soon as they lay hands on the unfortunate souls, and these people are fully at the horde's mercy. Their souls are in anguish, agony. Beyond rational reach. Some even resort to self-harm in their urgency to get noticed."

"But why?" Zach asked. "And why are they targeting you?"

Reverend Williams pressed his lips together. "They're not targeting me," he said. "They're targeting you."

"What?" Zach exploded, taking a sharp step back. "What are you talking about? I haven't done a damned thing up here—literally."

I couldn't help my smile at his dark humor, but I could tell his father didn't believe him. He glared at Zach across the table. "You're telling me nothing has changed in your situation in the past few weeks? Nobody new has entered your sphere, you've made no new friends...or enemies?"

That last question wiped the smile off my face, and my brows almost leapt right off my forehead, they climbed toward my hairline so fast. Zach, however, played it completely cool.

"Absolutely not," he said, with such assurance that even I almost believed him. "I don't have time to make new friends, and I sure as hell wouldn't do anything that would put anyone at risk."

"At risk for what, exactly?" Tyler asked, interjecting the question with such calm, levelheaded ease that Reverend Williams blinked at him. Tyler had been raised to dominate any room, and those leadership attributes had recently leveled up. It was a good look on him.

It also was something new. And exactly what Zach's father was talking about, I suspected.

The preacher blew out a harsh breath. "You want to explain it, Zach, or do you want me to?"

Zach's face darkened mutinously, and his lips curled. "I'm not you, Dad. What happened to you isn't going to happen to me—or to this team. Did the demons come here to seek you out? Is that why you left the school so abruptly after your freshman year, without confronting them in a place where you'd actually have help to fight them?"

"You still don't get it," his father snapped. "There *is* no help that matters for what we're dealing with. We sacrifice, and others survive. It's that simple. And we try to limit the damage as best we can."

"Ahh..." Tyler put in again, the other guys transfixed by the ping-ponging conversation, even Grim. Zach made a sharp, angry gesture with his hands.

"I'll tell you what Dad's concern is," he said, looking like he might reach out and throttle his father. "He's right about demons coming after our family. It's been going on for a long time now—generations. But there's a catch, and it's a fucking awful one. When we reveal our weakness, literal hell breaks loose, and the only way to stop is to make a sacrifice. We do that, and the demons go away, but only until the next Williams kid hits age twenty-one or so. Then they're back."

"A sacrifice," Tyler repeated. I glanced at him, taking in his set jaw, his steady eyes. "What kind of sacrifice?"

Zach flashed an ugly smile. "Depends entirely on the generation. My grandfather lost his wife. Dad, here—"

"That's *enough*," cracked Reverend Williams. I swung my

gaze back to him. He'd gone white with fury, his big hands curled into fists. He glared first at Zach, then Tyler. "He's right. The demons are coming. It's Zach's turn to face his challenge. But if he's not formed any overriding attachment to any one person or organization, if he doesn't place any of you above himself, then...I don't know what's stirred them up. Something triggered the horde, though. That's how they work."

"Well, we just finished our first official monster fight. That had to have put every demon in Christendom on notice," Liam put in, making Zach's father jolt with surprise. When the older man glared at him, Liam shrugged. "We're monster hunters, remember? That's kind of what we do. We can take down this demon once and for all."

"Exactly," Zach said through gritted teeth.

"We could have helped you too, Matthew." It was Frost's turn to speak, and Zach's father turned to him, his face shifting quickly through anger, sorrow—and then something else, equally profound. Resignation.

"No," Reverend Williams sighed. "No, you couldn't have. But that's water long under the bridge." He straightened then, and passed a hand over his face. "And ancient history, in any event. The trouble you're facing is here and now. There's work that needs to be done, especially if you're already seeing increased demon activity on campus."

"We're not seeing increased activity," Zach protested. "I had a demonology ceremony this morning. That's all."

"A ceremony that resulted in an unexpected reaction from the horde," Reverend Williams countered. "Don't let your pride make you foolish, Zachariah. It's a family trait that's gotten us in trouble more than a few times."

"And for the millionth time, I am not *you*," Zach retorted, his voice edged with ice.

47

"Hold up a minute." Tyler lifted a hand. "Let's say we are on the cusp of a demon attack—a real one, and not just our board going haywire. Where do we go from here?"

"*We* don't go anywhere," Frost said. "Reverend Williams and I will discuss this, work out a plan of attack, and inform you when it's appropriate. There's also an entire department at Wellington dedicated to fighting demons, and we'll need to loop them in. Furthermore, unless you've forgotten already, *we* are supposed to be keeping a low profile. That doesn't change with this information."

The advice seemed innocent enough, but the guys practically *erupted*.

"You can't be serious," Tyler began, turning on Frost.

"No *way*," Liam put in, electric with heat. "Those demonology guys are useless—Zach can kick their asses sixteen ways to Sunday."

"And it's *my* family, *my* problem. Not Wellington's." Zach stepped forward, his hands also clenching into fists. "You had your chance twenty-some years ago, *Dad*, and you said it yourself. The demons are targeting me. Well, if they come here, I can take them—our team can take them. For good, this time."

"And how exactly do you plan to do that?" his father shot back. "You haven't even graduated yet. You may have some basic demon hunter skills because of what we did back at the parish, but it is not like your friends here have had any of that training."

"Then I can teach them," Zach said, without hesitation.

"*No.*" Reverend Williams spoke with finality, in the manner of parents everywhere who were used to getting their way. Not only parents, I suspected, but preachers accustomed to leading a flock of wide-eyed believers. I got the impression that not too many people crossed Reverend

Williams—even though something about this entire scene stank to high heaven. Something was going on here, below the surface, nagging at me like a piece of seaweed wrapped around my ankle. "Commander Frost is right. Your job is to get your classes finished and to stay safe," the preacher ended heavily.

"If not us, who?" Zach pushed, turning to Frost. "Fighting monsters is what we're *supposed* to be doing."

"But you haven't *graduated*," Reverend Williams repeated. He scowled at Frost. "What sort of backup do you have, beyond these five students?" He emphasized students like we were barely out of monster hunting kindergarten. "Are there any fully trained resources you can tap?"

"Actually, no," Frost bit back, his beard twitching in equal parts annoyance and dismay. "Given what happened last week and the new reports of paranormal activity, the calls have gone out to past students. But no one has yet responded." He grimaced as Williams threw up his hands in disgust. "I know. That's not ideal for a couple of reasons."

"Wait a minute," I interrupted. "I thought monster hunters were on retainer for life. Like, the academy gives them a ton of money *specifically* so they're at your beck and call pretty much forever."

Frost's jaw tightened, but it was Reverend Williams who responded. "Now you understand why it's a problem that they aren't responding."

Liam's expression had grown more thoughtful during this exchange, and he spoke with a frown. "Well, that's something we can solve, right? Can we track them?" he asked. "Is it that they *can't* respond or simply that they're choosing to ignore the academy?"

Frost shrugged. "At this point, nobody outside this room and a few highly placed academy administration types know they haven't responded. Either way, it doesn't bode well. If the graduates' cohort is willfully choosing to abandon the academy, that argues for disbanding the program."

"And if they're not responding because they're already dead, that also argues for disbanding the program," Tyler said, as Grim grunted a laugh. "What a mess."

Frost passed a hand through his shaggy hair, making it stand even more on end. "So, it seems you understand the problem clearly. I would suggest you keep any discussion of the issue to a minimum. I don't need to remind you that the walls have ears, nowhere more so than in a magic academy."

He grimaced, looking more irritated than tired. "Finish your classes, watch each other's backs, and keep a sharp eye and shut mouth. You run into Dean Robbins, don't give him any reason to look twice. Especially you." He said this last to me.

Beside me, Tyler bristled. "What's that supposed to mean? Nina's part of our collective now."

"Your collective?" Reverend Williams asked. His brows lifted as he took us all in with a gaze that had gone slightly sharper. "What's that, exactly? We didn't have collectives when I went through."

"It wasn't a thing back in our year, not while you were here," Frost said smoothly. "Think of it as an informal study group."

"Which started when?" Reverend Williams pressed.

I held my breath, knowing exactly what he was after. But Frost merely shrugged.

"Earlier this year—much earlier," he assured the man, shifting his attention to Tyler. "Still, we need to keep a low profile. We don't need anyone paying too much attention to the collective or the minor, especially if we will be tasked with a demon fight. Make sense?"

Tyler backed down. "Makes sense," he agreed, and the rest of us nodded along, none of us looking at each other too closely. The collective was way more than an academy study group, and Frost knew it...which meant he was trying to hide the truth from Zach's father. But why? Had he learned newer, even crazier information about collectives that he hadn't told us yet?

"A collective..." Reverend Williams said again thoughtfully, and I felt his gaze on me as Frost outlined the basics of the collective for Reverend Williams, keeping it all very surface. He should keep it surface. There were certain aspects of the collective none of us had fully understood prior to undergoing the ceremony. I'd thought I was simply throwing my hat into the ring both to help the guys out and accept their protection as well. It turned out to be a lot more complicated than that.

Whatever the situation, the reverend seemed satisfied. "Very well, then. I'm glad they have you looking out for each other. We should all do more of that."

The tension in the room remained palpable, and no one said anything for a moment. Tyler straightened, gesturing to me.

"Well, I don't have any classes left," he said. "I'll walk Nina to class."

"I think I should stay here," Zach said.

"No," Frost and Reverend Williams said at once.

"Shouldn't you be tending to your finals, to stay on the right side of this Dean Robbins?" Reverend Williams continued.

Zach frowned at him. "Since when do you know my class schedule? Or care?"

For the first time, a flare of real irritation rose in the reverend's fair cheeks. His vivid blue eyes narrowed. "I will thank you to keep a civil tongue—"

"Whoa," Liam said. He stared down at his phone. "Asshole alert. Text from Robbins, incoming."

Zach sighed with real feeling. "Speak of the devil, and he shall appear."

7

Tyler and Zach dutifully whipped out their phones and swiped them on. I didn't, because as far as I knew, Dean Robbins didn't have my burner number. Grim didn't pull out his phone either, but I didn't know if he knew how to use a phone, so there was that.

"What does he want?" Frost asked, distracted by whatever he was reading on his laptop.

"I don't know, but apparently, he wants it with all of us," Liam said. "One after the other too. I don't like that."

That made Frost sit up straight, his heavy brows bunching together. "Really."

He turned and gestured impatiently for Liam's phone. Liam obligingly handed it over, and Frost scowled down at it. "Tyler, Zach, Liam, Grim. Not Nina. It's probably another review of your actions during the Boston Brahmin altercation the other day—or possibly something to do with the protests on campus. He keeps it open-ended, of course." He handed Liam's phone back. "You'll need to be careful."

"Another game of divide and conquer," Tyler said. "And I'm up first. Aces."

"Well, your family is the super specialist," Liam gibed, and Tyler shot him a dirty look. Those two had been friends long enough that their jabs at each other ended up being more joking than insulting, but that never stopped them from trying.

Tyler turned my way, clearly dismayed. I shooed him off.

"I can walk myself to class," I assured him. "I'm uniquely skilled at walking. I've been doing it most of my life."

"I can go with her," Zach said. A zing of panic sliced through me, but I managed not to blush. Smooth and subtle, that was me. "Just give me a minute to finish up here with my dad."

"Actually, you and Matthew can take over my office," Frost said, surprising me. He had an office? "Grim and Liam —I need you downstairs."

"But I—oh," Liam started, breaking off when he realized what Frost wanted them for. The basement of Lowell Library had turned out to be a hidden repository for arti-facts that sent his nerd heart pounding. If Frost was looking for a way to distract the guy, he'd hit the jackpot.

"Fair enough. We'll see you outside." Tyler reached for my hand as Zach turned back to his father. I couldn't say I was unhappy to have Tyler to myself for another few minutes, and I welcomed the touch of his hand against mine as we exited the library and reemerged into the bright late-spring morning.

"I don't like that Dean Robbins didn't ask to see you," Tyler groused as we moved off the steps of Lowell Library.

I blinked at him. "Really? I've been on campus for barely a minute."

"You're part of our team. A big part."

"A team he doesn't know about. And from what Frost says, the less he knows about me, the better. Besides, the way you guys talk, he's nowhere near as skilled as Frost when it comes to monster hunting."

"Massive understatement," Tyler scoffed. "That guy wouldn't be able to identify a monster even if it was in the process of eating him. How he got to be in charge of our minor, I'll never know."

"Hey!" We looked up to see Merry Williams trotting our way, her arms filled with poster board and stakes, but her grin wide as she swung her ponytail back and forth. One of the few students I knew at Wellington Academy outside of the guys, Merry was a self-contained tornado, bursting with energy. I'd met her when I'd first come to campus, bowled over by her enthusiasm and the speed with which she talked, which was almost a superpower in and of itself.

She also was a fervent believer in the equality of all creatures on this planet, up to and most especially including monsters. Tyler took in her poster board and fixed her with as dark a look as he could manage, given that he was trying to hide a grin of his own.

"Merry," he said severely. "There is no protest scheduled on the monster quad today. You've got your dates wrong."

"These aren't for you, I'll have you know," she sniffed, giggling a little at the end of her otherwise stern set-down. She believed enthusiastically in her causes, but she wasn't going to let it stand in the way of flirting with the cutest guy at Wellington. I appreciated that about her. "You should let the monsters you keep captive in their underground lairs go free, but there are all sorts of oppressors on this campus. It makes my head spin trying to keep up."

He grimaced. "Do I want to know?"

"Probably not," she said, laughing over her shoulder as she whizzed by. "Nina, if you ever want to drop these guys for a real major, veterinary studies is the best thing you can possibly do! I'm serious!"

"Okay!" I called back, laughing as she sped on, her long legs eating up the sidewalk.

Tyler shook his head as he watched her, but he hadn't forgotten his mad entirely. He slid his gaze back to me. "I don't like this whole separation thing Robbins is trying. It's not going to work. He's worried about controlling us, but he's going to have to get over that."

I studied him more carefully. Tyler had changed in the few days I'd known him—partly because of me joining the collective, though we were all still working out the why of that. But the changes were definite and becoming more obvious. While I suspected he'd always been the life of the party, the natural leader in any group, he'd gotten stronger, more forceful. Physically filling out, yes, but more than that, developing a sense of command no one could fail to notice.

"Do you think Dean Robbins realizes you've leveled up?" I asked quietly, as if the walls really did have ears—along with the trees and walkways of Wellington Academy.

"Maybe," Tyler sighed. Then he winked at me. "Though I can tell you right now, he'd *never* guess why."

I flushed, remembering what had happened before Tyler's transformation—him and me and a bedroom that looked like a bomb had gone off in it by the time we were done. Even kissing Tyler had made the world legit shake around us, but actual sex...

As if following my thoughts, Tyler changed direction and tugged me into a shady stand of trees, a few steps off one of the neat cobblestoned pathways that wound their way through Wellington's campus. We'd barely gotten into the shadows when he pulled me close.

That was all it took. A swift and unmistakable surge of

need erupted within me, the way it did whenever I got too close to Tyler. His lips came down on mine, and I met him more than halfway. Lifting my hands, I tangled my fingers in his thick, dark brown hair. I wanted to practically crawl inside him, and I groaned with real need as his arms went around me. He pulled up the hem of my shirt and pressed his palms against the small of my back, a low growl starting in his throat.

"Nina," he muttered, kissing me hard. His strength surrounded me, his muscles tightening as he held me close. In fact, *everything* on his body stiffened in response to our embrace, and I dragged my mouth away from his, trying to catch my breath as the trees began to quiver around us in earnest.

"Do we have time?" I found myself asking, blood rushing to my cheeks a second later. Had I seriously just asked Tyler if it would be okay for us to have sex in public? Did I have zero boundaries now?

He stared down at me, his own breath an unsteady whoosh as he sighed. "Not if I have any hope of getting to Dean Robbins before he expels me, no. I don't know how you do this to me, Nina. But it's freaking amazing."

I couldn't help myself, I let my hand drift down the front of his body, tracing the shape of his shaft through his jeans. The trees shook harder, the breeze kicking up as several newly blossomed flowers scattered around us.

Tyler shivered, a gust of wind making the trees shake in earnest, and I dropped my hand away. "I don't know why you have this effect on me, either," I sighed. "I don't understand any of this."

"Well, that works out. Because we're going to figure it out together—and it's going to be *awesome*. I know it." He kissed me again, long and deep, before stepping away. "I've gotta bolt. If you want Zach to find you, just put your hand over the mind-blocking bracelet. He can track you then."

"Oh." I lifted my wrist, my brain scrambling with renewed awareness of tall, vampire-beautiful Zach, all dark eyes and pale skin and mirror-bright energy. "Right. Zach."

"Don't give him a hard time, okay?" Tyler chuckled, shaking his head. "With his dad here, he may be off his game more than usual, and he's kind of the sensitive type. If he's picking up on our weird collective mojo, he may not know how to process it all that well. Liam hasn't said anything to him about the energy transformation thing we unleashed bringing you in, and neither have I. You can bet Frost hasn't spilled the beans either. Not given how cagey he was being back at the library."

"Right," I said again, trying not to wince. I needed to get a handle on all that "weird collective mojo" like, right now. Because if Tyler thought I was going to have the same strange, wild connection with Zach that I felt for Tyler, he was out of his mind. I didn't care what wild-assed magic or ancient collective lore there was in the books at Wellington Academy, or how randomly attracted I was to Zach. It wasn't going to happen.

"You know, you're beautiful when you're fierce," Tyler said, startling me back to the moment. And with a final kiss hard enough to send the trees quaking in their roots, he was off.

I squared my shoulders watching him go. I *was* fierce, I decided. And no more strangeness was going to happen. Not with Zach, not with any of the guys. Like Liam, for example, and dear *God*, not with Grim. I was in Boston to find my mom's family. I was at Wellington to learn how to fight monsters. That's *it*. That was plenty.

Chasing those thoughts away, I lifted my hand to get a

better look at the bracelet. The guys had given it to me the night we'd met, after it had become painfully clear to me that one of Zach's abilities was that he could read minds. As long as I had the blocking bracelet on, I was safe from him hitting up my brain on speed dial.

Unless I didn't want to be safe, that is, like when the poor guy had been assigned as my babysitter to walk me across campus. Maybe that was what Tyler meant about me giving Zach a break. I should make it easy for him to find me, not force him to work for it. I was willing to go with that.

"Earth to Zach," I tried, slapping my hand tight against the bracelet to press it to my skin.

My mind exploded.

8

_____

"*Who is she?*"

Zach's father spoke with such patent outrage, my entire body vibrated. I ripped my hand away from my wrist. Silence swamped me once more.

I didn't hesitate. Emerging from the trees, I made a quick scan of the quad to make sure Tyler was nowhere in sight, then beat it back to Lowell Library, running at top speed. Fortunately, Tyler and I hadn't made it very far from the building, and I was up the steps and into the main portion of the library in a few minutes.

Zach and his dad were still going at it, their voices only barely muffled by the thick walls. They were talking about me, obviously, but I had no idea where Frost's office was, and I didn't trust myself to connect to Zach directly by putting my hand on the bracelet again. Would he be able to sense I was listening in? I didn't want that.

Following the sound of their arguing, I angled back toward the war room in the corner of the main chamber of the library. I stepped inside the room, its lights now shut off, and strained to hear Zach and his dad. They'd dropped their voices to a more circumspect level, and I narrowed my eyes at the far wall. Was Frost's office seriously right on the other side of our monster hunter war room? If I tried hard, I could hear someone breathing in there. No wonder he'd hustled Liam and Grim downstairs.

What sucked for privacy made my job easier, though. I crept forward along the central table, pausing as Zach's voice rose again.

"For the last time, Dad, it's not like that. I don't *love* her."

My pause graduated to full-on frozen as my eyes shot wide. Um, *what*?

"Don't treat me like an idiot," his father shot back. "The energy between you two is obvious. I don't need to be a mind reader to pick it up. Give me some credit."

"You were picking up on her relationship with *Tyler*. Tyler, who is my *friend*," Zach insisted, and I winced. Truth be told, I did have some unexplained and highly inappropriate energy for Zach. I just hadn't thought it was that obvious. "What kind of asshole do you think I am?"

My lips twisted with chagrin as his Dad snorted something I couldn't quite understand, then I edged forward again. My hip caught the side of the table, and I flinched as the books piled on the table shifted. I blinked, glancing down.

Holy crap.

The Apocrypha was *right in front of me*.

Ignoring the conversation in the next room as it dropped back down to mumbling, I grabbed the second book down in the jumbled pile of texts, sliding it out and onto the table, my breath coming fast. The Apocrypha. There was no way I could read it all, especially with the freaking lights off, and the thing was way too big for me to smuggle out. Still, I had to do something.

I flipped open the book and nearly hissed in dismay. Frost had said something about there being pages missing, but for fuck's sake—the center of *entire chunks of pages* had been cut out of the book, leaving only the margins, as heavily inscribed as an illuminated Bible. While the book was closed, you'd never know anything was wrong with it, but once you opened it, the destruction was obvious—and devastating. I flipped through several of those excised pages, seeing nothing, until I got to a section that was still intact.

I didn't waste any time. I pulled my phone out and snapped picture after picture, page after page, only stopping when my eyes fell on the words *sexual congress.*

Hello.

"You cannot have any relationship with her, Zach. Any. Not if you don't want her to—"

Zach cut his dad off with a snarl of rebuke I couldn't quite make out as I jerked my head up, but the pull of the pages in front of me was even more compelling than the argument next door. I angled the phone so I could read more easily and leaned close.

Each sacred collective shall be formed with the express purpose of creating a unit stronger than the separate parts—and the key is the sexual center of that union. The flower from which all power blossoms. With her intimate touch, the collective grows and thrives. Without her, it shall wither. When the flower is also the harbinger, her gifts shall pour forth as a great river, flooding the fertile ground of all she touches.

I grimaced so hard, I thought my face might freeze that way. Seriously, who wrote this? I scanned through more cringeworthy sexual references, then slowed when I got to a passage that ended at the bottom of a page.

Each member who receives the blessing of intimacy— emotional, physical, spiritual—from the center shall surpass all previous strength. The blessed center shall gradually build in power as well, lifting all members of the collective until such time as she will destroy—

I turned the page, and flinched.

The next thirty or so pages had been cut out of the book.

I groaned audibly. "Oh, come on..."

"No!" Zach's father cracked out the word so loudly, I leapt back from the book, the wall beside me practically vibrating. I swiped off my phone in a panic as a door banged open, and watched with wide, mortified eyes as the steam-rolling locomotive of Reverend Williams left the station and pounded his way down the long stretch of the main library chamber. I didn't know where he was going, but I was happy to not be in his path.

Silence filled the space behind him.

I glanced back to the book, then to the far wall. Was Zach still next door? Had his dad actually choked him to death? I closed the book as quietly as possible and returned it to the pile, then drew in a deep, shaky breath. I covered the bracelet with my hand, pressing firmly. Silence flowed back to me...but not complete emptiness. There was something else there, a presence in my mind I'd never felt before. It made my heart kick up a notch, my breathing go shallow and quick. I actually suspected my eyes were dilating. Still, there was no sound.

"Zach?" I whispered, saying the word out loud, though I guess I didn't need to.

His response was immediate.

"Nina? Where—oh my God, you're here. You heard all that."

"I didn't..." I began, but cut myself off as steps sounded from the room next door. A few seconds later, Zach swung into the doorway of the war room, his lean runner's body silhouetted against the light from the main library chamber.

"I'm sorry—" he began.

"I didn't hear much," I insisted, stepping toward him as he shook his head.

"Right," he said with a rueful laugh. "How'd you get back in here anyway? My dad would have an absolute coronary if he knew you were listening in on all that." He turned and gestured for me to follow him, looking impossibly cute even though his cheeks still burned with embarrassment.

As I emerged from the war room, he moved ahead, walking quickly. His long, swinging gait showcased his athletic body, his fair skin perfectly contrasted his dark hair. Then he glanced back to me with those beautiful, purple-hued eyes, which now glinted with self-deprecating warmth as I caught up to him. "What's your next class, anyway? Since I'm supposed to get you there in one piece?"

I tilted my head, recalling the dizzying list of class titles and locations. "It's in Cabot Hall, I think. And you better not tell me you're student-teaching animal husbandry practices too, or I'll drop the class immediately."

"From that, at least, you're safe," he laughed, then sobered as we moved into the hallway and approached the front door of the library. No one else was in sight, and he breathed out a slightly steadier breath. "Look, I'm sorry about my dad. And me. And all this."

I bit my lip. Probably not the best time for me to tell him I was a sexual flower that could give him superpowers. "You think your family demons got stirred up because I showed up on campus?"

He waved that off. "Not so much you showing up as my reaction to you showing up. And that's really what I'm apologizing for, I guess. My reaction to you. I thought I had it under control, but...apparently not. I'll get it back under control, though."

It was a perfectly reasonable comment—especially since Zach having a crush on me might result in me becoming demon fodder—but I still felt stung. "Oh. Well, good. I guess I should get to animal husbandry. Because that seems important."

He snorted. "It apparently is to someone high up in the academy, anyway. That class is a standard requirement left over from the turn of the century. We all had to take it."

I slanted him a look. "Which century?"

"The 1900s. Back in the day, there was a belief that some monsters could be rehabilitated, I guess for lack of a better word, put to good use as stock animals or whatever for humans."

We were off the steps of the library and moving toward the main campus by now, but I blinked at him in genuine horror. "You've got to be kidding me."

"I'm not. It sounds ridiculous now, but a lot of the things we did in the early 1900s sound ridiculous today. Think of it this way—if you could, say, catch a griffin and use it for your personal hovercraft or whatever, wouldn't you want to try?"

"No. I generally prefer not to be eaten by my pony."

"Which is why the practice fell out of favor relatively quickly." He chuckled.

It was a nice laugh, different from Tyler's. Quieter, a little sad in a way, almost a commentary on the need to laugh in the face of sorrow as much as an acknowledgment of the humor of the moment. I internally rolled my eyes at myself. Nobody spent this much time analyzing anybody's chuckle, not even on a college campus where there were probably fifteen studies going on right now to get to the root metaphysical source of laughter.

I tried to return to the relatively safe topic of Wellington's syllabus. "But we still kept those farm-friendly classes around, just in case?"

"Yep. They've proven to be some of the most popular and useful courses in the academy, especially when monster hunting fell out of favor. There are a whole bunch of animal owners who would like to enhance their livestock, cure the mystery illnesses of their favorite pets, and in general get along better with their four-legged friends. That class sort of allows folks to combine spell work and channeling with straight-up vet techniques."

"Like you can become a real-life horse whisperer."

"Yep and donkey, and cow, and chicken. You haven't lived until you've chicken whispered."

I couldn't help myself, I giggled. It was such a ridiculous idea that I could see how it would gain favor. But we were almost at the main campus, which meant we didn't have a lot of time.

"So, um, back to your demon curse," I began, and Zach shook his head with a sigh.

"Yeah, back to that. Bottom line—you're safe, Nina. I swear you are. The curse basically requires us to sacrifice the thing we love, and, well..." he gestured curtly. "You're safe."

I rolled right past that tangled, knotted skein of a woman spurned. "But you love the team, though. So does that mean the guys are at risk?"

"It could, but the guys—even you as part of the collective —I can handle. I mean, to Liam's point, we're all monster hunters. If some old-assed bunch of demons wants to come and try to take a piece of all of us, we can take them. Or at least..."

"Or at least that's what your plan was," I finished for him. "That's why you stayed at Wellington. You knew about

66

the demons, that they would eventually come calling. You knew you'd have to face them."

"I knew," Zach agreed. "I just didn't think it'd happen before we graduated. Like, I thought that would be the trigger." He trailed off as we came around the corner of Cabot Hall, then he stopped abruptly again in the middle of the cobblestone street. "Oh no."

I glanced over at him, instantly on the alert. "No way. They're here? Already?"

He shook his head. "I wish," he sighed. "So, that mind reading thing? It's got its downsides. Like a lot of downsides, especially right this second."

"What...?" I looked around, and then I noticed them. Three underclassmen girls, including the redhead from this morning, standing in a tight circle. They weren't quite whispering and pointing, but even I could feel the flow of awareness rolling from them toward us, a tangible thing. In fact, I *really* noticed it, far more than I would've expected.

"Is mind reading something you can catch?" I asked, then winced at the stupidity of the question.

Zach shot a glance at me, momentarily distracted from his fan club. "What? Why?"

"Eh, forget I asked. I don't need to be psychic to realize those girls totally have the hots for you." I watched as the flush crawled up his cheeks. It made him, if possible, even more attractive, and I fought the eye roll. Not a half hour ago, I had *kissed Tyler* with enough passion to rock the freaking trees. How was I possibly attracted to another guy so quickly? Even if he was a hot-as-blazes mind-reading demon hunter, with his tall, strong body, his dark, mysterious powers, and a mouth I wanted to—

"See, this is why I'm glad you and I are teammates, nothing more," Zach said, the husky assessment somehow urging on my out-of-control libido, not tamping it down. "It makes things a lot easier."

I met his glance, and heat sparked between us. Alarm bells didn't just start ringing in my brain, they practically lit up my entire neocortex. "Yeah, right?" I hedged, struggling not to sound breathless. I darted my gaze to the canoodling couple approaching us from the side of Cabot Hall. *Not helping.*

Zach pressed on, apparently oblivious to my mounting panic. "Like for instance, straight up. How do you feel about me? Because I bet I know. I bet I can tell you right now exactly how you feel about me. No mind reading required. So hit me with it."

I swung my gaze to his face again, my mind racing. He couldn't pick up on my feelings, right? He said he couldn't read my mind. Could he read my body movements? Were my pheromones pheromoning out of control in his general direction? Was I emitting some sort of weird emo energy I didn't even know I was? I mean, I was going to school at a monster hunting academy. I'd been designated a sexual flower of power. My bar for normal behavior had gotten all jacked up in the past few weeks. But seriously?

"I—I don't really know how I feel about you," I said finally. "I guess I just want you to kiss me."

The words were out before I could stop them, but that didn't stop me from trying. I slapped my hand over my mouth in an impressive cartoon act of horrified dismay as Zach spoke over me.

"I mean, like, we click, we're friends and all, but—"

He registered the disparity in our words a microsecond later. His eyes shot wide, and he turned to me, so surprised, it almost edged over into horror.

"You *what*?" His words sounded less surprised than

intense. Fiercely intense. I practically tripped over myself trying to walk my words back.

"I mean nothing like crazy or anything, but I—I mean, it's this totally random feeling I have, probably something that happened because of the, um, collective thing, but it's nothing real, nothing serious, it's just sort of crazy, and—"

And then he did the one thing that I would never have expected from the son of a preacher. Particularly not in front of three underclassmen girls with obviously sexual feelings for him and barely twenty minutes removed from us all hanging out with my *boyfriend, for God's sake.*

He kissed me.

9

Kissing Zachariah Williams was nothing like kissing Tyler. The trees didn't shake. The world didn't tremble. I didn't feel the urge to rip his clothes off and crawl inside his body. Instead, time stopped —and we were swept away.

I blinked, stumbling back. Zach stood facing me no longer on the center quad of Wellington Campus, but on a flat and desolate landscape, broken only by a lone, twisted tree that hunched over us, its branches spreading like a spiderweb of shattered glass. A burst of hot, smoky wind flowed over me, through me. I stared at Zach, his impossibly beautiful face flushed and intense, his eyes like purple fire. As he lifted his hand for me, I flinched back.

That only made his eyes burn more fiercely, and a moment later, I was blanketed by the heat of that fire. I gasped, sucking in the sulfurous wind, letting it fill my lungs, my mind. I had the sense of being taken, possessed, entirely *consumed* by a power so much bigger than myself, a power that held joy and sorrow, forgiveness and condemnation, life and death in its unforgiving grasp, spilling both out in equal measure.

"*Mine*," Zach whispered, and a fragrant darkness spread through me like billowing silk, reaching into the hidden places of my soul that I'd never known were crying out for the night. Above us, the sun flashed white around a pitch-black center, surrounding us in a corona of possibility, lighting us up like torches in the night.

I jerked away, gasping, and Zach did too, and everything returned to exactly the same place.

Exactly the same.

The girls hadn't moved from their position. The coed couple approaching us hadn't edged forward. Zach and I remained in our original positions, staring at each other, as if time had clicked back thirty seconds. It was as if the kiss had never happened at all. Yet my lips still tingled with its heat, my heart still hammered.

Something else had intensified too. Now I really did want to rip Zach's clothes off and crawl inside his body, but my reaction was a half step too late.

He stepped back, shaking his head like a bear coming out of hibernation.

"I'm completely sorry I did that," he finally managed. "No, that's not true. I *apologize* for doing it. I shouldn't have taken advantage." He spoke in slow and measured tones, as if he was fighting to express himself clearly. His hands were clenched, his jaw set, and he practically vibrated with tension. He looked truly upset, and a pang of dismay swept through me.

Hadn't he just gone all lord and master fire king of the universe on me? Had I made all that up? Clearly, there'd been some sort of disconnect. Because my body and soul were practically vibrating with need for this guy, for his heat, his fire, his danger, his gothic-angel anguish, while Zach was...*sorry*?

What the hell was wrong with me?

Before I could say anything further, the pretty redhead lurched forward, almost as if she'd been pushed by one of her friends. She lifted her chin and marched resolutely toward Zach.

He went completely still, and I could practically feel his shields going up, phasers on stun before she got within six feet of him.

"Mr. Williams?" the girl asked, glancing between us.

"It's Zach," he said with an affable smile. "You're Wendy, right? You were at class this morning."

"Wendy Symmes," she said, nodding quickly. "I just wanted to tell you that you were really great. I don't know that I necessarily believed in demons before today, it was more, you know, an easy course to add as an elective. But I sure believe now. And I believe you can help keep the world safe from them. I think that's really awesome, and I wanted to make sure you knew it. And to thank you."

Zach smiled, and even if he didn't have psychic persuasion in his tool kit, it was a very, very effective smile. It was also a smile that subtly but definitively put space between him and Wendy Symmes, creating a thick barrier of protection between them. But protection for him—or her?

"That's kind of you to share that with me," Zach said smoothly. "A lot of going to college is about learning new things. Now, your friends are going to ask you about this, and I know it's awkward for you to come right out and ask directly, but yes, I have a girlfriend. This is Nina, and she's totally lit me on fire."

To my utter shock, he reached out his hand, twining his fingers in mine as he spoke, and then gave my hand a firm squeeze. It didn't take a mind reader to know he wanted me to go along with the show. And strangely, almost horribly, I *wanted* to go along with it. I gave Wendy my most reassuring smile.

"Oh," she said, blushing prettily. "Oh, of course you do. I'm sorry, I didn't mean to—"

"You're sharing your thanks with me, which is more than most people are able to do. Your grace is a gift, and you'll go far in this life with it," Zach cut her off, unperturbed. Which was okay, because I was perturbed enough for the both of us. "Thank you."

"No, thank *you*," Wendy said, and then she broke into the most beatific smile. "Thank you so much."

And she wheeled around and practically skipped back to her friends—leaving me standing there on the sidewalk, *holding Zach's hand.*

He turned back toward me and half-heartedly gestured us on, presumably toward my class that I had now absolutely zero interest in attending. I couldn't even remember the name of the class anymore, let alone why I should find it.

I didn't move.

"You're going to be late," Zach said, but his eyes flashed dark and hot. *Late,* I thought. I wasn't sure I trusted time anymore. I wasn't sure I trusted anything.

"Ah...so I should let go?" I asked in a low voice.

There it was again. The flash of darkness, of possession, completely in opposition to his soothing, quiet words. "I shouldn't have put you in that position," he admitted as he released my hand, turned with great deliberation, and started walking again. I fell in line beside him, surprise and embarrassment bubbling up at his unexpected reply. I didn't know what to do with my hand now that it wasn't connected to his anymore, so I clenched it into a fist. "It wasn't fair."

"Fair to whom, exactly?" I asked far too bluntly, the question coming out before I could stop myself. "Fair to Wendy or to me?"

Zach winced. "Nina..."

"No, I'm serious," I said, a surge of unexpected anger fueling my embarrassment. Ordinarily, I liked to believe I could play things at least somewhat cool, but now my emotions were raw, unvarnished, stripped away by that fiery wind. "You told your dad there was nothing between us, we both agreed there wasn't anything between us, but then you kiss my brains out and go and make some poor freshman with a crush on you *think* there's something between us? How does that make any sense?"

His eyes flashed with an irritation that matched mine, toe to toe. "I was handling the situation without hurting someone who didn't deserve to be hurt," he countered, completely skipping over the brain-melting-kiss part. "Would you rather I just told her the truth?"

"Yeah, I would," I came right back. "Especially since I have no freaking idea what the truth is. I told you that I wanted you to kiss me, and you kissed me, and then you *apologized* for it and said *you* were taking advantage of *me*. I'm the one who asked you to kiss me, remember? How could you be taking advantage?"

He winced. "You don't understand."

"Okay, well, why not try explaining it to me? I'm the kid of a college professor. I've probably read all the same books you have. Whatever super-complicated reason you have for rejecting me, I can take it, I assure you."

Zach's eyes flared. "Whoa—look, it's not that at all.

You're making this sound like I'm choosing to not, you know, want to be with you. It's not that way at all."

"Really? Because it sure does seem like that." I couldn't seem to get control of my runaway mouth, or the jackhammering heart that seemed to be fueling it. "I heard you with your dad, Zach. Maybe that was wrong of me, but I was right freaking there. You told him you didn't care for me, so this question should be easy for you. Do you have feelings for me or not?"

"I *can't* have feelings for you, Nina, okay?" Zach lashed out, anger jolting off him. "I can't. The second I officially have feelings for you, like real feelings and not just wanting you so bad that you make my head want to fall off, you *die*. That's the curse I have—same curse as my dad and his dad before him. You think that sounds like a fun way for our relationship to go? News flash, I don't. I'm sorry I kissed you. I couldn't help myself. I've been wanting to kiss you since Tyler hauled you free of that land worm, God help me, and I'm going to continue wanting to kiss you until the friggin' day I die, which is going to be sooner rather than later if I don't get my act together and demon hunter the fuck up. So this is the *end* of this conversation, and I'll do my damnedest never to breathe a word about my feelings to you again."

He stopped short, and I realized that our argument had carried us all the way to Cabot Hall. He jerked his hand toward the building, as if there was any doubt that he was about to leave me again. "There you go," he said, his voice cold, uninflected. "This is where your next class is. And now I've got to—"

"Wait," I blurted, and it was a testament to how strong the not-something was between us that Zach stopped midturn and looked back at me. His eyes were blazing now, such a deep, dark purple that he looked otherworldly, and his fingers straightened and curled into fists like a fighter looking for something to slug. The emotion radiating off him was palpable, and so was the desire. I just hadn't seen it before, swamped by my own anger and embarrassment.

But there was something he needed to know, dammit. About me, about us. Especially if demons were about to hit campus.

"I can help you," I finally managed. "*Because* I joined the collective."

He blanched and shook his head. "Yeah, not hardly. I wasn't going to give Dad the satisfaction, but I do think our Run is what finally triggered the bastards. I don't care—I wouldn't change it for the world, but—"

"No," I cut him off. "Just listen to me. I read about it in one of Frost's books. The fact that I'm a girl joining a group of guys—well, it changes things. It means that if *I* choose to create a bond with you—me, not you—I can make you stronger."

"Nina—"

"I'm serious," I insisted. "It's not about your emotions for me, okay? I run the show. If I'm into you, and you need my strength, just by us...well, connecting, I can help you. I just have to be willing to create some sort of intimate bond. That's it. And I'm willing to do that. More than willing. Like, I'm willing a whole lot."

By the end of my little speech, Zach was staring at me, which didn't lessen the deep crimson of my cheeks or the wincing grimace I couldn't wipe off my face. Could this conversation seriously get any more embarrassing?

Yup.

"What are you talking about?" he asked, sounding slightly strangled. "You want me?"

Oh my God. "It's not about that," I heard myself reply as if

I were standing over in the corner, watching some other girl make a fool out of herself and feeling really, really bad for her. "I'm just saying that I think it's a way around your, um, curse. Even if you end up deciding that you don't feel anything for me, we can still take advantage of the side effects of me being part of the collective."

"Like Tyler has," Zach suddenly said, as if it all had finally come together for him. "He's stronger now, isn't he? You did that for him."

I blew out a heavy breath. "I did that for him, yes. And I could—I mean, if you wanted it, I would totally do it for you."

I tried really hard not to think about the fact that I was trying to sell someone on the advantages of getting busy with me. Making it all about how it would help *him*, never mind how much I just wanted to wrap my arms around Zachariah Williams and never let him go.

Ladies and gentlemen, Nina Cross, humanitarian of the year.

It didn't seem to do the trick, though.

Giving me a long, measured stare, Zach stepped back, looking more stressed now than I'd ever seen him.

"Well, thank you. That's great," he said, though it didn't look like he thought it was great. His face was even paler than usual, and his hands had never stopped their clenching and unclenching. Sort of like my stomach right now, which was currently squeezing the life out of a million and one butterflies. "I appreciate that. Really."

I nodded, feeling like an idiot. "Um, you're welcome," I offered, unaccountably trying not to cry.

And this time when he turned away, I let him go.

10

How I got through the next hour and fifteen minutes of animal husbandry, I couldn't say. Apparently, the teacher had saved the last few sessions of school for breeding behaviors, and I was in no mood to deal with any creature's primal urges other than my own. At least nobody looked at me strangely, or more strangely than usual. I didn't recognize anyone in this section, but they all looked way younger than I was. I suppose everyone thought that about underclassmen.

Class let out, and none of the guys were waiting for me at the door. That surprised me a little, and then I became annoyed at how much it surprised me. I was capable of walking myself back to my apartment, thank you very much, or even all the way to my next class. Up until a few short days ago, I had been capable of entertaining myself in an entirely new city, all on my own. I held up my phone to see if anyone had texted me, but no go on that either.

I felt unreasonably hurt, like I'd somehow been abandoned. I didn't like it. I'd gone for a long time without really thinking much about anybody else but myself or Mom. I'd gotten used to that, and I'd never minded my own company. So why was I now so unsettled at the prospect of being left alone for a minute and a half? I needed to hit my apartment again, regroup. Maybe pick up the search for Mom's family, at least until I got word of Zach's apparently imminent demon attack.

As if my feet were listening to my brain without requiring further direction, I found myself heading for the edge of campus. With every step, I felt better. Maybe I needed to reset. I should go through the notebook I'd made of Mom's past, try to make a few more calls. I should focus on anything that wasn't Wellington Academy. And clearly, given what had transpired between Zach and me, I could do with the time-out.

I reached the walls of the outer campus without incident and breathed in the fresh spring air. I could understand why Mom had loved it here so much, especially in the springtime. From everything I'd read, Boston winters were murder, so spring always felt like a bit of a resurrection. The city was certainly putting on a show this morning, with chirping birds and blossoming flowers, pollen heavy in the trees. I took a deep breath and let it out again, already feeling better. Everything was going to be okay.

Something snapped behind me.

I whirled, my hands going out in a defensive posture, adrenaline jacking into the stratosphere. A squirrel sat frozen on the sidewalk, caught midtheft, a bright, shiny treasure in his tiny paws. We stared at each other for a long moment while my heart rate stuttered and slowed, and I shook my head.

"Sorry, buddy," I muttered. "I guess I'm a little on edge." He dropped what he was holding, chittered something that sounded vaguely offended, and bounded off, leaving his treasure behind. I stared down at the small round object. It seemed odd lying there on the sidewalk, so I took a step toward it, then squatted down.

It didn't look like a nut and, now that I thought about it, probably wouldn't be a nut this time of year. I also understood the sound that had distracted me. The squirrel had clearly been trying to crack the thing open by smacking it against the pavement, but it was never going to have succeeded. I picked up the shiny metal pellet, turning it over in my hands. It wasn't ammunition, I didn't think, but I also didn't think it was a piece of jewelry. There was nothing to string it on a necklace, and it would've made for a pretty heavy necklace anyway. The gleaming gray metal bead was about a centimeter wide and perfectly round—was it pure silver? Nickel? It felt a little heavy for nickel, but...maybe?

No guns shot pellets like this, at least not modern ones —no way. I pinched the bead between my thumb and forefinger, but that didn't help me figure out what it was. Were there any monsters that were *attracted* to silver? I didn't think so. I knew plenty of them that were afraid of silver, including demons, so maybe this was a good sign. I stood and tucked the bead into my pocket, resolving to ask Tyler or maybe even Liam about it when I saw them next. Tyler was the leader of our little collective, but Liam was the Encyclopedia Brown of monster hunters. If there was something important about little silver beads, he would be the one to know.

I continued on, feeling better with every step I took away from the academy. Did I really need those guys? It seemed wrong to even think that, especially now that I'd joined their group, but we'd done that without really thinking it through, and there were ramifications still unfolding from that action. Dean Robbins certainly wasn't a fan of mine, and I didn't think Zach's dad liked me all that much either, though he'd seemed really nice at first. Maybe too nice?

Zach, on the other hand...

I sighed—I really didn't know Zach well enough to pass judgment on him. All I knew for sure was—I wanted him. A lot.

My cheeks blazed with heat as I passed one of the pocket gardens that were among the things I loved so much about Boston. A mother and her young son sprawled on a blanket in the center of the green space, rolling a ball back and forth to each other. The perfect May morning, with summer about to burst into full flower. Even if the academy wasn't for me, I loved it in Boston. I wanted to stay here.

I stepped into the next shadow, and a surge of unexpected fear washed over me. Something was lurking, out there in the woods. I looked back. The young woman and her child were still on their tidy patch of grass, but though the area directly around them was bright with sunshine, everything else had turned dark and shadowed. And that darkness was moving closer to the woman. She laughed, her child laughed, but though they were only about fifteen feet away, the sound seemed far too distant. Like a faint echo from a TV show heard through a window, not something right next to me.

My hands went out again, and I turned in a slow, tight circle. I couldn't see anything, but there was definitely something wrong here. Something evil? Something strange, for sure. Moving as slowly and carefully as I could, I slipped my hand back into my pocket and pulled the silver bead free. An image flashed in my mind, the face of the squirrel as I startled him. Had I been the one who'd startled him after all? Or was my new shiny silver pellet the problem?

Slowly, with barely a twitch of my fingers, I let the bead

drop to the ground.

Light broke through the trees. The shadows scattered, and I gasped with audible relief. The woman looked up sharply, the baby's head swiveling toward me.

"Sorry," I said quickly, taking a few more steps away while she stopped midreach for her little boy, apparently comforted by my apology and the growing distance between us. "Sorry. I just remembered what I forgot."

The words made no sense to me, but the woman laughed. "I do that all the time," she confided. "Comes with having a baby."

"Too much to think about and too little time," I agreed, still walking away, wanting to put as many steps between me and the innocent young family that I could.

"What are you doing here?"

"Geez!" I jerked away from the harsh demand, but somehow still made the wrong decision with my direction, because I ran smack into a wall of muscle, my hands pressing against the broad, unforgiving chest of Grim Lockton. I could feel his vital heat through the thin blue cotton of his shirt, and I whipped my hands away, stumbling back a step. I really needed to stop running into the guy.

"Why do you *do* that?" I demanded. "Keep sneaking up on me, I mean. Can't you announce yourself from a clear distance?"

He didn't respond to any of this, merely studied me with his maddeningly cool eyes, dark in the gloom that once more seemed to gather close. Grim's thick white-blond hair, pulled back in its heavy braid, seemed particularly colorless in the shadows, and his pale golden eyes were catlike as he stared at me. My heart now bounced and skittered around, as nervous as the squirrel I'd surprised, but it wasn't because I was attracted to Grim, thank God. He merely pissed me off.

Right?

"What are *you* doing here?" I finally responded to his original question as he remained silent. "I live off campus. I have a reason to be out and about. You don't. What do you want?"

The words came out a bit harsher than I intended, but I was super stressed-out and the guy *did* have a tendency to sneak up on me. Monster hunter or not, it was a little obnoxious.

Grim smiled thinly. "We're having lunch, and the guys want you there," he said. "Tyler's been trying to text you, but you haven't responded. So maybe stop acting like a startled little girl and let's go."

He turned, clearly heading back to campus, and for a half second, I thought about telling him to go screw himself. But that was uncharitable. The guys had stuck their necks out for me, protecting me from my monster entourage the best they could, getting me into actual classes. Even if I was going to skip town sooner rather than later, I at least owed them my solidarity in joining their little lunch meeting.

"Well, why should anyone bother texting if they can just send the mighty tracker of the collective to come fetch me?" I groused.

As soon as I snapped off the petty comment, I regretted it. Not because it was petty. I was a big fan of pettiness. But because it caused Grim to turn and lift a cool eyebrow.

"You like me coming after you?" he asked, the question deliberately challenging.

I rolled my eyes. "Oh, shut up," I muttered. I had enough random emotions and feelings rolling around inside me to even consider adding Grim to the mix.

But, of course, he didn't shut up.

11

————

"What happened back there?" he asked as we strode back down Back Bay's cheerful streets, his long legs eating up the distance back to campus. "You were scared."

"First, I was *not* scared, and second, how can you make any sort of guess about what I'm feeling? You don't know me. I could've been worried about my animal-mating exam."

I winced internally at my unfortunate choice of words. *Smooth.*

Grim didn't seem to notice. "No. It was something more immediate. Did you see something in that park? Did you feel something?"

I sighed, letting go of my mad. He really was only trying to help. They all were. I needed to relax and accept that, especially with as crazy as everything was.

"I did feel something, I guess," I admitted. "It started with the stupid squirrel."

He nodded, but it was the kind of nod that you could as easily give to somebody you thought was insane as to someone you were legitimately listening to. A flare of irritation spread through me, but I struggled to remain the bigger person, even if Grim dwarfed me by a hundred pounds.

"A squirrel made a noise. I turned around, and saw it was holding a little silver bead," I continued.

To my surprise, he glanced my way, lifting one bushy brow. "Lead? A bullet?"

"That's what I thought at first," I said, feeling vindicated. "But it wasn't any kind of bullet, I don't think. It was just a round bead, about a centimeter wide. I picked it up and walked maybe half a block more, all the way to the park where you found me. And that's when I started feeling weird. Like there was something dangerous out there in the woods."

He snorted. "There were about thirty trees total in that park. I wouldn't call it woods."

"Really?" I turned around, peering into the distance. The park had seemed a lot denser to me when I'd come up on it. "Maybe...but anyway, I dropped the bead and I felt better, got away from the park, then ran into you."

Grim grunted but didn't say anything more, and after a second, I continued. "What? Do you know what that bead was? We could go back—"

"No. Not now," he said curtly. "It could've been nothing. It could've been your mind playing tricks on you. That happens, especially when you first get to the academy."

"Really," I murmured. I hadn't thought of that, but it made sense.

"And if it was something important, it'll find you again," he said, refocusing my attention. "Silver is one of the most spell-friendly luster metals. It does what you tell it to do."

I wasn't gonna lie, that all sounded pretty cool, and at least I didn't feel quite so nutso anymore. Grim didn't seem nearly as impressed with my silver-bead story as I expected him to be, though.

"So, finding a silver bead on the sidewalk was no big deal?"

Another shrug. "No more of a big deal than anything else you felt. How you react is the important thing. And you are a monster hunter, or at least monster bait. You have been for a long time. That means you already know you need to trust yourself."

That was one of the longest lectures Grim had ever delivered, and a legitimate one, which I wasn't really in the mood to receive from a guy named Grim. Fortunately, he seemed to have used up all his words, and we spent the rest of the walk back to campus in silence. When he diverted away from the campus entrance I was most familiar with, I shot him a look.

"They're at the Crane," he said.

I jolted. Had it only been that morning that I'd been at the bar? It felt like far longer. "Why do you guys all like that place?"

"I don't," he said, and kept walking.

I rolled my eyes at his back. He wanted to play hard guy, that was all right by me.

A few minutes later, we approached a small collection of bars and cafés right at the edge of Wellington's campus. "Hey, I noticed this earlier," I said. "Where's the wall? Like, this is protected ground, isn't it?"

He peered at me a little curiously. "Why would you think so?"

"Well, I mean, like the Crane bar. It's for magic people, or at least magic-adjacent people, right?"

He didn't answer me directly, but gestured at the nearest storefront.

"They incorporated the wall into the street, the side-walk," he said. "Not optimal. There are too many entrances to the campus. Too many ways to break down its defenses. Only the innermost areas of the campus are protected now, the core. Anything with enough time and interest in breaching those outer defenses can get in."

I frowned. "Who thought that was a good idea?"

"Who knows what people think," Grim muttered, and I had to smile. I couldn't argue with him on that.

Tyler looked up as we approached the table inside the White Crane, though I noticed that the woman from this morning wasn't there. Instead, the heavily paneled dark interior came complete with a tough-looking, leather-clad bartender polishing glasses in the corner, her dark eyes sharp beneath her fall of cherry red hair, while Zach and Liam remained focused on Liam's tablet.

"Hey! You rock, my man," Tyler said, pounding Liam on the shoulder as he stood. He drew me close and gave me a quick kiss. I felt the familiar chaos, as well as a sudden, sharp burst of brutal self-control at its edge, and I drew back from my stereo awareness of both Tyler and Zach as Liam started talking.

"All right, I'll make this fast, because if what I've discovered about Zach's dad is right, we are about to get seriously slammed. Like horde central."

"Wait a minute." I narrowed my gaze at him. "You found something out?"

"We did. Right after Dean Robbins's little one-on-one with us, or one-on-all, thanks to Zach's mind meld. He flipped it on as soon as he got into his sesh with Robbins."

"I forgot to mention it to you," Zach told me, his manner way too cool and businesslike for my jangled nerves. "I meant to tell you to keep your hand on the band while we were with Dean Robbins so you could hear me relay what the others were experiencing. Sorry."

"It's no problem," I replied, all too aware of Grim's sharper glance at me as Zach and I studiously avoided looking at each other. The big guy needed to stop with the keen-observation thing he had going on. "So, what's the upshot?"

"The upshot is Dean Robbins is fully aware that Zach's dad and Frost met up today. He's also caught wind of a potential monster attack, though he didn't mention anything about demons in the mix. We managed to continue to appear ignorant, but it's obvious he didn't get his information from bugs in the library; otherwise, he would have known far more than he did."

"How can you be sure?" I pressed. "The administration could have been tracking you all this time without you knowing it."

"I don't think so," Tyler said. "It's possible, and we shouldn't underestimate him or whoever is pulling the strings behind closed doors at Wellington, but I think his information is coming from somewhere else. Because he's not focusing on demons, and I agree with Zach and his dad. I think that's coming next."

"But what does that mean, exactly?" I asked. "I mean, that's fine that we think we're going to get hit...but how do you defend against an attack that could strike literally anywhere?"

The guys didn't have an answer to that at first. I started playing with the anti-Zach bracelet on my wrist as we all sat, pressing my fingers over its smooth edge. A soothing, intimate awareness flickered to life deep in my mind. Was that Zach? Could he sense me reaching out to him?

Liam broke in with a sigh. "Honestly? Until we figure out

our strategy, we're going to have to play this really cool, or we risk getting the demonology guys all up in our grill. We don't want that."

"So everyone keeps saying," I countered. "But they're demonologists. They can't be that terrible at this, right? That's their entire purpose in life. Why wouldn't we want their help?"

Zach took this one. "Ordinarily, we would—even if they're mostly a bunch of overeager Cub Scouts who chose this major to play at being Buffy the vampire slayer without having to deal with the larger challenges of protecting a congregation. But in this case, we're not dealing with random demons looking to pick off a soul or two and cause havoc to spit in the face of God. That's the problem."

I leaned back in my chair, finally beginning to understand. "Your family demons are different."

He nodded, but he wasn't looking at me—or any of us. His gaze was fixed on the far wall. He remained quiet as the bartender approached and set a round of beers on the table, then launched in after she moved away. "My line has always generated hunters, but the family demon problem was hatched during my great-great-grandfather's life, around the mid-1800s. He was an itinerant preacher, and he traveled up and down the East Coast trading sermons for food and shelter. He also did healings, weddings, funerals, and the occasional exorcism, and he was always interested in what he called the tools of the trade—crosses, vials of holy water, icons, and medals. Most of it crap, but some of it..." Zach shrugged. "One day, he picked up the wrong trinket, a piece of jewelry that'd been possessed. He could feel the power of it, the strength of the creature within. It tempted him—took over his whole life, really. He wanted to destroy the demon within it for good, not let it potentially be set free by some other, weaker preacher. He was a proud man, but not an idiot. He knew he had to prepare first."

"He eventually set it free?" Tyler asked when Zach fell silent.

Zach's lips twisted. "He didn't. Because things changed with that trinket. He changed. Got stronger, or so he told his trusted confidants. Better at fighting, killing demons. Better at knowing what others were thinking."

"Spelled," grunted Grim. "Right into his blood and marrow."

"Had to be. Anyway, he kept the thing, settled down as a permanent pastor, and started a family. His wife got tired of him staring at a piece of jewelry she suspected was a holdover from his wild youth or a gift from an old girlfriend and threw it in the fire one night. They awoke to the demon erupting into life, and shit got real. The wife threw herself at the demon. My great-great-grandfather stopped her, but this obviously distracted him. The beast killed them both, then escaped. The town went up in flames—most everyone outside the house died, and those that survived were seriously screwed up. Like straight-up insane."

By now we were all staring at him, even Grim. Liam spoke first. "If everyone...oh. Outside the house."

Zach nodded, his lips settled into a heavy line. "My great-grandfather Theodore was seven years old. After all the commotion ended, he ran from the house, never breathing a word of what he'd seen. Eventually, he was identified as the preacher's son, but no one knew the truth of what happened, and he wasn't about to tell them. Theodore could already read minds, the gift within his father's curse. Eventually, he grew up, lived a wild life, and was drawn to the family business of demon hunting. He stayed a loner well into his thirties, thinking that would keep him safe. Swore he'd never have kids. Then he fell in love."

"The demon came back?" Liam asked.

"Him and some friends, yeah. On my great-grandfather's wedding night. They laid it out plain—if Theodore sacrificed what he loved, the demons would go away. If he tried to kill them, they'd set the whole county on fire. His wife didn't give him a chance to decide. She sacrificed herself— ran right at the beast, and they all disappeared. Theodore collapsed, was sick for days, but he didn't die. Nobody died. By the time the neighbors checked on the newlywed couple, Theodore was severely dehydrated and too weak to walk, and they nursed him back to health. No one knew what happened—just assumed his new wife had poisoned him and skipped town. He was so moved by the community's care of him, and so guilty over his wife's sacrifice, he agreed to stay on as their permanent pastor."

"But..." I swallowed. "That's the end of the line, then. If the demons showed up on their wedding night, that means there were no kids. Which means..."

Zach's gaze was on his hands. "The next summer, a woman showed up at my great-grandfather's church with a seven-year-old boy who she claimed was my great-grandfather's. Theodore was all set to chase them both out of town, when the kid read his mind."

"Burrrrn," Liam murmured. "Nature finds a way."

Zach laughed darkly, then slumped back in his seat. "Yeah, well. When it was my grandfather's turn, he tried to fight the demons, and an entire town burned again, though at least there were a handful of survivors that time, including my dad. But my granddad was pretty broken. He gave my dad up in an open adoption to the local preacher, vanishing into the shadows after that, with nothing but a letter to explain what lay ahead for Dad, to be opened when he turned fifteen. Dad was raised by the preacher's family and eventually took over their congregation. He read the letter, of course. He knew the history. He deliberately married a woman he liked well enough, but didn't love. They married early, and though he'd never shared this part with me, he apparently came up here for a year to learn some skills, visiting home only occasionally before returning in the summer...to find out his wife was pregnant."

"Oh, no," I whispered.

Zach's lips twisted. "Yeah. When the demons came, Dad fought them all through the night while Mom prayed. The church burned to the ground, though no one was in it, thank God. When morning came, the demons were gone. He'd thought he won. And he had—just not the way he'd planned. Mom..."

He blew out a long, tortured breath. "Well, they said it was stress. That she was young, and that late-term miscarriages weren't unusual in her family. It was still devastating, of course. How could it not be? Then I came along a few years later, and Jeremy after me. And here I am."

"Here we all are," Tyler said, steadily. "We'll take these bastards out, Zach. Once and for all. It's not like they can get through all of us."

"It's the Run that drew them, isn't it?" Liam asked, and I jerked my glance his way to find him studying me. There was challenge in his gaze, and curiosity too, like I was some puzzle he wanted to solve, piece by piece. "That set the stage."

"Maybe, but it also helped us," Tyler countered. "Nina joining the collective solidified our bond as a team. We all felt it, even if the demons did too."

"It was the Run," Zach agreed. "Things have felt off ever since then, and then there was the sunrise ceremony. The horde is amped. They're looking forward to the fight."

Liam snorted. "Well, they should be careful what they wish for."

Tyler refocused on Zach. "What do we need to know to get ready?"

Zach blew out a long breath. "Honestly? This could go a few different ways. The infestation could begin with a place possession—or it could hit students. Or, if we get super lucky, we'll get a full-on horde sighting, complete with claws, horns, and tails. There's just no way of knowing until it hits. But I think when it does arrive, we'll know. I have a feeling it'll be really, really obvious."

At that moment, the chimes of ancient, degraded church bells echoed across the campus.

12

———

"**S**hit. That's coming from Bellamy Chapel." Zach knocked over his chair as he lurched up from the table, and my fingers spasmed over the bracelet as he clapped both hands to either side of his head. My brain served up the image of the pretty redheaded freshman as he spat out the words.

"Wendy Symmes—freshman student in Newton's demonology class. She's in the chapel. I don't know why. This is—not good."

"Bellamy Chapel?" Liam protested. "It's boarded up."

"Not any more—*shit!*" Zach said, his eyes still screwed shut. "I've got a lock on her mind. I connected with her earlier today, and she's...a little intense. The line between us is still open. She's hurt—fell, I think. She's not in a good place."

"Go," Tyler ordered, all of us getting to our feet as Zach raced out the front door. Tyler threw a pile of money on the table, gesturing to the bartender, who watched him without moving, as if this sort of thing happened all the time. "We may be back, we may not—keep the change."

Zach was already hauling ass across the street by the time we emerged from the bar. Grim raced after him. Tyler checked his pace for a half second, turning to me, but Liam shoved him forward. "We'll follow you," he said, pulling his bag around. "Go."

Tyler didn't need to be told twice. He turned back to Zach's trail, his entire body seeming to light on fire as he bolted forward, arms pumping, legs churning as he sped down the cobblestone street.

Liam barked a short laugh as he watched him. "Damn, that is some impressive amplification you rocked him with," he said to me. "Are you guys writing all this shit down?"

"We haven't really had time for journaling," I retorted, squinting as Tyler disappeared around the corner. "And how can Zach read minds from across the campus? How is that a thing?"

"I noticed that too—come on, we need to catch up." We started moving, picking up the pace as Liam yanked something out of his pack and waved it at me. "But Zach's not the only one with superpowers, yo."

He ripped the small container open without breaking stride, his grin going wide. "Go," he said, but I understood it wasn't an order this time so much as the name of what he was currently squeezing out of the snack tube, shaking his head hard as he swallowed it down. He turned to hand off the remainder of the packet to me. "Like a caffeine or sugar jack, but with an extra kick. It'll help you keep—"

"Got it." I took the packet willingly and squeezed some of the chocolate-flavored paste into my mouth—instantly feeling the jolt to my system. Liam and I both lurched forward as if we weren't quite sure of how to use our legs, but after a few windmilling steps, we settled into a stride that was about three times faster than any speed I'd reached before. I shot him a look, wide-eyed, and his grin told the story more than words ever could. Liam had done a ton of research to fill up that backpack of his, and I had no doubt these little packets were not something you would find on the shelves of the local convenience store.

We raced on, the campus falling away like a dream as we pounded through it. I had the vague sense of students watching us with curiosity or surprise. Either they hadn't heard the church bells ring or they didn't know the significance. The crowds thinned out considerably as we got through the main quad and turned toward the older section of campus, where Bellamy Chapel was located. By the time we burst into the courtyard of the old church—now bathed with sunlight and looking like a charming country idyll, not the site of some dire demon attack—no one was in sight. We slowed to a trot, then stopped entirely in front of the chapel.

"Where?" I gasped, belatedly realizing my lungs were heaving as Liam gestured to the front door.

Liam turned to me and gestured with his fingers over his left wrist. I immediately understood, and covered Zach's bracelet with my hand. Once again, I was flooded with images—and more this time. Zach's calm, reassuring, almost mesmerizing voice sounded in my ears, as the images he saw flickered to life inside my mind.

"You don't have to do this," he said, power crackling beneath the easy declaration. "Fight me, if you want to fight. Leave the girl alone."

I shot Liam a startled look as a guttural snarl erupted from deep inside the chapel. Liam nodded me forward, and together, we walked several careful steps toward the front door. It had been practically wrenched off its heavy hinges, and was now hanging open.

"Oh, your fight is coming, boy," Wendy said, only she

didn't sound like Wendy, certainly not the girl I'd met earlier today, bubbly and self-aware, the prettiest girl in the room. This Wendy was tortured, low, and angry. And a dude.

"So I keep hearing. Maybe you should run back to your masters and tell them we're ready." We stepped quietly into the chapel, startling a brace of mice trying to make their escape. They reversed direction and scampered away, clearly terrified.

"Like your *daddy* was ready?" Wendy sneered. "Because he wasn't. He still isn't. We know he's run up here to warn you. So sad about Samuel. But there's always a sacrifice. Just maybe not the sacrifice you want it to be."

Zach's response lashed across the room, all the more unnerving because it was delivered in the same low, controlled monotone. "You will not say that name again, or I will rip you apart."

Now it was Liam's turn to look at me with some surprise. Apparently, this type of declaration was unusual for Zach. I could only guess that Samuel was the name Zach's parents had given to the baby who would have been Zach's older brother. The unborn child lost when Reverend Williams had attempted to take on his family's demons. I wondered if the demons knew about Zach's younger brother, Jeremy, living a normal life, unaware of the family curse. If Zach failed...would his life be ruined as well, along with the lives of everyone he loved?

Either way, we weren't in some tent revival in northern Georgia. We were in Boston, Massachusetts. Demon possessions were not a good look for Wellington Academy, and they were in particular not a good look for Wendy Symmes, whom I could see through Zach's eyes.

Liam and I breached the side door of the chapel, moving

slowly. And I got my first good look at Wendy, unfiltered by Zach's perception.

Zach could have a future in Photoshopping. In his view, even under duress, Wendy still remained the young, vibrant coed she'd been a few hours ago. But the reality, or at least the reality I now perceived, was vastly different. Where before her hair had been a bouncy rich ginger red, perfectly highlighted to catch the sun, now it was lank and greasy, her skin sallow as she stood with her feet planted wide, her shoulders hunched. She stared out at Zach with hooded, sunken eyes, her head rocking slowly, as if suspended from a string that was constantly being tugged to and fro.

I took an errant step, and a board creaked beneath me. Only the slightest sound, but it was enough to draw Wendy's attention. Wendy or whatever was inside her.

She turned her head toward me, the crackling sound of her bones beneath her skin making my skin crawl.

"So, it is true," the demon within her sneered, delight threading through the words. "The harbinger has come. Oh, they're going to *love* that."

"You don't have to do this," Zach said again, only this time, his words were met with a hideous guffaw on the part of the demon, as Wendy threw her head back and laughed.

"I don't have to do anything," she agreed. She smoothed her hands down her body, a grotesque caricature of a young woman assured of how good she looked. "A nice, fresh body like this one, unspoiled and unbroken? The things that I can do to a body like this, a mind so easily shattered."

In that moment, Wendy convulsed, her head snapping up as her eyes flew wide.

"Mr. Williams!" she pleaded. "Zach, you have to—"

She drew in a harsh breath. When she spoke again, the voice had changed completely.

"I like it when they beg. Don't you? Or, no, that's right. Never have you taken of the flesh promised to you by your blighted birthright. Never have you dipped your bursting cock inside a right and willing well..."

"*Enough*," Zach said, and the temperature in the room seemed to drop by twenty degrees.

"Zach..." Liam interrupted, his voice low and soothing. And I instantly got the impression something had gone wrong. "You're good, man. You've got this," Liam continued.

"He's got it, but he doesn't know who he's up against. Not really." Wendy's dark inhabitant smirked. "You've been dealing with the most pitiful of the horde up to this point, veritable children caught outside after bedtime, too dumb to know when to quit. Has that made you confident, Zachariah, like it did your father? Are you the Big Man now with all your academy training, too afraid to even enjoy the bounty of all that lies before you before it's ripped from your grasp? Such a waste."

Once more the demon drew its hands down Wendy's body, its fingers curling around her collar, dragging it down to expose her neck and collarbone, the soft curve of her breast. Tyler shifted on the other side of the room, but the demon inside Wendy only had eyes for Zach.

"The rest of us are not so stupid," she crooned. "We come prepared to use the chattel that has been given to us. It's your time, Zachariah. Your time to give us what is duly ours. The whole of the horde knows it."

With that, Wendy tilted her head back, her mouth opening wide. Her peach-glossed lips parted at an unnatural angle, and then continued to stretch. Something shifted in the gloom, a puff of mist that seemed to emanate from her throat.

"Look sharp," Tyler said, and the guys all reacted, their

hands going up, their stances widening. I had no idea what we'd do once we all assumed the jumping jack position, but I obligingly lifted my hands as well. Never let it be said I wasn't a team player.

"No," Zach murmured, the word barely audible, but it seemed to resonate through the room, shifting the air in the space. "You cannot. You dare not."

"With all of us fixed on you now? You'll find there is no end to the things we are willing to dare, preacher boy." Wendy spat.

No, seriously—she spat. From her mouth emerged a horde of flying creatures, each as big as a human hand, horned and winged and clawed, spewing out into the chapel in a rush of screeches and howls.

"*Scati!*" Zach shouted.

They attacked.

13

The tiny flying demons scattered to the four corners of the room and immediately attacked Liam, Tyler, me, and Grim. But even as I threw my arms up in front of my face, my mind spinning with the fact that I'd never fought a demon before, I realized the small creatures weren't attacking Zach.

I dimly registered how bad that likely was, then they were on me. I dropped to the ground, grabbing my knife, but Liam was right there, knocking the knife out of my hands and replacing it with a silver cross, only not your ordinary silver cross. This one had spikes sharpened on each of its ends, and I flipped it around, the long end serving as a blade worthy of Wolverine. Liam spared me only enough time to grin, then he whirled away, slashing at his own flying horde.

I slashed and hacked as well, but I had to get to Zach. Because now Wendy had gotten much closer to him, and he stood stock-still, his hands up. A curious radiance surrounded his body, as if he were standing in a flicker of sunlight, though no sun had reached the inside of this building in generations.

I'd barely made it through the first wave of creatures when Wendy leapt for Zach—something I'd never witnessed before. The battering array of the creatures fighting us was horrifying enough, but Wendy didn't so much attack Zach as *engulf* him, flowing around him, her hands spreading, her arms lengthening, her body stretching out long and thin and flat to wrap him up in a mounting tide of darkness. In my fighting fury, I'd taken my hand off his bracelet, but now I hit the floor, rolling into the pews, and grabbed the bracelet tight. I needed to see what Zach saw. I needed to understand.

What I saw rocked me back against a wooden kneeler. Zach still saw the Wendy he knew, but she hung as limp as a rag doll in the hands of a creature one and a half times her size. Great horns curled back from a broad forehead, and thick muscles bulged from neck to shoulders to beefy, corded arms to the meaty paws that held Wendy's body. Held it and pierced it through, blood dripping down now, pooling beneath her.

"This piece of meat is *dead*, Zachariah. She's not enough to serve as a sacrifice. She hasn't *earned* it."

"You don't have to do this," Zach said for a third time, irritating the crap out of me. *Seriously, that's all he has?* I scrambled up to see him, furious that this was all he was going to offer this creature, the sum total of his verbal game—

A horrific crack sounded above us, and the demon jerked up his gaze, clearly surprised. Zach shot forward. His hands swept out, his face stretched into his own snarl, and with a vicious swipe, he reached out and yanked the body of Wendy Symmes out of the demon's grasp, holding it close.

As I watched in horror, every piercing in her body, every defilement, faded from her and reappeared on Zach. Suddenly, it wasn't Wendy with sallow skin and matted hair and dozens of puncture wounds and bruises, it was Zach. She remained perfect and pristine, while he took on her injuries as his own.

In that moment of surprise, the horde of flying demons scattered, and all three guys moved in perfect symmetry. Grim barreled into the demon from behind, while Liam and Tyler positioned themselves in front of it, their hands up high, gripping their weaponized crosses and driving them down into the creature's upper chest.

Another resounding crack sounded above us, and the demon howled. It staggered backward, only to fall over the beast that was Grim. As it sprawled to the side, Grim plunged his own cross into the creature's gut, then wrenched it free, an arc of gore spewing up out of the demon's belly. With a final furious snarl, the demon disintegrated into a pool of greasy ash and smoking entrails.

Silence hung in the room, not even the mice daring to breathe.

"That...I guess went well," Tyler began as I lurched forward.

"*Zach,*" I managed, falling to my knees beside his body, still wrapped around Wendy's.

"Hang in there, my man, hang in there." Liam dropped beside me as Tyler disentangled Wendy from Zach's grasp and pulled her away.

Wendy's eyelids fluttered, her lips parting as she finally gave voice to her words. A quick startled muttering of the

Lord's Prayer floated around us as Tyler stood, lifting Wendy easily in his arms.

"I'll get her out of here," he said, and without another word, he turned and strode out of the building. I dimly understood that he was doing what needed to be done, that he was looking at the larger picture. But all I could focus on was Zach.

Zach, whose wounds weren't getting any better, whose breathing grew ever shallower, even as Liam put his hand over his forehead and started murmuring the Lord's Prayer. But I knew it wasn't enough.

Grim crouched beside me, his mouth at my ear. "You don't have to like it, but you know what to do," he growled, the words low, reluctant, and feral, sounding like the last thing he wanted to say. "You want to help him? Then act. Now."

I turned to him, my eyes wide, totally confused. "What?"

But Grim had already moved away from me, executing a sideways shuffle that looked almost animalistic and took him all the way to the pile of refuse that was what remained of the demon. He stuck his head close to the entrails, inhaling, that sight so disturbing that I wrenched my gaze away and back to Zach. His eyes were open now, but unseeing, and Liam's voice had risen slightly, the only outward sign of his distress.

Grim's snarl echoing in my ears, I remembered the Apocrypha, the painfully awkward language hinting at the power I brought to the team as a female, a harbinger. Tyler had leveled up after we'd had sex—but I wasn't going to jump on Zach as he bled out in a chapel. There had to be some sort of halfway point that would still be effective.

I leaned forward and grabbed both sides of Zach's face, then pressed my lips to his.

Time stopped.

14

This time when we kissed, Zach and I didn't end up on a barren plain, buffeted by sulfurous smoke. Instead, we sprawled in a sea of satin sheets, my hands going out from underneath me as I fell heavily over his trembling form, spread-eagled awkwardly on the enormous bed. He was on fire, but there was no longer a mark on him, and I drew in a shaky breath as I took in the full magnificence of his body. Everything was sculpted almost to perfection, lean muscles rippling down over his arms, chest, abs, and farther—

I drew in a sharp breath as Zach's shaft slipped free of the covering sheets, as perfect as the rest of him—but then Zach groaned, and I ripped my glance away to focus on his face. Definitely his face. His face was much safer.

"Nina," he managed. His eyes flared wide as he took in our surroundings—the bed, the sheets, the satin curtains ringed around us. "No, no, you can't be here. *We* can't be here—"

His entire body seized, and I slipped again, face-planting into his chest. The scent of burning embers swamped me, and I scrabbled up, realizing belatedly that I was naked too. Then Zach's arms went around me, hugging me tight as he flipped me over. It was the most natural thing to do for me to arch beneath him, my body lifting to mold itself to his. Heat arced around us, crackling with manic intensity, and Zach's eyes blazed with purple fire as he leaned forward to plunder my mouth.

Mine, he groaned, or I thought he groaned. The word seemed to manifest as a physical thing around us, ripped from the depths of his soul. I felt an answering fire leap up within me, and I gloried in the darkness of his cry, the fierceness of that single claim. I didn't understand it, but I didn't need to understand it. All I needed to know was that I could give Zach strength and he was willing to pull that strength from me, demanding it as if it was his birthright—as if I was his now, forever, and always, and no one would dare to suggest otherwise.

He breathed a deep, ragged sigh, and I felt his shaft press into my belly. A wild, desperate need erupted within me as Zach fixed me with his wide and desperate gaze, equal parts need and horror.

"I can't do this," he panted. "You'll die."

"I'll die if you don't," I heard myself gasp back, an undeniable need for completion filling me with a longing I'd never experienced before. This was wrong, this was dangerous, this was *not* the time—and none of that mattered as Zach groaned again, his entire body shuddering as he kissed me hard, sure, lifting his body away and shifting down those precious few inches—

The room fell away.

With a jolting thud, we were back in Bellamy Chapel, my heart racing, my body frozen, my lips still pressed against Zach's. A chill raced through me as I jerked back from his bloody battered face, and I stared down at him as he lay on the stained and grimy floor. His eyes moved beneath his closed lids for a second longer, his mouth twitching.

"Hey, that worked," Liam announced beside me, way too loud. "He's better. Do it again." Ignoring him, I sat back on my ass, lurching to the side as Zach bolted upright. He pushed Liam's hands away from his face.

"I'm okay—seriously," Zach said, peering around as I gaped at him. He exuded straight-up, normal Zach in the midst of wide-eyed confusion, with not even a hint of the fiercely intense guy who'd been damned near about to... wait, what had actually happened just now? Images converged in my mind, running together in a sea of heat and satin. Had I...had we...?

"What happened to Wendy?" Zach asked, further scattering my thoughts.

"Tyler got her out," Liam informed him. "She looks in way better shape than you do, for the record."

"Thanks," Zach said drily. He lifted a hand to his forehead, and I realized it was still shaking.

I cleared my throat, going for casual. "Ah...what exactly was all that? Like, what just happened? Here, I mean."

Zach didn't seem to notice my confusion, though Liam shot me a curious glance.

"That was two levels of infestation," Zach said grimly. "Congratulations, you've passed the first half of your semester in one morning. The small demons, the *scati* is what we call them, those are generally place demons. They infest buildings, rooms, basements. They're the creatures responsible for knocks in the walls, creaking staircases when no one is there, and that scattered tap-tapping of running overhead. Vicious little bastards, but they don't really hurt you. They're mainly there to distract you from what's really going on, the deeper evil that's leaching into a place. They're sort of like flies and can sometimes show up that small. You ever walk into a house that's teeming with flies, you know that's probably not a good thing." He shook his head. "I'm babbling, sorry. Bottom line, they were part of the problem, but not the big issue. The big issue was—"

"The big scary horned demon that had its spikes in Wendy? That the big issue you're concerned about?" Liam put in.

Zach blinked at him. "You could see that? Normally, you see only the afflicted."

I held up my wrist and dangled the bracelet. "We all could see it if we were linked up to you. Did you recognize it? It seemed to know who you are."

"We've got company." Grim's sharp voice sounded from several feet away. He no longer hovered over the remains of the demon, but stood at the front door of the chapel.

"Who?" Liam asked, moving to help Zach stand. He scowled down at the demon corpse. "Yo, this thing isn't disintegrating fast enough. We don't need anyone to see me get rid of it. Who's out there?"

His question was destined to go unanswered, though, as Grim slipped through the door and out into the sunshine.

"Helpful," I deadpanned.

"I'm fine. Really, I'm fine," Zach said again, shrugging off Liam's aid. "I should try to look as normal as possible when we go out, you know?"

"Good luck with that," Liam said, but he let Zach take a few steps until he faltered again. As he listed to the side, Liam posted up to his right and I stepped to his left. I reached out to hold Zach's hand as if it were the most natural thing in the world, and Liam coughed a quick laugh.

"Whoa," he said, leaning forward to peer around Zach at me.

"What?" I frowned at him.

"Your touch—it was like a current of energy going through me. You felt that?" Zach asked Liam, still seeming the wondering neophyte and not the hard-and-sure demon-hunting lover he'd been...wherever we'd been. *Had* I imagined all that?

"I felt it," Liam confirmed, studiously looking forward, and not at either one of us anymore. "You guys have definitely amped up your connection after that little mouth-to-mouth, which is something to keep in mind going forward, for all of us. How're you feeling now, my man? Better?"

"Yup. Better," Zach said, though I winced at the wheels that were obviously spinning in Liam's mind. I suspected he was making way too many connections for his own good, and if I ever found where he was journaling about all this, I'd probably need to set those pages on fire. "I feel really good, actually."

"Great," Liam announced. "Then you can feel good all the way out the front door while I clean up the mess you made."

Liam let go while Zach squeezed my hand harder, and I shelved all my questions and held on for all I was worth as we made our way out of the chapel into the bright sunshine.

Grim had been right. There was now a small clutch of students in front of the chapel, gathered around a remarkably radiant-looking Wendy, whose eyes were fixed on Tyler like he was a superhero. As far as I was concerned, he kind of was a superhero, but my strange and screwed-up feelings for Zach notwithstanding, Tyler was *my* superhero. I narrowed my eyes at Wendy as we approached, and Tyler looked up.

"Oh good," he said with the overbright smile of someone who was about to spin a line of complete bullshit, his words carrying over the suspicious-sounding creaks and whooshes from the chapel behind us. "I was worried that fallen timber was going to give you more trouble. Are you guys okay?"

"Couldn't be better," Zach confirmed. He dropped my hand, but not before trailing a long, sensual finger down my palm. My entire body electrified with sudden need, and I jerked away from him as he continued talking, calm as you please. "I'm glad you got Wendy out."

"God, *Tyler*, you were amazing," Wendy said, with such fervency that I found myself blinking with a whole new spurt of confusion, wondering what she'd experienced that I'd missed.

She looked around as if noticing her audience for the first time. "I was just being stupid, I guess," she said. "I don't know why I had the weird compulsion to enter the chapel, but I couldn't get it out of my head after this morning's demonstration and when I got here, the door was, like, standing open. I figured it was a sign, you know? I thought I'd take a peek around and see what it really looked like inside. It seemed like it had been really pretty at one point, and I was sad that nobody else was there to pray inside it anymore."

"That's very compassionate of you," Zach murmured, and she lifted startled eyes to him, then colored.

"I'm so sorry," she said. "I knew you'd tell me to stay away, I wanted to see it. I went inside, and it looked like it'd been a sweet little chapel at one point, and then...I don't know. I got lost in the shadows, all turned around. I must have bumped into something. I remember falling, like there was a hole in the floor. Did you see a hole?"

"There hasn't been maintenance on that building in

probably fifty years," Zach said, which didn't exactly answer the question, but Wendy didn't seem to mind. She widened her eyes.

"Oh my God, so are you okay? You look really beat up." All eyes turned to Zach, which wasn't really fair because he was looking a hell of a lot better than he had inside the chapel. He laughed.

"I hurt my pride more than anything," he said easily, and everyone around us seemed to relax another notch, whereas I remained amped to the max. I thought again about Zach's ability to read minds, and about the hot-as-hell guy wrapped up in piles of red satin sheets, looking like he might eat me alive and have me suggest he help himself to seconds, and schooled my face to remain neutral. Zach couldn't read my mind when I was wearing the warding bracelet, I reminded myself. I just needed to keep from giving my thoughts away more obviously.

Zach shifted beside me, sending me a sharp glance. A flicker of fire seemed to reach out to me from him, and I froze. Bracelet or no bracelet, could he read my thoughts when we were touching like this? I felt a rush of embarrassment rise in my cheeks and was grateful when he didn't seem to react.

"So, what did you see in the chapel?" one of the students asked Wendy. "Was it super creepy or just, you know, old?"

"I..." Wendy's eyes fluttered again, and her smile brightened. "It was mainly old, not creepy. Sad more than anything."

A general wave of agreement filtered through the group. It *was* sad, everyone seemed to agree.

"Some old buildings just need to rest," Zach said, and there were more nods, the Wellington Academy students happy enough for an explanation they could understand. A way to connect the dots that didn't look like a tangle of silly string.

"Still, you could have been really hurt," another student said. He stared uneasily at the building, and there was something about the way he regarded it that wasn't quite right. He seemed less dismayed than excited. "Monster hunters," he muttered darkly.

"Well, we should get going," Tyler said, standing and reaching for Wendy. She slipped her fingers into his hand like a princess and allowed him to pull her upright.

"Thank you again," she said breathily. "I was so scared, and so grateful when you showed up...I mean you and Zach..." She broke off, and I had to work harder to hide a smile. Her mind was no doubt struggling with what exactly had happened in the chapel. I wondered briefly if that was going to be a problem.

Liam chose that moment to come striding out the chapel door, looking supremely pleased with himself and fairly crackling with latent energy.

"Hold up a second—it's Wendy, right?" He pulled a bottle of water out of his bag. "Take this. You're probably a little dehydrated."

Wendy took the bottle gratefully and checked the seal, clearly satisfied with its pristine condition, then cracked it and took a deep draft. She sighed with genuine pleasure.

"Oh, that is better," she said. "Thank you."

Liam gave her a broad smile and hitched his backpack higher on his shoulder. "It's what I do."

We walked together as a group back to the main campus, with only Tyler and Zach peeling off for Fowlers Hall, the guys' dorm. Zach muttered something about needing to get changed, while Tyler offered to make sure he made it without passing out. Grim, of course, had already slipped away into the shadows, which left me and Liam accompanying the students to the center of campus, where they all dispersed happily enough for other destinations. When we were alone, I gave him a shrewd glance.

"So...what was in the bottle?"

He laid a hand on his chest, his river-stone eyes filled with mock indignation as his lips twitched, trying to smother a grin. "What are you talking about? I would do nothing, *nothing* to artificially enhance the experience of another student here at Wellington Academy. That would be wrong."

I snorted. "She won't remember?"

"She'll sleep like a baby and be amazed at her strength and bravery in entering a dilapidated old building on campus and coming back out virtually unscathed," he said, the broad smile finally breaking through. "She's really quite impressive when you think about it."

"Then I'll try my hardest not to think about it," I said. We'd walked only a few more steps when Liam's phone rang. He looked down at it, frowning, and I shooed him on.

"I'll catch you later," I said. "That was pretty cool what you did back there, and the performance supplement you had in those little packets is amazing."

"Somebody should really patent that," he agreed absently, lifting the phone to his ear as he turned away.

I watched him go, my right hand stealing over to my left wrist almost of its own volition, tracing the delicate line of the warding bracelet. If I pressed my hand to it and brought to mind the images of Zach and me together—would he remember it too? Was the line between our minds now open for him to connect with me, like he had with Wendy all the way across campus? She'd only had a crush on him, after all. Zach and I had kissed. More than kissed, we'd—

"Ms. Cross. Shouldn't you be in class?"

I wheeled around in surprise to see Dean Robbins standing in the shadow of the classroom building, peering at me with stony disapproval down his long patrician nose. He was a tall, thin man in a suit that looked like he'd spent maybe fifty dollars on it off a rack at a department store, but there was still something about him that breathed old money—the kind of old money that stayed in the family because nobody could think of anything worthwhile to spend it on. This was the first time that I'd encountered him without one of the guys present, and I straightened my shoulders, forcing myself not to step back.

"I'm good for the next hour or so," I said. "Why? Is there something you needed? Something I could help you with?"

Dean Robbins curled his lip into what I suspected he intended as a smile, but came across more as a sneer. "I can assure you, if there was anything that I needed from a member of the monster hunter minor, I would not be asking you for it. You have barely begun your studies here at Wellington Academy, for which you should be profoundly grateful. You would do well to take as much advantage as possible of the classes that we are so graciously providing you, and not spend your time daydreaming. You never know when such an opportunity for education might be stripped away."

The threat was clear, and kindled a new fire within me. "Why do you think so?" I asked. "Aren't you the dean of the program? Shouldn't you want to see it continue?"

"My role with the academy is to ensure the success of the school as a whole, not the existence of one particular course of study over another. Wellington Academy has long been one of the premier institutions of magic in the United States, even the world. You, of course, would have no way of knowing that, not being a legacy student. Again, I hope you appreciate the extraordinary circumstances that have allowed you entrance into these elite halls. It is not something you should take for granted."

"I don't," I assured him, but a contrary heat built within me, eager to tweak the thin-faced man into revealing his cards. "In fact, having watched the success of the monster hunter minor in action, taking out the real, genuine monsters that plagued the campus just a few days ago, I'm completely impressed with everything you've done here to train the guys. I would think that once word gets out about that, there might be more students who would want to join, and more funding for those students from the families who'd like to see Wellington Academy returned to its former position of power."

Robbins didn't rise to the bait but merely stared at me more disdainfully. "You should be aware there are other families who are interested in seeing Wellington Academy evolve beyond its former position as a school for thugs and killers," he said with a twist to his lips. "In any event, such discussions are far above your station in life. Your mother was a teacher, right? Some small college down south?"

He spoke with a derision that sent a spike of irritation down my spine. "A professor. She taught around here too when she was younger. I'm not sure exactly where, but she always loved this area. How about you? What brought you to Wellington Academy?"

"Duty," Dean Robbins said darkly. "Something your generation knows little about. Good day, Ms. Cross. I hope you enjoy the academy while you can."

He turned away, and I did too, not knowing where I was going, but eager to get away. I felt uneasy, off-kilter, my nerves all jangled up. Because of Dean Robbins and his empty threats? I didn't think so. This was a heavier feeling, an anticipation of dark, heady danger I couldn't quite shake.

Then I glanced down at my hand, which I now realized had been grasping my left wrist the whole time I'd been talking to Dean Robbins, covering the bracelet.

Uh-oh.

"Zach?" I whispered. In response, I heard Zach's laughter echoing from a far-distant place—once again with a dark edge that took me right back to our kiss, the enormous shadowy bed with its red satin sheets, and his hard, flashing eyes as he'd hovered over me, staring at me that long moment out of time, challenging and fierce. *Did he remember?*

"*I remember,*" he murmured right back, the words slipping and sliding through my mind. "*Everything. And when you're ready, I'll be waiting for you.*"

I whipped my hand off the bracelet.

15

I ran my hands through my hair, momentarily at a loss. I should go back to my apartment. For the first time, it felt way too removed from campus, too distant. This would be a liability if things heated up here quickly, or, say, a demon attack hit the school. How would I know if that happened if I wasn't here? How could I be sure I'd get back in time?

Maybe I should stop living off campus after all. Maybe I should take Tyler up on his suggestion and get a room in Fowler Hall?

I felt the blush rise in my cheeks as I thought about that possibility. Coed dorms were nothing new. We'd had them back in Asheville when I'd attended my first two years of college. But coed dorms with four guys I'd bonded with in a weird, arcane ritual suddenly seemed like maybe not the most brilliant idea I'd ever had. Just imagining a typical Saturday morning, shuffling down to the kitchen for coffee and running into multiple guys in various stages of undress was enough to make me hyperventilate. Especially if I couldn't predict whose bedroom I might just have been in.

My cheeks burned at the thought. "That is so not happening." I needed to figure out how to shut down my insane attraction for anyone other than Tyler right now... well, Tyler and maybe Zach, anyway. But that would require a conversation with Commander Frost, and I didn't really have that in me. Not yet.

Maybe I should just head back to my own apartment and figure out how to make that work? Off-campus housing was popular for a reason, and when I wasn't so distracted with the craziness on campus, I could focus on my search for Mom's family. I hadn't been spending nearly enough time on that—and shame needled its way into my thoughts. Why did I keep allowing myself to get distracted? What kind of daughter was I?

Then again...why had Mom hidden me away? Was she that embarrassed by me? We'd always had enough money. We'd always made do. And this was the age of cyberstalking. If her family had really wanted to find her...they could have. Which meant they didn't want to see me either. Was it even worse than that? Had they *asked* her to take me away, bury me in the countryside, and never mention my existence again? Was that why she'd written those letters she'd never sent?

These unhappy thoughts dispersed somewhat as I headed out into the early afternoon of what was proving to be an absolutely gorgeous Boston day. Never mind that I was an embarrassment to my family and I'd already sustained two demon attacks today—things were improving. I crossed the campus and exited the main gateway of Wellington Academy, looking up almost with fondness at the faces etched into the archway, ghoulish guardians of the academy and all who lay within.

I was surprised at how sentimental I already felt about

the campus, as if I were a returning journeyman and this was my alma mater, not a place I'd called almost home for less than a couple of weeks. Still, I moved into the tree-lined streets of Back Bay with a lighter heart. As I walked under the leafy boughs of the blossoming trees, I wondered again about what my mom had loved so much here. She'd always referred to this area with a smile, but when I'd pressed her for more stories, she'd simply shake her head and inform me that that was a long time ago.

It couldn't have been all *that* long ago, but I guess when I'd finally gotten around to asking her about it in more detail, over a decade had passed since she'd been a young woman here. She'd been a teacher, I knew. Were her family members teachers too? My father, maybe?

The question pulled me up short, and I stopped in the middle of the sidewalk. My mom had been the sole person I'd connected with as a child, the sum total of the family I'd needed. I'd always known it was just her and me against the world. I'd never asked about my dad because I knew from a very early age that was an off-limits topic and that he wasn't part of our little family.

But why had it never occurred to me to ask about grandparents, aunts and uncles, cousins? How was it that I'd simply assumed so easily that Mom and I were all alone and that was simply that? There'd been a time when I'd fanta-sized that Mom had survived some sort of cataclysmic accident where everybody else in her family had died...but then I found the letters. Was it something totally simple? Like she was the black sheep of the family, cast out for, I don't know, maybe getting pregnant? It seemed like the most obvious reason, but was it the right one?

And why hadn't *any* of these questions occurred to me until after she'd died? How weird was that? A few days ago, I wouldn't have thought it strange at all, but now, surrounded by four guys who were pursuing monster hunting as a legitimate minor at a magic academy in the middle of a gorgeous section of Boston that was apparently chock-*full* of magic academies, I was beginning to get an uneasy feeling. And then, of course...there were the extra scars I carried. Something else I'd never thought to push on, to try to understand. Something else my mother had never bothered to explain.

I started moving again. It wasn't fair of me to conflate the two ideas, this possibility or strangeness of not pushing for more information from my mom about her family, coupled with not fully understanding where all my scars had originated. Not even that, not fully *thinking* about the ones that remained on my body or how odd their existence was when most of them had faded.

Grim had pointed out the ones on my shoulder right off the first night I'd met the guys, and obviously, Tyler had seen them. I had to assume Zach and Liam had glimpsed them as well. They simply were a little politer about it. But why couldn't I remember what had caused those scars? What had I buried so deep that I couldn't dredge it up again, even when the evidence of something happening was clearly written upon my skin?

And why hadn't I ever asked about my mom's family?

I'd started walking more quickly, and within a few minutes, I saw my apartment building up ahead. I slowed my step as I approached, however, as I recognized my landlord on the front stoop. A sudden panic grabbed me. What was Mr. Bellows doing here? Had I missed a rent payment? Surely not. It'd only been a few weeks since the last time I'd paid, and I'd deliberately paid a couple of months in advance in case I ever got forgetful...or hurt.

At that moment, my landlord turned and looked at me.

He smiled widely, lifting his hand in greeting. A surge of relief washed through me, though I didn't know why. I hadn't done anything wrong. I moved toward him, glancing around to make sure that nothing else was following me or watching from the shadows. The habit was so ingrained in me that I wondered if I would ever shake it. Clearly, not today.

"Nina," Mr. Bellows said. "I happened to be in the neighborhood and wanted to check on you. Everything okay with the unit?"

There was enough loud cheeriness to his voice that I went on my guard. "The apartment is great," I said brightly. "If you've been up, you may have noticed that I have a couple of extra locks installed, but that's more to do with where I came from, not here. I hope you don't mind. I can get you the keys if you do, of course."

"Oh no, no, no problem at all," he said. "At the end of your lease, whenever that might be, I'll ask for your keys or get the locks rekeyed myself. But I never have a problem with a tenant wanting to be safe." He looked at me more carefully. "You do feel safe, right? Nobody's been bothering you?"

"Not at all," I said blithely. I racked my brain to remember how I'd left the apartment. It had been spotless a few days ago, but had something happened to it? I really should have come back sooner to check on it again. "Is there a problem? Someone say anything?"

"Not at all, I was just talking with one of your neighbors, Mrs. Pendleton, downstairs. She's a bit of a homebody and she mentioned she hadn't seen you around in a few days. She was a little worried."

I lifted my brows. Mrs. Pendleton? I honestly had begun to wonder if the apartment building was empty besides me, as there'd been absolutely no activity when I'd been coming and going. To be fair, with my random hours at the academy and searching for my Mom, it probably shouldn't have surprised me that I had neighbors I'd never seen.

I plastered a relieved smile on my face. "Oh, how nice of her," I said. "I honestly haven't met her, but if I see her, I'll wave. I guess if you rent to a lot of students, she's probably used to them coming and going all the time."

"You're not wrong." Mr. Bellows chuckled. "I've had great success renting to students in this area. It sort of attracts the good ones, you know? The ones who are serious about school, I mean. Learning is so important."

Learning was important, but it seemed a strange thing for a landlord to say. I'd found Mr. Bellows through the most basic of online searches for apartments, but this was the most we'd ever talked after he'd confirmed I had plenty of money to pay the rent and didn't appear to be a serial killer. Now, though, as I was starting to feel truly nervous, he smiled and gave me a little wave, trotting down the steps past me.

"Well, I'm glad you're good. I hope you enjoy your stay in Boston, how ever long it is, and who knows? Maybe you'll stay here forever." His smile was wide and gracious, but I couldn't help the tremor of dismay that passed through me.

"Maybe," I said cheerfully and waved as well, waiting until he turned away before I headed up the stairs. It took everything I had not to glance back as I keyed open the front door and stepped inside. Had he turned to watch me? Was I under some kind of surveillance? Who was this Mrs. Pendleton? That sounded like an old name, a name vaguely familiar...maybe someone Tyler knew, a high-society connection?

Even as I entertained that thought, I chased it away.

Pendleton wasn't exactly an unusual name, especially in the Northeast. And she was an old lady living in an apartment in Back Bay, Boston, not in some gracious old mansion. I was imagining things that weren't there.

I climbed the stairs to my apartment, hastily going through the ritual of the keys until all the locks were disengaged and I could step inside. I paced all through the bright open space, my gaze darting everywhere, but I could tell at a glance that nothing had been disturbed.

My chaise sat in the center of the main room, tidy and tweedy and bearing just enough rust-colored threads that any errant bloodstains were easily hidden after a particularly bad monster attack. There was nothing else in that room but my cheap electric clock and a couple of extra pillows. My bedroom looked even tidier, since I'd rolled up both the plastic tarp and the sleeping bag and pillow and tucked them against the wall.

My iron box in the armoire was still locked and the clothes arranged perfectly around it, wrapped and rewrapped to my specifications—no one had touched it. The bathroom was pristine, and the kitchen as well, down to the slightly chipped and now no-longer-complete dish collection, a victim of Tyler's first visit to my apartment. When he and I kissed, the world literally shook. When Zach and I kissed...

"Don't think about Zach," I ordered myself. Especially don't think about kissing Zach. And even more especially, don't think about kissing Zach and ending up on desolate open plains or an enormous bed of red satin, his body stretching over mine, poised and ready to—

Stop thinking about that, I insisted, more firmly this time. But I knew it was a losing battle. And why was I fighting this so hard? I didn't have to jump Zach in some back alley like some crazed nymphomaniac, but what would it hurt to understand *him* a little bit more? In fact, I probably *should* understand him better. He was my teammate. We would be fighting together, presumably. Heck, we'd already fought together. Knowing him better would help me be a better teammate, was all.

Yeah, right.

I peered around the space, suddenly feeling out of sorts. Almost like I didn't belong here, which made no sense. This was my furniture, my supplies. All I really owned in the world. Even the few mementos I'd kept from back in Asheville, which hadn't been much, now that I thought about it.

Why had I kept so little?

I frowned and stepped back into the bedroom, moving over to the armoire. I carefully unwrapped the folded clothes to reveal the chest, a two-foot-by-one-foot iron case with an iron clasp. With monsters literally coming out of the closet to say hello at all hours, I hadn't wanted to take anything for granted.

Now I popped open the lock, which didn't require a key but a code. It opened easily, and I stared down at the few things I'd kept from my childhood home, which I'd shared with my sweet, careful mother for twenty-four years...right up until she'd died far, far too young.

There was depressingly little. Mom had only had one piece of jewelry that she'd worn every day, and that was a necklace with a teardrop stone surrounded by diamonds. Citrine, she had told me once, and the diamonds looked real enough to me, though of course I hadn't ever had it appraised. That piece lay in its velvet bag, along with one of her handmade pairs of earrings, shards of sea glass that she'd twined thin metal strips around. Otherwise, there were financial records, insurance documents, and maybe a dozen photographs of her. She hadn't been much for digital photos, but these had been with her letter to her family... though not in the same envelope.

I sighed now as I settled on my heels, setting the carefully unsealed letter to the side, then paging through the photos. My mother looked nothing like me, or at least not enough, I'd always thought, with her bouncy brown hair and sparkling blue eyes, her wide smile and happy countenance. Getting to my feet, I carried the earliest-looking snapshot to one of the few pieces that had come with the place, a heavy, stand-alone wrought iron mirror positioned between the bedroom's two windows. I held the picture up next to my face. If I squinted hard, there was some resemblance, I thought. Maybe.

I'd never thought Mom had adopted me, but now a strange kind of disquiet snaked through my stomach, curdling in my belly.

Pinching the photo between my lips, I turned to the side, and lifted my shirt. The ugly ragged scar was still there, puckering my skin. It was the largest of my mystery scars. I ran my fingers along it, surprised at the chill that slipped down my spine. As with all the scars that had refused to heal, I had no recollection of this particular monster fight, but it had happened a long time ago, I knew. I'd carried that scar with me for most of my life.

The phone buzzed in my pocket, so loud I yelped in surprise and jumped back, spitting out the picture. I bent down to pick the photo up off the floor before even swiping for the phone—I had my priorities straight—but it had slipped behind the mirror's base, of course. I had to angle myself awkwardly to reach it, my gaze instinctively scanning up the wall to fix on a point just beneath the window sill.

Which was how I discovered the camera in my bedroom.

16

The phone blared again, and I jerked up, banging my head on the mirror. "Ow!" I yanked the phone out of my pocket, then fell back on my ass and scooted away from the camera.

The photo. I lurched forward again, pulling up the photo before retreating entirely out of the bedroom and sinking down against the wall of the corridor. Who would have put a camera there? Given its position—low under the window, facing the door—the only thing you could see with any amount of certainty would be someone crossing in front of the bedroom door to head to the bathroom.

Depending on whether or not it was a wide angle, you couldn't even get a decent view of anyone above the knee. So what was someone trying to see? And where was the feed going? My apartment backed up to another apartment, I was sure, but I had never heard anyone there in the few weeks I'd been here. Was this some sort of Peeping Tom situation? Was it Bellows's camera?

Dimly, I realized the phone had stopped ringing. I looked down at the screen and scowled. Though I'd managed to swipe the device on, I'd missed the actual call, which maybe was just as well. I sat with my back against the hallway wall, my lungs heaving. I should just contact Mr. Bellows, I thought. Or simply cover the damn lens. If Mr. Bellows didn't know about it, then he could continue not knowing about it until I moved out. I didn't really feel like having anyone else in my space right now.

My phone rang again, the same number. This time I picked up.

"Hello?" I asked sharply.

"Nina, where are you? What's going on?"

I blinked at the worry in Commander Frost's voice, then modulated my own. "I'm at my apartment."

"You're on campus?"

I shook my head, though of course he couldn't see me. "No, the one I have off Newbury. I'm on a short-term lease."

"You know you can stay in Fowler Hall. It'd be better to have you on campus."

I grimaced and leaned against the wall. Now was as good a time as any to wade into this mess, and it would distract me from the flat lens I couldn't stop seeing in my mind's eye, even if I'd scooted out of view of it.

"Yeah? You really think me moving in is a great idea given everything that's going on with the guys now that I've joined the collective?" My blunt honesty came out almost harshly, and Frost breathed out a long, careful sigh. He knew what I meant.

"Yes...I do," he said heavily. "The collective was created to ensure the absolute power of any hunters willing to dedicate themselves to each other as a team unit with an unbreakable bond. It was designed to *protect* the individuals, not put them at risk, and I believed—wanted to believe— still believe—that you were safer as part of the collective, or

I would never have allowed the five of you to complete the process. Tyler leveled up after you and he, err..."

"Had sex," I helped him out as he hesitated, and I could practically feel Frost wince over the line.

"Yes. But you should have leveled up after that as well. It's only when you didn't that I realized I didn't have all the information, and what's worse—I *still* don't have all the information. There seems to be a legitimate value to you, ah..." Frost broke off again, but I was all in at this point.

"Hooking up with all four guys," I stated flatly. "Yeah. I read through the Apocrypha."

"You..." Frost broke off, clearly trying to process that piece of information. Meanwhile, I didn't know whether to laugh or cry, but the butterflies taking up residence in my stomach had woken up during this conversation, and appeared to be fully on board with the idea of me getting cozy with Zach, at a bare minimum. They were practically playing Twister in a hurricane by the time Frost continued.

"Well, yes. From what still remains in the Apocrypha, if you choose to connect with the other team members, it will help them. Help you too, though that part isn't quite clear."

"Yeah, about that. I read the section where I'm supposed to destroy...something. Then it was cut off. Please tell me you know something more about *that* little piece of crazy."

"Unfortunately, I don't," Frost said. "Furthermore, I'm not sure that actual physical connection is required in every instance. It's possible that an emotional connection is enough. It would need to be a profound emotional connection, but..."

I sat up sharply, my butterflies leaping up with me, their spinning making me dizzy. There had been something about an emotional link. How had the book put it? "Yeah? You think so?"

"I do. That said, we know precious little about any of this, and every new revelation leads to two or three more questions. This magic is very old, and the older the magic, the more the people who were wielding it tended to keep things simple and, frankly, primal. Which means..."

I grimaced, not needing him to complete the sentence. It meant the writers had sex in mind, full stop. It also meant that not only would I need to act on my irrational and irresponsible attraction to Zach...but to Liam as well. And *Grim*.

All the butterflies fainted.

Frost again hammered home the data point of past collectives imploding, and his theories about how we might avoid that slice of joy, but I couldn't quite hear him anymore. Instead, I saw my mother's face, white with fear, her orders regarding four men in a collective harsh and overloud in the small room. *If you ever see them—you run. Promise me!"*

"...and that takes us back to where we started from. Which is knowing too damned little to do any good," Frost finally muttered, and fell silent. I wanted to give the man a break, but I didn't know how. We had to figure this out.

"Okay, well, let's look at whatever comps we have," I offered. "Liam said this kind of, um, relationship is normal at your sister school or whatever, Twyst Academy? How do they handle it?"

"Twyst is an entirely different scenario," Frost grumped. "Except for those Trials teams who actually win—which is precious few—the teams are temporary constructs and their participants are *not* required to physically bond in order to win. It helps, without question. But it's not required. With Wellington collectives, it's not only not required, it appears to be the most dangerous course you can take, regardless of the upsides."

I winced. "And you haven't figured out any workaround yet."

"I haven't. Every trail leads to the same response. You engage in some sort of intimate interaction with another member of the collective, they level up. You should have as well, but since you didn't, I suspect you will only level up to a significant degree *after* you engage with all of them. And what that transformation will look like is unknown."

"Right." I sighed. "This is some seriously twisted magic you guys have going on here, if you don't mind me saying so."

"On that point, we agree," Frost said. "Which gives us something else to consider. This is an old book, and old books are given to absolutes, and they are often written by, frankly, socially inept old men. So perhaps I *am* mistaken in what's truly required. With everything going on, I haven't had time to research it more thoroughly. I should put Liam on the job."

I grimaced. "That's okay. I don't know that I necessarily want Liam thinking too much about...all this."

Frost snorted. "Good luck with that. I have a feeling he's already undertaken plenty of research on his own."

Heat flashed through me, equal parts dismay and...okay, pretty much only dismay. I didn't even know what to do with that information, so I pushed on. "Why did you call, anyway?"

Once again, Frost hesitated. "I was concerned about you. Dean Robbins stopped by the library to discuss your conversation with him. He wasn't sure you were as appreciative as you could have been regarding your recent change of circumstances. He also pressed me for more information about your mother."

I sat up straighter. "What did you tell him?"

"Exactly what I know for certain, which is very little. Janet Cross disclosed to you that she taught in the Back Bay area of Boston, but we've found no record of that. If she did teach here, which seems likely given her mentions of the area to you, she may have changed her name upon relocating to Asheville. Or she could have been making up that history to lead you down a false path."

"But that's..." I frowned. Frost didn't know about the letter Mom had written to her family. I hadn't told him, and the guys who knew about it had kept my secret. It was a secret I couldn't keep for much longer, though. "She lived here," I finally said. "I've got some of her things I can show you. Maybe you can make some sense of them."

"That would be—hold on." Frost broke off for a second, then was back. "Ah...are you checking your messages? Tyler is looking for you."

"Oh." I pulled the phone away from my head and saw that I had several messages flagged in my text app. "Yeah, I'm not used to checking it. What's up, do you know?"

He sighed. "I do not. Robbins has had me cornered for the past two hours. I think he's shifted his attention to you, which, frankly, does not make my day, but he doesn't seem like he's got a specific agenda. You'll probably have eyes on you, though, from here on out. Be careful."

I frowned, my gaze shifting to the bedroom. "What do you mean? Like surveillance?" My conversation with Mr. Bellows leapt in my mind—who was the woman he said had noticed my comings and goings? Was that camera a new addition to my apartment, or had I somehow stumbled into some high-rent neighborhood-watch situation with the blue-blooded, blue-haired first families of old Boston? "Does Dean Robbins know where I live?"

"You should assume he does, to be on the safe side,"

Frost said, winding my nerves tighter. "As to surveillance—probably nothing majorly high tech, but I don't want to take anything for granted. Keep your eyes sharp. I know you've been asking some questions about your mother... Maybe ease up on that until Robbins makes his next move."

I made a face, then bent to retrieve the photograph of my mom that I'd let fall to the floor. "You haven't found out anything about her, even if it wasn't for certain?"

He sighed. "Not a damned thing. It's like Janet Cross never existed. There's no reference to her on any archived social media, and there are no property records attached to her name. There are Crosses in the area, and I'm working through those, but it's been slow going."

"I don't get it," I muttered. My mom had been a teacher at an accredited college in Asheville, and even though she'd been an adjunct professor, there had to have been *some* criteria for that. She wouldn't have been given the job based solely on her good nature. "Do you think she could have been lying about the whole thing?"

"I don't," he said, surprising me. "You're a monster hunter, Nina. There's only one monster hunter academy in the world—and it's in Boston, where your mother said she had family. You said you had some of her personal items? At this point, that would help."

I twisted my lips. "I do. A letter she wrote but never sent, some photographs. I don't know how *much* they'll help, but they can't hurt, anyway."

"Agreed," he said. "Bring them to me whenever you can."

I tried to stuff down my apprehension of turning my few mementos of my mother over to anyone, even someone trying to help. Maybe I needed to start my search again in earnest. The PO Box she'd provided on the envelope had turned out not to be tied to any post office in the area, but maybe she was from somewhere else in Boston? Or maybe... I didn't know. There'd been no postage affixed to the envelope either. Almost like she knew...

I blinked. "Hand delivered," I said aloud as Frost continued.

"If you want you can photograph the items and text them to me, or—what?"

"Never mind," I said quickly. I needed to think more, but I felt...knew I was right. Mom had never intended to mail her several-page, several-*years*-long letter. She'd hand it off to someone she trusted. Someone who would understand what to do with it. So, the PO Box listed on the envelope was, what? Some kind of clue? I needed to do more research. "I'll bring you the stuff I have later today. Maybe you can scan it then?"

"Absolutely, and you should head back to campus anyway. This morning's demon attack has left everyone unsettled. That might be why Tyler is asking for you, now that I think about it."

"Yeah?" I asked, sitting straighter against the wall.

"Yes," he said. "Zach's...taken a bad turn."

17

I froze, the phone pressed to my ear. "What do you mean?"

"Liam mentioned that you had some kind of connection building with Zach. Something *not* intimate, mind you," Frost added hurriedly, and I barely kept from laughing.

"Yeah, okay, but what about it?" I asked, not sure if Frost would count the kiss in the chapel, but pretty sure Liam hadn't mentioned it. Liam had already been forced to explain my relationship specifics once, and I suspected he wasn't too stoked to do it again. There were downsides to being the brainiac researcher of the group. "Did Zach ask for me?"

"He didn't, but I don't think you should read anything into that. He hasn't been able to talk."

Gripping the phone, I scrambled to my feet. "What are you talking about? Why hasn't he been able to talk? I left him only an hour or so ago. He wasn't hurt that bad."

"The attack he sustained from the demon left a series of marks down his torso. Did you see them?"

I scowled, picturing Zach's perfect abs as he'd lain ensconced in the red satin sheets. "No. No, that's not right. Zach wasn't the one who was hurt. Wendy was attacked, punctured, and Zach sort of adopted her injuries for his own, but only temporarily. I don't think the demon ever touched him."

"Well, something did," Frost said. "Liam took photographs of it, and Zach's father..." He paused.

"What?" I demanded. I moved through my rooms quickly, ripping a backpack out of my armoire, stuffing clothes inside. I couldn't stay off campus anymore, I realized. I couldn't be this far away from the guys. Not if they needed me. No matter how weird it was, if they needed me, I had to be there for them. I eyed the metal box, thought about the camera beneath the mirror. Was my stuff safe here anymore? I didn't want to lug it over to campus now, but...I needed to. Soon. "What about Zach's dad?"

"He fainted at one of the library tables," Frost said summarily. "I found him slumped over his research materials. I didn't want to rouse him at first, and when I finally made the attempt, he reacted violently. I think he may be caught in the same thrall that's holding Zach."

"That sounds pretty awful," I slung my backpack over one shoulder, heading for the door. I hadn't taken the time to cover the camera in the bedroom and certainly not to search for anything more, but I didn't care. If there was nobody here, then whoever was watching on the other side wasn't going to get much of a show.

"Is Zach in Fowler Hall?" I asked as I rattled out the front door, locking all the locks. I turned and trotted down the stairs.

I barely heard Frost's affirmative before I hit the front steps, shoved the phone in my pocket, and took off running.

The campus was only fifteen minutes away—I made it in about five. When I reached Fowler Hall, Tyler was there, all Big-Man-On-Campus gorgeous in his blue polo shirt and jeans, his hands lifting to block me before I went bursting inside.

"Hey! Hey, hold on, breathe," he ordered, and there was a resonance to his voice that did more to slow my pounding heart than even the feel of his hands on my shoulders, the reassurance of his presence.

"Is he okay?" I asked brusquely, and Tyler studied me for a long moment, something in his eyes I'd never seen before, at least not from a guy. It was something bound up with love or affection, but not solely that. *Pride,* I thought suddenly. He was proud of me.

He leaned down and kissed me softly on the lips. "He will be now that you're here," he said with such positive force that it nearly bowled me over.

"Jesus," I muttered as he turned toward the front door of Fowlers Hall, gesturing me to follow. "Are you throwing spells every time you talk now?"

"You like it?" Tyler grinned, and I punched him in the arm...an arm that was decidedly more buff than it had been when I'd first met him. "I can't even seem to stop myself anymore. It just sort of happens."

"Well, try harder."

He laughed and carded us through the entryway and the foyer door, then took off across the marble floor, moving quickly but not running, giving me time to calm my breathing and refocus.

I'd only been in Fowlers Hall a few times, but it was already starting to feel like home. Never mind that it looked more like a castle then any reasonable sort of residence hall. Marble floors, tapestries, inlaid wood designs, and stained glass panels hung from heavy chains in the main areas, which we strode by to climb the staircase to the second floor, then the third. Actual bedrooms were on this level, but Tyler kept walking for what felt like a football field more, three or four turns away from where I knew his rooms to be, before finally stopping at another door, this one cracked slightly open.

"You guys like to give each other your space, at least," I said wryly, trying to quell my mounting nerves. There was no sound from inside the room.

He smiled. "It just sort of worked out that way. Liam's in there, making sure Zach doesn't hurt himself, but go on in. The last time I entered, it didn't turn out so well. Same with Grim."

I blinked at him. "What do you mean?"

"Let's just say there was a lot of screaming and obvious pain on Zach's part. You'll be awesome, though. I know you will. He needs you."

For once I didn't bother arguing with him. The bizarro of my developing relationship with the guys was something I could figure out later. Right now, I needed to see Zach.

I knocked softly on the door, but didn't wait for a response before stepping inside. When I did, I blinked hard against the fumes in the room—sulfur, I thought, so much sulfur. My eyes burned with it, and I barely made it across the wide expanse of the chamber without choking to death.

"What's going on in here? What is that stench?" I rasped, but Liam merely turned to me, his thick brows climbing his forehead as he narrowed his concerned hazel eyes at me.

"What are you talking about? It's fine." He gestured to the windows, and I could see they were open to the outside, but the atmosphere in the room didn't lighten. If anything, as I got closer to Zach, it grew thicker and more difficult to breathe.

By the time I reached his side, I was wheezing. I reached out for Zach even as Liam stood, knocking his chair over in his haste. Strange, I thought distantly, but I didn't pay any attention to him. I reached for Zach's hand, while Liam's mouth opened, his eyes going wide.

"*No!*" I heard faintly, but it was as if it was a different Liam—a person shouting at me from a movie screen or the pages in a book. Time was away and somewhere else.

Fire.

I was surrounded by fire, and Zach—beautiful gothic angel Zach, all dark hair and fair skin and beautiful, purple-hued eyes—hung in front of me, burning alive. Or what was left of him, anyway. His wrists were lashed high to two metal posts, his body encased in flames as it twisted and writhed. His head lolled to the right, eyelids blackened, the skin little more than char, his mouth stretched wide in a rictus of pain.

The most horrifying thing I could imagine was kissing that mouth, but it was the only thing I'd done before that seemed to help. All this had to be an illusion, right? This couldn't be real.

I stepped forward, through the solid wall of heat, and got right up on Zach. He stank of burned meat, and my stomach pitched, gorge rising in my throat. Before I could jerk away from him, though, I lurched forward and pressed my lips to his.

Suddenly, I was the one on fire. I was the one burning black. I was the one taking on the pain, the searing torment. Zach was nothing more than a hollowed-out shell, while I staggered under the impossible, bone-melting horror.

The chittering of a thousand voices called Zach's name,

mocking him, suggesting the most foul and despicable abuses they would delight in inflicting upon everyone he held dear. Including me, I thought, but all that was lost in a wave of pain that seemed to dissolve my bones and send a stream of jagged shards ripping through me.

Somehow I managed to frame what was left of Zach's head with my hands. I pulled him closer to me, deepening the kiss, and with a horrifying clicking noise, his eyes shot wide. But they were no longer the beautiful purple irises I'd come to treasure so much. Instead, his eyes burned black with hate, a crimson flame burning deep within, stoked by an endless terror. This was what Zach stared into, I realized, when he saw into the heart of a demon. This was what he had to save people from. This was why he had to make the sacrifice he did—and why I needed to sacrifice too.

Knowledge and terror flooded me even as fire erupted all around us. Zach convulsed and came apart in my hands, his body becoming its own firestorm. Leaning into him despite the howling wind, I managed to keep my hands pressed tight to his temples, and I leapt onto him much like the demon had attempted to leap on him earlier in the chapel, wrapping my legs around the burning husk of his body.

He screamed.

Or...maybe that was me.

18

The scene shattered into a million pieces, and then we were back inside Zach's dorm room in Fowlers Hall. With a snarl of rage and pain, Zach shoved me away from him, sending me tumbling into Liam's arms.

"I've got her! I've got her," Liam said, as if Zach were simply handing me off and not rejecting me outright. I didn't so much mind the rejection this time. I flopped over onto my hands and knees, my lungs bellowing for air.

"*Nina,*" Zach moaned finally. "Tell me you didn't do what I think you did. Tell me."

I turned back to see him lifting his hand to his face, his very normal-looking face, no longer filled with sunken eyes and charred skin. He looked like he'd just recovered from a two-day bender, but there was no blood, there was no...

"You're not burned," I managed, not knowing if that would make any sense to him. It barely made any sense to me.

He slowly shook his head, his gaze turning mournful. "You could see all that. You *saw*. Dear God in heaven."

Zach's door burst open. Tyler rushed in first, striding

over to me and pulling me around, inspecting me. I opened my mouth to speak, to reassure him, and a thin wisp of smoke puffed out.

Tyler's eyes shot wide. "Whoa! Are you okay?"

I nodded, and he half turned to Zach, who paid him no attention. Instead, his gaze was locked on me, fierce and resolute. I stared back just as fiercely, wanting that connection, *craving* it. I didn't miss the flicker of heat in those purple-hued eyes. That heat had nothing to do with the scourging fire he'd endured at the demons' hands...and everything to do with me. In his reflected gaze, I relived my decision to push through the flames and gather him close, the moment where we touched, soul to soul. I shivered as Tyler started talking.

"We all tapped in via our tattoos, but we couldn't see much. Only that it seemed like Nina reached you and pulled you back from wherever you were. It looked like a lot of fire."

Zach chuckled grimly, the sound like gravel over crushed glass. "Yeah. There was a lot of fire. It wasn't real, technically." He gestured with noticeable weakness to his body, clad in a T-shirt and gym shorts that were soaked through with sweat and striped, charcoal-like stains. "But the body doesn't always understand the difference between what is happening in the real world and what is happening in the mind. I've never spontaneously combusted, but...there's always a price to pay for work in the darker realms."

I swallowed, Zach's words jangling harshly around my skull. A price to pay. The demon had said something about that earlier today. But hadn't he already paid enough?

Liam stared at Zach for a long minute with narrowed eyes, then rocked back on his heels, and stood. "I think we need to let Zach grab a shower and crash—if you can, now? Can you sleep?"

Zach nodded, grimacing as he pulled his shirt away from his body. "Yeah. They won't bug me again for a while. Not like that."

"Good. Because we've got our own work to do," Liam said, still studying him. "You've been out for a couple of hours, and there's something you should know. Frost texted all of us, and if we've got the timing right, your dad fainted probably right around the time that you did. Does that happen often?"

"Dad?" Zach's face cleared, the question serving to focus his attention. I suspected that was why Liam asked it more than anything. "That's...no. That's not how it usually works. We're honestly not linked at all. I mean, there's no bad blood between us or anything like that, but it's not like we have some sort of active psychic connection unless he's fully in the mode of exorcising somebody's demon. He can't read my mind—we're safe from each other in that way. More or less ordinary, if you can call it that."

"Could be his proximity to you, here on campus," Tyler put in, and Zach blew out a breath. His color was returning to normal, but he still looked unsteady on his feet.

"Maybe. Is he okay now?"

"Unknown." Liam held up his left hand, flashing the small tattoo of interconnected symbols that laced his wrist. "As soon as we know something, you will. Unless I miss my guess, he probably broke out of his faint right around the time you came to. So even if you don't normally hook up mentally, whatever is happening now is definitely linking you together. We've got to do some research, find out exactly what this thing is. I have a feeling your dad is going to be a little bit more forthcoming this time around."

Zach grimaced. "Don't count on it," he said. "Dad has made a life out of not telling the truth if he feels that people can't handle it."

"Yeah, well, Commander Frost has made a life out of hunting monsters, and since it's now Bring Your Family Demon to Work day, he can't let that slide, no matter how private your dad wants to keep the fight. He'll get what he needs to know."

Tyler nodded, and Zach sighed, both of them clearly accepting the truth of this. I wondered again about Commander Frost. Despite looking like Paul Bunyan, he was an academic, not a fighter. Had he really fought actual monsters? Or just the holograms they served up to students at Wellington Academy these days, all flash and no fang?

"Okay, let's head to the library," Tyler said. "Zach, try to get some rest. Ideally without setting yourself on fire."

Zach laughed a little weakly, but as we turned to go, he spoke up again. "Nina, could you stay for another second? I want to go over...I want to double-check something," he ended lamely.

Liam instantly perked up, but Tyler put a firm hand on his shoulder and steered him toward the door.

"Absolutely, my man," Tyler said. "Nina, we'll meet you at the library, okay?"

I nodded, but I didn't trust myself to say anything further. There was something in Zach's expression that unnerved me a little. Like someone desperate to tell you something you equally desperately didn't want to hear.

Zach sat as the guys exited, more a collapsing of his bones, and I wondered how exhausted he really was. I moved forward instinctively to help him, but he stopped me cold with a swift jerk of his head. Slowly and carefully, he put his hands on his knees and simply breathed. I breathed too, drawing in the faintly sulfur-tinged breeze, my lips pursed together as my panic grew, but nothing else happened. Zach waited until after the guys were gone a full two minutes, and then he finally shifted his gaze from his hands to me.

"How bad was it?" he asked quietly.

I lifted one shoulder. "You were caught on fire, looking like you'd been strung up that way."

He winced, then set his jaw, his expression hardening. "Strung up, like in a noose? Or hanging from the ceiling?"

I shuddered a little, trying to recall. "Your hands were held high, lashed to poles, I think. And you were on fire. You looked like you'd been that way for a while, but you were still alive. When you opened your eyes, they weren't your own."

He wiped a hand over his brow, shoving his hair back. "Did I look like a devil was inside me, a demon?"

"I'm not sure about that. You just looked like you were in a lot of pain." I tried to recall more details, but they were already slipping away. I frowned. "It's already fading. Is that normal?"

He snorted, sounding impossibly tired. "None of this is normal. You shouldn't have seen any of that. You shouldn't have been able to come into my private torment."

I flinched back a little, and he lifted a hand that was blessedly intact now, none of the slender, calloused fingers broken. "I don't mean it like that, I mean it's just never happened before. It's really dangerous, and you came right up to me and plunged in. That's a little scary—not for me, but for you. I don't know how to protect you."

It was almost like he was talking to himself, not me, his words low and wondering, a distracted professor working out an unexpected calculation.

"Well, have you considered that maybe you're not *supposed* to protect me?"

He looked up at me, startled, but I pushed on. "I mean, Zach, I know the whole point of me joining the collective was to protect me. And I really appreciate it because I need a lot of protection," I said, trying to go for levity as he grimaced again. "But maybe I can help protect you guys too. Maybe that's part of the reason I was drawn here, and why Frost went forward with us becoming a collective despite his reservations. Maybe I'm supposed to help."

"I can't imagine Frost would be happy with the idea of you being in danger," Zach countered.

"But, you see, that's not the way it works," I said. "I fight monsters. I have my whole life, and I don't see that changing anytime soon. So I was going to be in danger anyway. If I'm near you guys, I at least have a fighting chance to knock back anything that comes after me. If I can return the favor, well, honestly, that makes me feel a hell of a lot better."

Even as I said the words, I realized how true they were. I *had* helped Zach today. Not only here, but earlier in the chapel. I'd been his strength when he had faltered. That was new for me, different. I'd done a good job of protecting myself all these years, keeping others safe, but this was maybe the first time I'd helped protect another hunter. I realized I'd moved closer to Zach only when I saw my hand reaching for his, lying half open on the bed. When I touched his palm, there was no denying the zing of electricity there, the leap of awareness.

"I don't understand what this is between us," he muttered.

I drew in a deep breath, ready to try to explain further.

But Zach's eyelids drooped as I tried to figure out how to begin, and he sank back into the pillows, boneless.

"Man, I'm tired," he murmured. "I need to grab a shower, but...not yet, I don't think. I'm wiped."

I squeezed his hand, perfectly happy to avoid the *oh, now that I'm part of the collective, there's something you need to know* conversation. "You should rest," I agreed. "That's your number one job right now. I have a feeling that whatever we find in the library, you're going to be our go-to to handle it."

"Yeah," he murmured, but he was fading fast. As his eyes drifted shut, I leaned forward and dropped a soft kiss on his forehead. He smiled, half asleep as I drew back.

"I think you're seriously great," Zach mumbled woozily. "I really don't want you to die."

He passed out.

19

I made it to Lowell Library in just under ten minutes, quickly making my way to the conference room, which had become our unofficial headquarters. Books, scrolls, and various laptops lay open around the space, Liam moving from one to another, muttering like a lunatic. Tyler looked up when I arrived, his smile broad.

"I couldn't really get into it when we were with Zach. He was pretty traumatized by the whole thing. But Nina, you were *awesome*."

"So you did see us?"

He shook his head. "Not exactly, but I could figure it out. You totally marched right in there and ripped Zach out of the teeth of the demon. Not caring about any damage to yourself, not stopping because of the pain. And there was a friggin' crap ton of pain."

Now it was Liam's turn to stare at Tyler, his river-stone eyes turning speculative. "You could feel what she felt?" he asked, beating me to the punch. Tyler blinked, then nodded, smiling broadly.

"I sure as shit could," he declared. "Which makes it even cooler, for those keeping score. I like being this connected. I think it's helpful."

"I'll remember that the next time I have a migraine," I snorted.

Liam's gaze dropped back to the computer he was holding. He jolted. "Hey, this is what I was looking for, Tyler. I knew I'd read about it somewhere. I just never thought it'd made it to computerized files."

Tyler turned to him. "Hit me."

Liam started pacing up and down the room, speaking quickly as he read from his laptop screen. "High-level demons don't travel in packs, like what Reverend Williams said, even if they have bands of *scati* that show up on their heels to wreak havoc, and *timore* that follow them around like scavengers, waiting for a strike. But they can attract other high-level demons to their battlegrounds—especially if they feel like they have something to prove."

I wrinkled my nose. "Something to prove? Like if one of Zach's family demons has a pitchfork to grind?"

"I think so. I think that's why we're seeing this uptick in activity, both with the demons on Wellington's campus and the sightings that have been reported all up and down the coast—maybe they aren't such bullshit after all. It's Zach's time to shine. Maybe it's his demon's time too. Remember, if you do subscribe to the whole idea of Lucifer as first fallen, the prime reason given for his downfall was..."

"Pride," Tyler said, cutting him off. "Demons are proud. They may not care about much, but they do care about being respected."

"Yep," Liam said. "I think what we're dealing with here is a demon who's been disrespected, and he's out to prove that

that was a very bad idea. He's stirring up the horde to come watch the show."

"And that show will play out on campus in real life. Not just in Zach's mind?" Tyler asked.

"Definitely in real life." Liam blew out a breath, tilting his head, the blue-white glow of the laptop reflecting off his deeply tanned skin. "What I don't know is what will happen once they all converge. Will the other demons chip in to help take out Zach—and us, by extension—or are they just coming for the popcorn? Honestly, we need to talk with Reverend Williams."

"Yeah, I'm sure that's going to go well," Tyler scoffed. "You see him anywhere around here? I don't, and that pisses me off. There's something about that guy that bugs me a lot."

I blinked at the very un-Tyler-like anger in his voice. "Really?" I asked. "What do you mean?"

He shook his head. "You saw the way he treated Zach. Even beyond his disdain for the academy, you'd like to think he would have an appreciation for everything his son has done or can do. And hell, we all saw to varying degrees what Zach went through with demons today. We heard it too. Not only did his dad not give us the intel we need to fight these assholes, but—"

"The demon said Zach's dad wasn't ready to fight," Liam said, recalling the words from Bellamy Chapel, earlier in the day. "Yeah. I remember that too."

I lifted my brows. "Zach's dad hasn't told us everything he knows."

Tyler finger gunned me. "Exactly. I'm going to text Frost. I expected him to be here already, him and the good reverend." He pulled out his phone and shot off the text.

Frost answered immediately...but not in a way Tyler

expected. The commander's heavy boots sounded down the hallway, and a moment later, he swung into the room, bushy brows drawn together, beard jutting out.

"All of you get to class, now. And look sharp. It's time to put on the show."

I blinked, surprised not only by the demand, but by how quickly the guys were reacting to it. "Put on the show?"

"This freaking sucks," Liam muttered, moving around the table, shutting laptops and closing books, stacking everything away in record time.

"It's friggin' bullshit is what it is," Tyler protested. "They can't do this to us so randomly. We've got work to do. Where's Reverend Williams? Do you even know what just happened to Zach?"

Frost's mouth tightened. "Zach's injuries will be explained away in one of a couple of different ways, and I left Matthew resting in one of the study lounges. He's awake, but groggy and a little disoriented. No one knows he's on campus yet. Let's try to keep it that way. That means Nina, you're up for this demonstration too."

I stared at him, thoroughly lost. "Up for *what*?"

His bushy beard quivered with irritation, and he folded his arms over his broad chest. "Showing our respect for the families that pay our way. Every once in a while, Wellington's board of directors wants them to know that their hard-earned money is being put to good use. The timing for this demonstration is curious, but that doesn't change the facts. It's happening."

"But what is it?" That seemed reasonable enough. Tyler and Liam had already started for the door, but I hesitated, looking between them and Frost. "Are we going to show people how we hunt monsters?"

Liam cursed under his breath.

"That would be a no," Tyler said drily. "It's way worse than that. C'mon."

20

―――――

"So this is how it goes," Tyler said as we left the library and began walking swiftly across the campus. "The academy gets a lot of money from donors in very high places. That money funds our tuition in small part, and then our lifelong stipend in large part."

"Right," I said. "Which pisses everyone off to varying degrees."

"Pretty much. But all that money talks really, really loudly, and as a result, the board of directors has deemed it perfectly acceptable for us to serve as ambassadors for any of the donor families, basically at their beck and call whenever they might come to campus. Apparently, this is one of the days we have to pay the price of our entitlement."

Pay the price. I grimaced. "You guys are seriously screwed up here."

"Don't we know it," Liam said, laughing. "But wherever your next class is, look for the fourth horseman of the apocalypse—yours might actually be a horsewoman. Either way, you'll know who she is—old, rich, annoying. Try not to piss her off, answer her questions, and let her study you like a bug. It gets easier over time."

"Study me like a—"

"Gotta roll. I'm all the way across campus." Liam peeled off, and, after a quick kiss that left the nearby trees shuddering violently, Tyler did as well. Without any other option, I headed to my Akkadian language class...and found my assignment waiting for me at the door. A thin-faced, sharp-eyed old woman, with her steel-gray hair wrapped back in a severe bun at her nape, her clothes heavy and layered despite the warming day.

"Margaret Pendleton," she announced without preamble, clicking her tongue in dismay as she took in my jeans and T-shirt. Clearly not the Wellington uniform, but the Wellington Academy skirt-and-blouse uniform was optional the last time I had checked. Not to mention impractical by any stretch of the imagination.

I blinked at her. That name...

Then it came to me. "*The* Mrs. Pendleton, from my *apartment*?" I blustered. "You've been watching me?"

"The same. Though rest assured, that's not my actual residence. And yes, I've been watching you traipse between Wellington and your apartment for the better part of a week now. You may enter your classroom. I'll follow behind."

"So that camera is yours?" I demanded, but Mrs. Pendleton merely flapped her hands at me.

"Cameras," she scoffed, making me blink. *Cameras, plural*? "Fat lot of good those are doing with that blocker you've set up. Half of them are useless. Bellows is a fool, but at least he had the good sense to alert us when Tyler Perkins brought you home. That's when we started paying attention, and not a second too soon. Now *go*. People are staring."

My cheeks flaming, I entered the classroom, sitting

several rows away from the professor, toward the wall. My iron-jawed senior tagalong drew several curious stares, but fortunately, no one said anything.

As it turned out, I actually enjoyed this class, which made it almost possible to ignore the old woman beside me. I'd taken Spanish in high school and understood it well enough to test out of it for college, but I'd never really given much thought to the value of learning a second language...especially one not spoken in millennia.

But Akkadian flowed more naturally to me than I would have expected, and though I'd only taken a few classes, I was able to converse in halting sentences with the instructor, who fell all over herself with surprise and delight at my attempts. I didn't know if that was, in part, to impress Mrs. Pendleton, but I was still grateful that she made me look competent. By the time class closed, the old woman's face had softened ever so slightly, but I still wanted her gone. How often did the guys have to deal with this? And when would it end?

The other students dispersed, and I stood up, gathering my things. I couldn't stand the tension anymore and turned to Mrs. Pendleton.

"So did you get whatever you needed? Watching me here?" *Watching me anywhere?*

"I did," she sniffed. "And you should be glad of it. As sponsors of the monster hunting minor, we must ensure the students who receive our patronage are properly vetted. Our vigilance is for your protection as well as ours. Not every student who passes onto our campus has what it takes to be a hunter."

"I'm sure," I said, already tired of the lord-and-master act. Did the guys have to put up with this on the regular?

That would get old fast. "Is there someplace that I can walk you to, or, ah, something that you'd like me to do?"

She peered at me down her long nose as if she totally saw through my veneer of courtesy. "What I would like is for you to comport yourself in the manner to which a monster hunter should, Miss Cross. You and your fellow students should *own* this campus. Instead, you've been degraded to a shadow of your former selves. Given the givens, I suppose it isn't reasonable for me to have lofty expectations. However, the *least* that you can do is not be so dismissive of your own skills. You clearly have been fighting on your own for some time. Stop apologizing for that."

I narrowed my eyes at her. "I've never apologized for it."

"Haven't you? You second-guess your every move on this campus. Time was, there was more to being a hunter than sticking a knife in some creature's throat. And not every monster comes from a fairy tale."

I blinked at her words—I'd said something similar to Grim the first time I'd met him. There was no way Margaret Pendleton could have known that, right?

Either way, she drew herself up stiffly. "I'm not a hunter, nor is anyone in my line, but I'm well aware that this academy was put in place to ensure the full extent of your services would be made available to my family should we ever need them. I must say I am chagrined to find you not as prepared as one would have hoped."

Embarrassment leapt up inside me. "But—I've only just started here."

"And you've been a hunter your whole life." She raised a sharp hand, cutting me off. "Enough. I have stayed quiet for all these long years, we all have, as Wellington Academy has tried to stamp out hunters once and for all. It will not continue. It's beyond time for us to act."

Um...what us? I gave her my best smile. Mrs. Pendleton might represent the money behind the monster hunter minor, but that didn't mean she wasn't crazy. More to the point, I didn't care what she said about some of the cameras in my apartment not working—that meant there were more than the one I'd found, and even one was way too many. I was getting my crap out of there, pronto.

"Sounds good," I agreed, all cheerful acquiescence. She smiled thinly back at me, making it clear once again she wasn't buying my act.

"Who is your family, Nina?" she asked. "Specifically?"

I jolted—less with surprise at the question than at her narrowed eyes, which rendered her into something more like a bird of prey than a grumpy old woman. Still, if anyone would know about my family, it had to be a woman who commissioned surveillance cameras on unsuspecting students. Which I was pretty sure was illegal, at least everywhere that wasn't connected to a monster hunter academy. The fact that Mrs. Pendleton had to ask the question, however, made me think that maybe she didn't know as much as she thought she did.

All that having been said, however, I was still trying to shake loose any information about my mom's family I could. If this busybody could help... "My mother was a teacher in North Carolina, though she started here," I offered. "Janet Cross."

She hmphed. "That's not a name associated with Wellington Academy. I would know. Who's your father?"

"I don't know," I shot back, unreasonably stung. "I never knew him. He wasn't part of our lives."

Mrs. Pendleton leaned forward, her nostrils flaring. "Oh, I think he was more a part of your lives than you may have realized, if your mother was that good at hiding you away," she murmured. Then she straightened. "Either way, you are no longer a child playing an adult game. It's time that you started acting like the hunter you truly are, and to own your birthright. Whatever line you've come from, we're glad you're back in the fold."

We? "I'm—what?"

Mrs. Pendleton flicked nonexistent lint from her sleeve and gave me an arch look. "We will be in touch. And don't worry, I'll give Dean Robbins a full report on how helpful you were, the miserable little toad. But we've work for you to do, and plenty of it. Never mind campus politics, young woman. Don't stray too far from your team. Ever."

While I was still grappling with how to respond to that, Mrs. Pendleton turned smartly on her heel in the middle of the corridor and marched off.

I was happy to let her go. I wasn't sure how long I stood there staring as students flowed around me, but eventually, my phone buzzed again.

I pulled it out of my pocket, then stared down at the text from Tyler. *Keep moving. Go to class. Eyes on you.*

As coolly and calmly as possible, I pocketed my phone and headed down the hallway. My next class was animal husbandry, but for once, I didn't dread it. I just wanted to duck out of sight for another hour.

By the time I emerged from the next class, however, Liam reported in with news that made me scowl down at my phone for an entirely new reason. Reverend Williams had already left the academy, heading back home to deal with urgent matters of his congregation—effectively leaving us holding the demon bag. Frost was in a foul mood over a raft of meetings that he'd been scheduled into with the first families roaming the campus. He wanted us out of sight—

unless we wanted to be roped into more dog-and-pony shows.

No, thanks. I exited the classroom building, momentarily at a loss as to where to go. I was uneasy about returning to my apartment, but frankly, I didn't want to spend the night in Fowler Hall either. That was a level of crazy I could do without in my life, at least not tonight. I was standing uneasily at the arched opening to the campus when I heard a slight shuffling beside me. I turned sharply, and there was Grim.

"You shouldn't leave campus," he said, as if he'd somehow smelled my desire to flee. His preternatural tracking ability should've unnerved me, but I was getting used to it—and his warning reminded me of Mrs. Pendleton, which almost made me smile. Then he continued. "Not alone. Zach will be here soon. He'll go with you."

"He'll...how do you know that?"

As usual, he didn't respond to me directly. "You're nervous. Why?"

I shrugged. "It's nothing. My off-campus apartment sort of freaks me out."

He grunted. "Then you shouldn't go back there."

"Well, that's a cute idea, but I need to sleep somewhere, and I don't suppose you're offering up your couch." The quip was out before I could stop myself, and I winced, feeling the blood rush to my cheeks as he studied me long and slow.

"Don't answer that," I said, when the silence dragged out too long. "My mouth gets ahead of my brain sometimes."

To my surprise, he drew in a sharp breath and hesitated —almost as if he was going to say something...then another voice sounded in the distance.

"Hey," Zach called out as he jogged out of the trees in runner's gear. "Nina. And Grim, what're you guys..."

Grim shot me a sideways glance, his mouth going flat. "That's my cue to leave," he said, and so quickly that I almost couldn't track it, he faded into the shadows.

———

21

"Where's he off to so fast?" Zach asked as he stopped beside me. He'd turned to peer after Grim, giving me a second to recover from monster hunter whiplash. Where Grim's energy was all feral and fierce, Zach's was a combination of beauty and darkness that seemed to weave a spell around me, whispering of possibilities and danger in the night—and his black running pants and deep crimson shirt left very little to the imagination. My imagination really didn't need any help on that score, and I swallowed, trying to ignore the line of perspiration that trailed down between my shoulder blades.

"I honestly think I freak him out sometimes," Zach continued. "Which is like the night freaking out the wolf."

I shook my head hard as images of Grim loping though the shadows scattered, leaving only Zach. Gothically gorgeous Zach, looking as perfect as when the angels first made him. Which...*wait a minute.* "How are you even upright?" I blurted, swinging around as my feet started moving again. I needed to walk. I needed to move. "You weren't doing so great when I last saw you."

"Yeah?" He eyed me as he fell into step beside me, his brow furrowing. Then his face brightened. "Oh! That's right —Liam said you were there at the very end, the first time. Was it bad? When I woke up, I mean?"

I shot him a hard glance. "You don't remember me being there?"

He winced, then rubbed a hand across the back of his neck. "Not all of it, not by half. I had the usual shitty nightmares, getting attacked by demons, caught, set on fire. That happens more than I'd like."

"Nightmares," I echoed weakly. My own skin felt like it was on fire again, and I dearly hoped I wasn't flushing. "Ah... How'd this one go?"

"Better than usual, in the end." He brightened. "Normally, I have to tap something I don't want to trigger, an anger deep inside me, and then I explode and the dream stops. Not this time."

"Yeah?" For the barest moment, I fantasized about what Zach thought had occurred in the thrall of his demon fight. Had I been an angel, racing forward in a blur of white light? A fierce warrior with a winged helmet and silver armor, battling back the creatures of darkness? "What happened?"

He huffed a short laugh, shuddering. "One of the demons broke through the flames—ugliest piece of shit you've ever seen, and old—so old. Coming straight for me. He got near enough to me that I didn't have to dig deep. I reacted out of pure instinct and blasted my way right out of the... You okay?"

"Totally good," I said, nodding rapidly, then glancing away, scrambling for a saner reaction. "You were...delirious when you woke up the, um, first time, I guess."

"I guess so. I remembered Liam being there, but not you. When I woke up for real, he was gone, but when I contacted him, he told me what had gone down. He texted me a shit ton of directions on what pills to take from the stash he'd left behind. I ignored all that, because, well, I wanted to find you."

"Me," I said, sounding remarkably less crazed this time. Almost like a normal girl. *Go, me.*

"Yeah. It was awesome that you came to... I don't know. To help. Liam said you were on hand, right along with Tyler. That you were worried about me."

"I...well, sure," I said. "I mean, you'd been through a demon attack already, and then you were getting hit again—in your mind, anyway. Of course I was worried."

As I kept talking, Zach's gaze sharpened on me, something shifting in his purple-hued eyes. "Did something—actually, forget all that," he said. His face cleared, and I found myself sighing with relief. "It's a gorgeous evening, Frost has cut us loose, and I'm glad I found you. Where are you headed?"

My tightly wound nerves finally unraveling, I peered around. We were already a few blocks away from Wellington Academy. No wonder I'd started feeling better.

"I was thinking I'd go back to my apartment off campus." I winced, belatedly remembering what awaited me there. "I don't suppose you know anything about electronics?"

"Are you kidding? Who do you think had to keep the church running all those years out in the middle of nowhere?" Zach laughed at my surprise. "Oh, come on. It's not like I planned to become a full-time exorcist my whole life—though I knew from the start that preaching wasn't for me. I pretty much thought I'd go into engineering, thank you very much, before we got the scholarship announcement from Wellington the fall of my senior year. Up to that point, I was the church's main handyman, especially when it came to tech. I dealt with all the computers in the house and the electric crap around the property, figured out how to manage the tent's portable lighting and heat during all kinds of weather, even jerry-rigged the surveillance cameras to work with sat phones when our cell service crapped out. Which was often. Why? Did you blow a fuse?"

"Ah...something like that. Mind walking me back to my apartment?"

"Absolutely." He agreed so quickly, a shiver of awareness slid through me before I tamped it down again. Zach was my teammate, nothing more. Kissing him to give him strength was part of the job—as insane as that was. Besides, when I'd blasted through the flames of his terror to rescue him...he'd thought I was a hideous monster. I needed to play it cool, was all. I could do that.

"So...I thought you were living on campus now?" Zach asked as we turned the corner onto Newbury Street. "Or maybe coming to Fowler Hall?"

"I've been thinking about it. It looks like you have the space."

"That's for sure. Hell, you can have a whole wing to yourself, which matters. If I had to see Grim on the regular, I don't think I'd be okay."

I laughed and felt relief all over again as we continued away from the academy. This was the first time we'd really chatted, I supposed, at least not when there was the prospect of a demon lurking around. It was good. It felt right. "So really, you were heading to engineering school? Do you still want to go?"

"What, you mean after my illustrious career as a monster hunter is over?" Zach cocked a self-mocking brow. "Nah. I think part of me always knew I'd end up doing something like this. I just didn't want to do it in a backwater congregation in the middle of nowhere Georgia. It takes a certain kind of person to want to live in such a remote place, and I'm not that guy."

"Yeah? Where would you rather be?"

He gestured around. "Bright lights, big city, I've loved it here in Boston. There's so much noise and chatter that you don't get caught up in the thoughts of people so much. It makes a huge difference."

That made me think. "Can you hear people's thoughts all the time? Or do you have to focus on it to make it happen?"

"It used to be something I couldn't control." We'd stopped at another light, and he had his hands in his pockets, rocking back on his heels. In the half-light of the street-lamps, he looked even fairer than usual, his jet-black hair curling around his face, skimming his neck, and his purple-hued eyes almost otherworldly. "Now I can dial it back to sort of a dull roar, unless I'm trying to parse somebody else's thoughts out, and assuming they aren't warded against me."

He smiled and pointed to the bracelet dangling around my wrist. "Liam really knows what he's doing when it comes to magical trinkets and gadgets. He's absolute shit when it comes to real-world electronics, don't let him tell you otherwise, though he knows his way around the internet and the dark web like nobody I've ever seen. The components he used in that bracelet and the magnetized ink he found for the tattoos are top shelf. Really good stuff. So as long as you're wearing that, you're safe. But if you ever need me, don't wait and think you're going to have time or the presence of mind to keep your wrist covered. Rip the damn thing off, and I can find you. We can always give you another bracelet. Liam can make them out of damned near anything, and Tyler can now recite every spell to activate them he's ever looked at, chapter and verse. We can get you set up."

"Good to know." Another rush of emotion zipped through me, warm and comforting, and I blinked. "But you can't read my mind at all when I'm wearing it, right?"

He made a face. "Absolutely not," he assured me, then slanted me an intrigued, more assessing glance, holding my gaze. We'd stopped—why had we stopped?—in the middle of the sidewalk, the few other walkers moving around us like leaves skirting rocks in a stream. "Why, do you want me to?"

"Oh, of course not." I swallowed, then heard my own words as if they were coming from far away. "That would be crazy."

He didn't drop his gaze for another second, maybe two, his eyes seeming to reach inside me, searching, exploring. I felt myself shift toward him without consciously trying to, my breath catching in my throat—

Then he grinned. "Well, we're all a little bit crazy here, right?"

The moment of tension between us flashed away as quickly as it'd arrived, and we started walking again. Had we stopped? We had to have stopped, turned toward each other, but now we were facing forward again, moving easily, and the flow of people around us felt unchanged. That strange time-displacement thing had happened before when we'd kissed but—we hadn't kissed this time.

Right?

Our chatter returned along with our movement. Zach asked me about my search for Mom so far, my classes. I pointed out my favorite coffee shop as we passed, and we moved on, almost like normal people. We reached my apartment a few minutes later, and without a word, I led Zach upstairs, pausing only briefly to disengage all the locks. He made no comment, but as he opened the door and stepped inside, he looked around, startled.

"Do you live here with somebody else?" he asked.

I snorted. *Only Mrs. Pendleton, staring at my feet.* But I got the feeling Zach meant a real person. "Not at all. I mean, Tyler was here the other day. Is that what you mean?"

"No, this doesn't feel like Tyler. I know his energy."

I gave him another sideways glance. "Ah...is that a thing? Knowing energy?"

He shrugged. "You know how I can read people's thoughts, right? Well, sometimes they leave, I don't know, a sort of residue behind. That...probably sounds strange, now that I think about it. But there's something off here. A ward maybe? I don't know."

I blinked, remembering Mrs. Pendleton's comment. "Actually, I may know what you're picking up on. At the risk of sounding pushy, wanna check out my bedroom?"

Zach's grin was immediate and broad, but I turned away, laughing before he could get in a full eyebrow waggle.

"It's back here." He obligingly followed me down the hallway—but we didn't make it far. He stopped in front of the bathroom, moved forward...then backward. Then he leaned down and peered toward the toilet.

"Do I even want to know?" I groaned as he fished out his phone.

"You fix things for long enough, you see things that shouldn't be there. It's ninety percent of figuring out what's broken. And you, my friend, have something that damned sure looks like a surveillance camera where it absolutely shouldn't be, under the tank."

"A camera. Under the *toilet.*"

"I know, right? You'd be surprised at how many apartments have cameras now, but...generally not where this one is." He continued scrolling through his apps. "Lemme check this other thing..."

He pointed the phone into the room, scanning quickly. "Just the one, looks like." He glanced back to me. "I don't suppose you're trying to keep track of how many times you go to the bathroom?"

"No." I choked off a laugh as he handed me the phone, then entered the bathroom. He angled his long, lanky body to the side, bending down until he was eye level with the camera. "Huh," he said.

"Huh, what? What does huh mean?"

Zach wedged himself closer to the device, and I sent up a prayer of thanks that I kept the entire apartment reasonably clean. "It doesn't appear activated. The indicator light isn't covered or anything, it's just dead."

"Oh." I breathed out a sigh of relief. "That's good, then, right?"

"It's less bad, anyway. This is better." With a discernible pop, he pulled the camera off the wall, then straightened, handing over the small device. "This isn't top of the line, and it isn't new, but it's not like it's ancient either. Someone installed it, though I can't imagine why they put it here."

He shot a glance along the line of the camera trajectory and shook his head. "It's not a wide-angle lens. All that camera's going to get is foot traffic. And seriously, we're talking *only* feet."

"Well, feet are important." I opened the medicine cabinet door and tucked the camera inside the pristine shelves. Meanwhile, Zach poked at the rolling bins I'd set against the wall by the toilet.

"That's a lot of gauze for one girl," he noted, and as I

winced and turned back to him, he looked at me with something different in his eyes. Something darker, more focused. "Good thing you're not just any girl."

My breath died in my throat, and the errant thought struck me again. Had we kissed, out there on the sidewalk? Had I somehow forgotten? My cheeks burned, and I forced myself to stay focused.

"I...so, that's kind of the electronics concern I was getting at earlier. There's more cameras. Like one in my room, for sure. Probably more. Apparently, the benefactors of Wellington had my landlord put cameras in my apartment either before I showed up or at least before I got all my own locks installed. The old lady I had assigned to me today on our campus tour project came right out and told me they'd set the things up, but for some reason, they weren't working. She thought I'd warded myself somehow, but I didn't even know the cameras existed until earlier today. I found one by mistake."

Zach narrowed his eyes at me, their blue-purple depths sharpening. "Today," he echoed. "You discovered a camera in your apartment the same day we all got called onto the carpet for the first campus meet and greet we've had with donors since Christmas...and the woman you're assigned starts chatting you up about them? That's not a coincidence."

I winced as he laid it out for me. How had I not made that connection? "You're right," I agreed, feeling sick to my stomach. "That meant they did see me find it. The cameras do work."

"Well, not that one," he said, poking his thumb at the bathroom again. "But there's no other way..." He ran a hand through his thick black hair, the movement straining the running shirt against his pecs. Zach wasn't as built as Tyler and nowhere near as big as Grim, but he was no slouch in the muscle department. "Did you say anything to anyone else about them? Frost or any of the guys?"

"No. I was going to tell Frost about it when I brought him some of Mom's stuff I was storing here, but—I never got around to that. You were having a near-demon experience, and that kind of distracted me."

He made a face, his expression rueful. "Yeah. And I appreciate it. We need to talk about all that but first..." He waved around. "We should probably see what other welcome gifts your landlord left for you."

"Ugh," I agreed, shivering. "I can't believe people were watching me all this time and I never knew it. I mean, what were they looking for, anyway?"

"Could be anything. They could have a perimeter set up around the campus that only gets triggered if someone special moves in, like a motion-detector camera, but set for magic." He glanced down the hallway, his gaze turning speculative. "This is a pretty nice apartment, actually," he said, and I blew out a breath.

"I thought so too," I muttered. "Now the whole place freaks me out."

"Not for long," he said easily, as if having my apartment bugged wasn't the creepiest thing that could possibly happen to me. As if he could simply wave a magic wand and make it go away.

"Something like that," Zach said with a wink, though I was sure—pretty sure—I hadn't said anything out loud. "Let's go take them out."

22

It took Zach about two hours to search and debug the apartment. My small toolbox was put to good use as he unscrewed vent covers, checked into cabinets, angled my small flashlight into every nook and cranny. By the time he'd gone through the entire apartment, he'd uncovered ten different cameras. Only four of them appeared to be working, which should have made me relieved, but instead left me curious.

"Go over with me again how you landed this apartment," Zach finally requested, after we'd laid out all our ill-gotten goods on the kitchen table.

"It wasn't anything special." I spread my hands, trying to remember what exactly I'd done. "I did your typical Google search and found it online, through like a neighborhood site kind of thing. I don't remember the name now. I used a laptop at the library to do the search. Mine had fried again, and I hadn't gotten it replaced."

"So you didn't use Apartments.com or Zillow or anything like that?"

I shook my head. "I'd planned to double check on one of

those sites to see if all the photos of this place were the same in multiple listings, but the apartment was adorable and available and exactly where I wanted it to be, so I just went ahead and contacted the owner, a guy named Mr. Bellows. He took my information, contacted me within a couple of days, and that was that. It was a really easy process, and I started packing. I rented a U-Haul with the few pieces of furniture I needed and showed up here...maybe a day early? I mean, he said I could move in any time, but I did come earlier than I'd thought I would." I looked around the room with renewed dismay. "Do you suppose I just caught him off guard?"

My gaze shifted to the door. "Oh my God. The locks."

Zach looked back to my reinforced front door. "What about them?"

"I put them in right away. It was something I didn't want to wait on. I didn't ask Mr. Bellows if I could either. I did it right after I moved in, so no wonder they weren't able to come back in and finish wiring everything up...if that's what they were doing. Like, assuming these weren't left over from the last tenant or whatever."

Zach nodded. "Well, it looks like the only ones still active were the one in the kitchen, the main room, and down the long hallway through the opening in the vent. Still pretty comprehensive, and then you've got one on the front door facing into the living room. The one in the bathroom, the two in your bedroom, and the second one in the kitchen were installed and hidden, but they got fried."

"But I noticed the one in the bedroom. If that one wasn't working..." I frowned, glancing back to the hallway. "I scooted right out of there, I guess. Sat on the floor, obviously freaked out. Maybe they figured out what I'd seen from that?"

He nodded. "It's the only thing that makes sense. They knew they'd been made, and they needed you to know the truth so that you...I don't know. Maybe they didn't want you to start asking too many questions of the wrong people?"

I winced, the warning from the bartender at the White Crane coming back to me. "But who would I ask?" I gestured to the table, trying to quell a spurt of hysteria. "Do you have any idea what the feed goes to? Like specifically, who owns these?"

He reached out and touched one of the smaller cameras, barely larger than his fingertip. "I don't. You have to assume Mr. Bellows is behind it, but then again, it's at least theoretically possible that he had no idea they were there. Even the one behind the trash can was pretty well hidden. If he wasn't the one cleaning the apartments or inspecting them thoroughly, these things could have been there for a long time. Well, not too long," he said, checking himself. "They're all pretty new components."

"But they're disabled now."

"Yep. In part, courtesy of your impressive collection of scissors, I should say. Not too many people have scissors that are capable of cutting straight through wire, but good to know that you do. And the entire bunch of them can now enjoy their new home inside the bathroom cabinet."

"I don't know why anyone would be so interested in me in a damned near-empty apartment..." I winced. "Good Lord, they've seen me cleaning myself after an attack. They saw when Tyler brought me home. That's so *gross*."

"It's beyond gross," Zach agreed. "It's bullshit and it's wrong, and we will find out who's doing it, I promise you."

But I'd already turned away, crossing my arms close to my stomach, hugging myself as I paced. "This whole thing is stupid. Dangerous. I can't believe how clueless I was coming here."

Zach sighed behind me, and I could feel his gaze on me, warm and concerned. "You know, you should really be staying at Fowlers Hall. It's a really big place. I promise you you'll have your privacy."

"A heck of a lot more than I had here, clearly," I said ruefully, tightening my hold on my arms. Why was I suddenly so nervous?

"Hey."

Zach had stepped up soundlessly behind me. He turned me to him, tucking his hand beneath my chin and lifting it. "I know this has to be really weird for you. Scary, even. But it's going to be okay. If somebody is tracking you, there's a reason why, and we'll find it. Period. You don't have to worry that you're not safe. That's why you joined the collective."

My heart gave a fluttery thump at the intensity in his eyes. "But none of this makes any sense." I sighed. "I don't know why anybody would go to the trouble about me."

"Oh, I don't know," Zach said, his mouth kicking up at the corner. "You're pretty special, I'm not surprised at all."

It was the most intimate thing he'd said to me, and it caught me strangely off guard.

I blinked up at him, trying to ignore the swell of heat that seemed to be rising up around us. Instead, I gave him an awkward smile. "Well, you're kind of special yourself," I said. "Probably the most special demon hunter I've ever met. Especially when you're not strung up, and—"

I broke off, realizing too late what my idiot mouth was saying and trying desperately to figure out a way to back-track. But Zach's hand turned to stone beneath my chin, his gaze going diamond-hard. I froze, caught in his glare.

"What?" he asked softly, his dark blue eyes now deeply

purple. The question slipped beneath my frantically scrambling thoughts, piercing any attempt at an easy lie. "What were you saying?"

"Nothing," I tried, but I couldn't keep the tears from burning in my eyes, a single drop breaking free to track down my cheek. Images flashed through my mind so quickly that I couldn't catch my breath—so much fire and pain, Zach stretched, bloodied and broken...

Unable to help myself, I lifted my hand to his, and he caught it, his fingers slipping beneath the mind-blocking bracelet.

"Do you want me to take this off?" he asked, the words still soft, but so self-assured, they almost felt mocking. Like he knew what I was thinking, even if he couldn't read my mind. "Is that what you need to be honest with me?"

"What—*no*." I shook my head hard, trying to unseat the dizziness that swept through me. I already felt this much, and I was still protected from him. Protected from myself? The heat was replaced by rolling shivers, and I fought the unreasonable desire to swoon in the arms of this gothic angel looming over me, his skin smelling of cinnamon and smoke, his hands firm and steady as they gripped my trembling body.

"What did you see in my room, Nina, that I knew once, then forgot?" Zach whispered again. "What did you do?"

I opened my mouth to lie—I truly did, but as I met his gaze, the groan that burst from me sounded like it had been dredged up from the depths of hell itself.

"They'd caught you," I whispered, the words nearly a sob. "They'd caught you and were burning you, over and over again. Your skin was charred and bloody—your face..."

I was shaking harder now, one wrist in Zach's grip, while he pressed the other to his chest. Beneath the thin cotton of

175

his shirt, I could feel his heart beating in steady, rhythmic thumps, completely unlike mine, which was trying to jackrabbit its way out of my rib cage.

"They'd strung me up. How?" he asked.

"T-two poles." And though I was staring at Zach's face now, his preternaturally perfect features pristine and whole, that wasn't what I saw anymore. I saw the sunken eyes, the ravaged cheeks, the mouth lolling open with its blackened tongue slipping to the side. The face of a desperate warrior fighting—fighting—

"What did you do?" Zach asked, and his hand pressed flat against mine, against his quickening heartbeat that thudded harder and faster now as he took my panic as his own.

"I d-didn't know what to do," I stuttered, my words tumbling too quickly now. "You were so hurt, so burned. I didn't know how to help you except what I'd done before, in the chapel, when that demon jumped you, and I—I just—"

"Show me." The words were wrapping around me and threading through my mind, and I couldn't think anymore, could hardly breathe. I stepped up on my tiptoes and pressed my lips to Zach's—his mouth nothing like the gaping maw it'd been before, with matted blood and ash and—

"*Nina.*" Zach gasped in what sounded like genuine horror, releasing my hands and hauling me up high into an embrace tight against him, my legs going naturally around his waist as he turned me around and pressed my back against the wall. He plundered my mouth as I lifted my hands to tangle my fingers in his long, lush black hair, my legs resting on his hips as his legs spread wider, bracing me. He broke away from my mouth and burned a trail of kisses along my chin, my neck, up to my ear.

"What were you *thinking*?" he growled in my ear. He pulled his right hand out from behind my back and slid it up the front of my shirt, dragging the fabric high. The other hand splayed beneath my ass, tilting me into him. He was hard and ready, and I groaned as he pressed me close to him, rocking his hips rhythmically. When his right hand closed around my breast, heat blasted through me, and I sagged against him as his growl lengthened into a ragged, fierce moan. "You could have *died*."

"But I didn't," I assured him quickly, following him as he lifted his head away from me, getting only a glimpse of his eyes as I leaned up to find his lips with mine again. I kissed him, and he shuddered hard, shoving me back against the wall and grinding into me. "I didn't die," I said, peppering my words against his mouth as I covered his lips with kisses, desperate for him not to let me go. "I was meant to help you. I *wanted* to help you. I wanted to k-kiss you, to be with you, to make you whole."

"*Mine*," Zach gritted out, or I thought he gritted, but he was moving again, turning me around so that his back was against the wall and I was able to pull away and look at him —his chiseled jawline, now flushed and tight, his lushly carved lips, his winged eyebrows, and his purple-hued eyes, shot through now with licks of white-hot flame.

"I want you," he rumbled. "I want to rip your clothes off right now and pound you right through the floor. I want every single inch of you."

The air died in my throat, and my mouth went totally dry. I started to shake again as Zach continued. "But you— you're with Tyler, and—"

I blinked, jerking back in surprise. The anguish in his voice was so real, so visceral, that it shook me out of my fugue with the horrifying realization of the truth. He didn't know about the sacred flower of sexual power-tripping or whatever the hell it was. He didn't know.

Oh my God. Was he even truly attracted to me? Or was this some screwed-up collective ritual, forcing us together?

"Zach," I tried again, feeling the blood rush to my cheeks and holding on to my embarrassment as the only thing that could save me now. Zach's hand splayed beneath my ass again and hauled me close, and I lost myself in a renewed spiral of need, then fought my way clear. Zach didn't know. He didn't know this was maybe possibly not real attraction, but some sort of artificial weirdness between us. That it wasn't real.

I *wanted* it to be real. I wanted it to be everything. More than that, though, I wanted it to be honest. "You—there's something you have to know," I finally managed.

"What," Zach growled, but as he refocused on me, his elegant brows crashed together. "*What?*"

"This—this isn't easy to explain. Maybe you should put me down."

"No."

I bobbed up my head, meeting his gaze, which had gone cold, almost haughty. The look of a man who wasn't going to let go, ever, I thought, then chased that idea out of my brain before it could get too comfortable.

"No," Zach repeated. "You either tell me what's going on, or let me take off that bracelet." His lips kicked up in a harsh smile. "Better be careful about that second choice, though."

My heart leapt with twin surges of fear and excitement, and it seemed way less scary to tell him the truth and not find myself laid bare before this man, this hunter, this *warrior* who'd looked roaring demons in the face and raged right back at them, trading blood for blood, blow for blow.

So...I started babbling.

23

———

"The way you feel about me—the way I think you feel about me, anyway..." I began, my words tumbling out way too fast, Zach rolled his hips beneath mine, reminding me exactly of how he felt, and I flushed again. "It's possibly like, a magic thing. Something that happened when I joined the collective."

He stiffened, and not in a good way, sending all the butterflies dancing in my stomach into free fall. "What are you talking about?"

"I can't really explain it, because no one knows what's going on, exactly, but something strange happened between me and all the guys. Like we sort of, uh, got attracted to each other and that was on purpose, according to Frost."

Zach grimaced in surprise, his brows shooting up. "Frost *knows* about this? How come he didn't tell us? Or warn us, even? How is it I'm just finding out now?"

I winced. "I think he was hoping it was something in the old stories that wasn't actually true. He seemed pretty unhappy when I explained to him what was happening. Actually, it wasn't even me, it was—"

"Oh my God, no," Zach cut me off, his horror only deepening. "Do not tell me that *Liam* was the one who figured this out. Have you and he...?"

"*No*," I said, my cheeks thoroughly on fire now. "Absolutely not. I feel kind of weird around all the guys, but the only one other than Tyler I seem to be hyperfocused on is you. And, like, you don't have to do anything about that, like we can just stop this—"

"Well, hold up there." Zach hadn't let me go yet. He settled his legs more widely, bracing me as he peered close. "So you're saying you're attracted to me."

He shifted his hips again, and I grimaced, trying to keep my cool and failing. Miserably. "I...am," I confessed.

"And you think it's because of you joining the collective."

"No." The rejection of that idea was quick and absolute, making a corner of Zach's lips curve up again.

"What if I don't believe you?"

I held up my wrist with the bracelet on it and gave it a little shake. "Wanna see for yourself?"

"Oh, I do," he assured me, and the fire flickered in his eyes. "But not yet. We'll save that for later. For now, though..."

Zach abruptly leaned forward, his lips claiming mine with a deep, searching kiss. My mind scrambled, visions popping into my brain and disappearing just as quickly—smoke and fire, a moonlit vista, stars dancing in the sky—

He pulled back again, his eyes wide and wild, the dark, needful energy leaping within them as his entire body trembled. His mouth curved into a hard, possessive smile, and for the very first time, I was scared. Deliriously, gloriously scared, and I wouldn't trade this feeling for anything.

"*Mine*," he muttered again as he pushed himself from the wall, still holding me tight. He strode across the room until we reached the multicolored chaise, then tossed me down on it hard enough to send the clock and pillows bouncing off it, tumbling to the floor. Zach came right after, pausing only long enough to pull off his shirt.

My own need surged within me, sharp and bright, and I reached back for him, every bit as frenzied, pulling at my own shirt, then reaching for the hem of his pants, our hands tangling in our haste until we were both kneeling on the chaise, facing each other like two Olympic wrestlers, naked and breathing heavily. The clock ticked loudly in the sudden silence, and I glanced at it. 8:02 p.m.

"Nina," Zach whispered, startling my attention back. He was staring at me. "My God, you're perfect."

I flushed as I shot a rueful glance down my body. "Well, I'm hardly...um, wait a minute."

This was wrong. This was all wrong. Something had changed about me in the last few seconds, something bad. Except obviously, Zach didn't seem to see it that way. In the haze of our sudden embrace, the scars that I'd carried on my body for so long had resurfaced. Not just the ones that never went away, the ones that I couldn't quite remember acquiring, but every tear, every brand, every bite and scrape and scratch. They shimmered on my skin like a record of the past, a beacon marking every trauma I had ever endured.

"Oh my God, seriously. I'm not this messed up, I swear, I'm not."

"It's okay." Zach laid a hand on my thigh, where a dark and angry welt remained, the memory of a monster's grip long since passed. I felt something shift in my body, cool light flooding me where his hand touched. And I realized what he was trying to do—take my injuries for his own, my pain for his own.

"*No,*" I said, pressing my hand over his.

Zach's head snapped up, his eyes meeting mine. And I saw a line of fire trace itself down his cheek, flaying the skin open, I felt a similar heat along my jaw, quick and hot, the fire of absolution ripping through me.

I blinked. I'd never been injured with fire before, not like that. I'd never burned my face. So how...

Zach figured it out before I did.

"*No,*" he blurted. "Nina, no. You can't." But he seemed frozen in a kind of shock, and I took both of his hands in mine, and for the next breath of time—a second? An hour? An eternity lost in the space that only Zach and I could occupy, we held each other. Sharing each other's pain, torment. Breaking down each other's long-held wounds. Living and feeling and surviving—all at once, an intense explosion of sensation, a throat-closing gasp of agony—and then it was gone, and we were on to the next violation.

Only certain scars never rose up to take hold of us both, I realized dimly, like a distant lighthouse in a furious storm. The scars I had never been able to identify—or remember receiving. But even those were finally obscured by the rushing gale of all that had come before and after. Not only mine, but Zach's as well—his caused by slicing demon claws and grinding teeth and fire...so much fire.

Tears were running down my face by the time we broke away, sprawling on each other, exhausted. My gaze found the clock again as it clicked to the next digit. 8:03 p.m.

Dear God. Only one minute had passed.

"What the hell was that?" Zach moaned, and we half laughed, half groaned as we instinctively rolled back together again on my chaise, both of us trembling. I lifted myself up on my arms and stared down at him, his gaze immediately going to my side.

"I couldn't heal that one," he murmured, and I glanced

down at the ragged mark that some unknown creature had left behind on my rib cage long ago. A long, puckered scar, marred by teeth marks. "Or the one down your back. Or—"

"You did enough," I cut him off. Actually, I didn't know exactly what he'd done, I only knew I felt better than I had in years. Like all my exhaustion had suddenly slipped away, falling off me like rainwater. I looked down at him, his pristine perfect body, and felt the thrill of excitement course through me. "You're also exceptionally naked. It seems like we should do something useful with that information. Since, you know, we can't help ourselves."

"I mean, it seems like we don't have a choice," he agreed somberly, though he couldn't quite hide the smile. His beautiful purple eyes met mine once more. "I know you heard what the demon said earlier today, in the chapel," he said, his words low but not quite embarrassed. More matter-of-fact.

I stared at him, and then the scene came back in a rush. I'd honestly forgotten all about it. The demon, leering and taunting Zach, mocking him for being a virgin. "There's no *way*," I protested, casting a glance back to the wall. "You seemed like you knew what you were doing."

He grimaced. "Yeah, well...demons are assholes. What he meant was, I'd never actually had sex with anyone I— well, that I really liked. That's really the key—for them, for everyone. The emotional connection."

"Ahhh..." I said, then draped myself over him, reveling in the touch of his skin against mine, his every curve and ridge. "So the physical isn't important?"

Zach breathed out harshly as I shifted against him. "I wouldn't say that..." he began, but I was already moving down his body, exploring the slope of his sleekly muscled pecs, the ripple of his abs as they slipped down to the vee of muscles that pointed to his shaft. With every sight, taste, touch...I wanted more—needed more. But as I drifted a line of kisses over his hipbone, Zach's hands tightened on my shoulders.

"Nina," he began.

"Just the tip..." I promised. Then I took his shaft between my lips and slid my mouth over him.

Zach's body convulsed, every muscle going absolutely rigid as he bit out a curse. I licked and kissed and teased for as long as I could bear, but my own body was rebelling against any delay in experiencing more of Zach, in claiming him for my own. I released him and moved up his body again in one quick movement, positioning myself above him. His hands dropped to either side of my hips, gripping me, as his eyes locked on mine. I held his gaze as I lifted myself up the final critical inch and welcomed him inside my body.

Zach's mouth opened on a gasp as I sank down, seating him deep within me in one slide. He filled me completely, but I was lost in his gaze, the world around us shifting first to a desolate scene of smoke and fire, then to an open, grassy plain beneath a starlit sky, and then to the red-satin-covered bed he'd taken me to earlier today. It all swirled around us as we moved, rocking against each other, exploring every nuance of each other's bodies, our hands questing and exploring the skin whose wounds we'd just shared and suffered over. The sense of impending climax built within me, impossible to ignore, but I pushed it off as long as I could.

A growing thunder sounded far on the horizon, but I didn't know if that was a storm coming to Boston or just to Zach and me as we wrapped ourselves around each other and became one person more completely. The thunder loomed closer, crashing around us, electrifying the air. The tension tightened, quivered for a long, torturous second, then burst out of control, leaping higher and higher. Zach whispered something that I couldn't make out. I snapped open my eyes to meet his wide gaze, his eyes wild and fierce.

"*Nina,*" he gasped, and with my name on his lips, we both exploded, a surge of absolute rapture transporting us once more through all the varied landscapes of Zach's mind before crashing us down again upon my multicolored tweed chaise. I blinked blearily across the space as the clock, still on its side, clicked over to its next digits.

8:02 p.m.

24

Waking up next to Zach in my apartment was entirely different from waking up with Tyler. For one, Zach remained wrapped around me, warm and comforting, a slight scatter of energy glistening along my nerves wherever our bodies connected. I opened my eyes, and a breath later, he opened his, blinking as if he'd been disturbed from a deep sleep.

"Hey." His easy smile stretched into a grin, faltering only as he blinked around in the early morning haze. He glanced over my shoulder. "What time is it?"

"Hey, yourself." I huffed a laugh, then squinted at the clock as well. "Apparently, it's eight in the morning. Which means we slept for, like, twelve *hours*. Have you done that recently? Because I haven't. Not for a seriously long time."

"What? No way." Zach levered himself up on one elbow, which only made him look more like a reclining angel carved out of marble. His tousled hair dropped in waves over his forehead, his purple-blue eyes stared soulfully out from his beautiful face, his perfect skin stretched lovingly over cheekbone, jaw, and...

Hold up there, Sparky.

"Oh, my God. You've already *changed*," I complained, rolling off the chaise and stalking toward my bedroom, where the full-length mirror stood.

"What? What do you mean?" Zach called after me, but I didn't stop. I planted myself in front of the mirror, my hands on my hips, still scowling at my reflection when he strolled into the room, a sheet slung haphazardly low over his hips.

"Seriously?" I protested, turning away from my own image to flap my hands at him. "You're going full-on Greek god now?"

"What are you talking about?" He strode over to me as I gestured him toward the mirror, then squinted at it. "What's changed?"

"Are you insane? Look at yourself. Just look."

He leaned forward, but I could see in an instant he had no idea what I was talking about. Stupid boys. "Ummm..." he tried. "I mean, I look rested...?"

"No. *I* look rested. You look like you've just spent a week at the Heaven's Blessing spa, turning your already superhot everything into something that would make Michelangelo cry. You went from cutey-patooty yesterday morning to having your face fried off to looking like you'd been to hell and back so many times, you needed a frequent flyer card, and now..." I gave up and sighed, gesturing helplessly. "Angels are weeping right now. Tell me you can't hear that."

He made a face, then looked at me with real worry. "I seriously don't even know if you're joking anymore."

"On this count, I'm not." I ran my hands through my hair. "I need a shower."

Zach instantly brightened and dropped his hands to his sheet. "I think that's a really good idea."

"Oh, no, you—" But I was too late. He stepped out of his

sheet, and I barely held back a sob of pure, unadulterated awe at the gloriousness that was his body. Unlike Tyler, he hadn't bulked up, exactly, but every cut of his muscles, every curve and dent as he spread his arms wide, was pure perfection. Even the dark swirl of hair that veed down toward his shaft looked like it had been threaded to lie in perfect symmetry.

"...*damn*." I managed, because there wasn't really anything else to say.

"Language," Zach chided in a tone that sounded so much like his father that I visibly jerked—and then he was lunging for me, chasing me around the room in all his naked fabulousness until we made it into the bathroom. Whooping, he slung his arm around me and with his other hand, turned on the spray full tilt, then carried me, still kicking and squealing, into the shower.

The moment the spray hit me, wrapped in his arms, something unlocked within me, though. I sagged, nearly boneless, as he huffed out a startled breath and tightened his hold on me. "Nina?"

"Oh my God," I whispered, but I couldn't do anything more than cling to him, hanging on for dear life as a door opened up deep inside me and what felt like a lifetime of grief I didn't even know I was carrying tumbled out. I began crying—weeping—with deep, racking sobs.

"*Z-Zach,*" I managed, but I couldn't offer him any more explanation as my body convulsed and shuddered, smote by wave after wave of pain. Dimly, I realized he was patting my back, speaking soothingly to me, but I couldn't respond for what felt like several long minutes, the tears flowing down my cheeks, mixing with the water to swirl down the drain.

"What's h-happening?" I asked, surprised to hear my teeth chatter as he wrapped his arms around me.

"Maybe you're changing after all?" he asked, but I laughed shakily, leaning back in his embrace to stare up at his absolute, breathtaking beauty.

"I don't think so," I said. "I think your natural, nonmagical gifts of reassuring those around you, your sense of knowing what to do, what to say, whatever—I think it's now on steroids. You're like the Mentalist without even trying to be. Only cuter."

"The who?" he asked, and I chuckled, shaking my head.

"Never mind. It was a show my mom used to love— whoa." Something shifted in my chest, a fizzy burst of happiness, and I lifted my hand, blinking. "I think...I think my little outburst may have had something to do with my mom."

I spoke with such wonder that Zach cocked an eyebrow at me. "You were thinking about your mom while you were standing in the shower with me?"

"What? No!" I batted him away, but he didn't let me go, merely laughed with pure, unfettered joy—the first time I'd ever heard him do so. "I mean, like, your super mojo powers pulled that grief out of me—a lot of it, anyway." I looked up at him, blinking as I put a hand over my heart. "I feel different."

"Good different?"

"Oh, yeah." I smiled, drawing in a deep breath of steam. "Definitely good different."

"Well, if you're feeling good and I'm feeling good..." Zach shifted slightly, and I realized that something else on his body had achieved ultimate perfection.

When he lowered his face to mine, I met him more than halfway.

· · ·

189

Two hours later, we locked the doors of my apartment behind me, my head feeling so light and fizzy that I thought it might float away from my shoulders. Zach trotted down the stairs in front of me, my iron box in a tote bag slung over his shoulder, but I couldn't look at him without my brain starting to spin. I needed coffee—desperately—but there was nothing in the apartment. We had to head for the Crazy Cup, or back to campus. Weirdly, campus sounded better to me. I didn't feel like sharing Zach with anyone new. Not yet, anyway.

Stepping out into the bright sunshine, I glanced out of habit at the park beside me.

"What is that place?" Zach asked. "It seems a little off. Watchful, almost."

I squinted back at him. "You can sense that? Like, more than usual?"

"Maybe?" He shrugged. "But between that and the cameras in your place, I'd say it's time for you to give up your lease."

"Agreed," I sighed. And there was no mistaking the sense of relief that simple decision gave me. If I was going to be a part of the collective, whether for the next month or until I found my Mom's family and figured out what I was going to do next with my life, I might as well go all in. With Mr. Bellows creeping me out and possibly spying on me, and the spooky park next door, I shouldn't have any reason to stay in this apartment. It still felt a little odd, though, stepping off the stairs. After the extreme emotional deluge I'd suffered in the shower, which had left me oddly hollow and out of sorts despite Zach's firm and reassuring presence, it felt like saying goodbye.

"Hey," Zach said, lifting his hand to tuck an errant strand

of hair behind my ear. "We'll be back, you know. It's going to be okay."

I wanted to believe that he was right, but it wasn't an easy sell. Still, when he reached out his hand for mine, I took it willingly. We'd gone only a few steps before Zach started up again. "We need to talk more about the curse. Since, well, you're totally at risk now."

I squeezed his hand. "It's okay, honestly. I've been monster bait my whole life, as it turns out. Now I get to be demon bait too."

He snorted and ran his free hand through his hair. "I'm serious, Nina. With Dad, he'd planned so hard to avoid losing anyone, he thought he had it all figured out. He didn't, though. The demons found a way to make him pay, and he's never forgiven himself for that. I don't know if you were paying attention to my little history lesson, but a lot of times, the victims tended to sacrifice themselves for the greater good, even when the demon hunters in my family wanted to protect them. I know you're going to pull that shit too, so don't even fake like you won't."

"Okay, then, get used to the idea." A small tremor shivered through me, a lick of genuine fear, but I chased it away. "I do know how to fight monsters, you know. I just need to upgrade my demon-smiting skills."

"Everyone on the team does," Zach shook his head, the sun hitting his hair and turning it into a blue-black fall of night. The guy really and truly needed to look into a modeling contract if this whole monster hunting thing didn't work out.

And I'd done that to him. For him. Me and the whacked-out magic of the collective, anyway. "It's going to be okay," I said, echoing Zach's words at my apartment, and though the words weren't in direct response to anything he'd said, he seemed to understand.

"More than okay," he agreed. "We're going to show them all."

We'd only made it a few minutes toward campus before both our phones pinged, and Zach pulled his out of his pocket, eyeing it. Relief flitted across his face. "It's Mom."

A blade of unexpected sadness knifed through me—when was the last time I'd talked to my mother? The last time she could recognize my voice, before she slipped away completely? Tears sparked in my eyes again. I knew Zach had no idea how precious the gift of that text was. Hopefully, he wouldn't have to learn that lesson for a long, long time.

"Well, good," I offered. He'd told me only the tiniest fraction about her, and that referenced back to when he was a little boy. "Is she okay?"

"Oh, yeah. I've been thinking about her the last couple of days, with Dad here and everything. Normally, he doesn't leave the congregation for too long without taking her. She doesn't like to be alone."

"That would be hard, I think." For so many reasons, not the least of which was living in what I suspected was a super-creepy clapboard house in the middle of the North Georgia forest. "But he's back, right?"

"Yup. He got a call and went home as soon as he could stand upright. It sounds like someone's pregnant daughter got sick, and everyone is convinced it's demons. Mom says it isn't, but Dad can't stand for fear to take root again, so he needed to be there to calm everyone down, exorcise some worry goblins, as he likes to call them. Anyway, she just texted to tell me he was safely home, and everything's fine. So that's perfectly reasonable, but...it still feels like she's worried."

I nodded. If the good reverend had spilled the beans on what was happening up here, his wife's worry didn't surprise me. "Does she text you a lot?"

"Not really. I mean she checks in once a month to make sure I've got everything I need and that school is going okay, but she isn't a helicopter parent. She kind of was of the mind that college was something I needed to do to get away."

He frowned. "In fact, those were her exact words, now I think about it. That she wanted me to get away. I never really thought about that before now, and I've been here three years. But those were strange times in the run-up to coming to the academy. I thought I was going to go to engineering school, like I told you, when the welcome package came in the mail for Wellington. My mom got it before Dad could see it, and showed it to me, but there was no keeping a secret from my dad, of course. He acted like it was a big surprise, though now I know that was bullshit. I guess...I guess he just wanted me to be prepared. To learn to fight the evil that's out there, waiting to trip up everyone who isn't watching out for it. I think he suspected I wasn't cut out for being a preacher." His lips twisted. "I can't believe I never figured out that he'd been here himself. I never even asked where he went to school—which is crazy."

"Yeah." I could relate, of course. "There's all sorts of things that I didn't talk to my mom about. And then one day she got sick, and it seemed like all we discussed was how she was going to get better and all the things we were going to do after."

Zach reached for my hand, and it was the most natural thing to do to curl my fingers into his palm. I looked forward, but my vision blurred, images of my mom surfacing in my mind along with the press of tears behind my eyes.

"Those conversations gave her hope," he said quietly. "That was important to her."

"It was," I nodded, trying to even out my voice. It sounded almost strangled. "But I can't help...I mean, there's so much I don't know. So much I didn't think to ask. Setting aside an entire family I never knew I had—that almost bothers me less than not knowing what her hopes were when she was a little girl. Her dreams. Had she always wanted to be a teacher? She was a botanist. Did you know that?"

He squeezed my hand, and my throat tightened. "I didn't," he said. "That is pretty cool, though. Did you use plants as medicine, or—"

I coughed a short laugh. "That's what she told everyone," I sighed, thinking about the fairy-tale garden behind our cottage, everything bunched together in a riot of colors, shapes, and sizes. That garden was my mother's pride and joy. She'd always been happy there. "But she confided in me that she mostly planted what she thought was pretty. I never knew whether to believe her about that or not."

"Moms generally tell you what they want you to believe, if they can," Zach said, laughing softly. "They protect you even when you don't need protecting, I know from experience."

"Yeah?" I glanced up at him, happy to turn the conversation away from my own regrets.

"Oh, yeah," he said, glancing down at me with a smile, his dark eyes deep pools of warmth. "For the longest time, she gave me Bible verses to tuck into my pocket every time

Dad trooped me out to an exorcism, even though he always did the heavy lifting. She was petrified I'd be called to fight and not have the shield of God to lift up high."

I chuckled, liking his mom better for it. "She sounds pretty sensible to me."

"She's the best. And though Dad refuses to admit it to himself—he does love her. Maybe he kept himself from falling hard at the start, but you can tell. He'd be lost without her, hates to leave her now, really, despite the tough-guy act. And she loves him right back. Always has. We don't talk much about her miscarrying Samuel, but she never once blamed Dad for that—at least not in any way I could tell. Samuel was a gift she couldn't keep for very long, was all. And for both Mom and Dad, the parish means everything. Folks come from all over to hear Dad give his sermons. He does good work. Needful work."

I nodded. "You sure you don't want to do that same work?"

"Not even remotely." He grinned, and I felt my own grief lessen in the lightness of his expression, the warmth of his hand in mine. "I came to Wellington to learn how to take demons out, once and for all...and now it looks like I'm going to get my first chance. But this is all reminding me of a few things I haven't been focusing on enough. If things are about to go down, and I do think they are, we need to get busy."

"We do?"

But Zach merely dropped my hand, focusing back on his phone to text something new. A few seconds later, my phone buzzed. He gestured me to look, and I obligingly pulled it out.

How to Kill Your Demon 101, his text announced. *Training field in thirty. Bring your favorite weapons, but no crosses required. Promise.*

"Let's go," he said, and he reached for my hand.

25

To my surprise, Zach didn't head immediately for the monster quad, but cut across campus toward the academic buildings. He only slowed when we reached Cabot Hall.

"It probably would be better if you stayed out here, but screw that," he said. "I don't like leaving you anywhere right now. Not with the shit that's about to go down on campus."

I shot him a glance as we entered the classroom building, the murmur of teachers and students rising and falling from behind closed doors.

"You really think demons are just going to jump out of nowhere? You think they're that close?"

"Honestly, I don't feel them yet, but that doesn't make sense. They're here, and they're waiting. I don't know where they're going to come out, but it's just a matter of time. I don't want to leave you hanging around like..."

He reddened a little, and I snorted. "Like bait. You can say it, I'm getting used to the idea."

"Not for long," Zach promised. We moved quickly up the stairs to the second floor of Cabot Hall, which I already knew was the demonology department. There was nobody up here from the looks of it, and Zach answered my unasked question.

"Classes are done for this semester for these guys. The sunrise ceremony is sort of an unofficial capstone every spring, and then they've got finals next week. Believe me, I wish they were all already home and off campus completely. It was never my goal to involve them in any of this."

"You don't think they can help you at all?"

He sighed. "It's not that they can't help me, it's like what I said back at Lowell Library. These are my family's demons. They are very specific. All the usual tricks and tools to exorcise a demon, to remove it from plaguing a person or a space, are all great, but they're only the beginning of what's needed. Honestly, that's why I think our team of monster hunters has a better shot at these guys. You guys won't get hung up in expecting all the traditional solutions to work. They'll help, without question, but they're mostly going to be useful to keep the demons trapped long enough for us to finish the job. We're not looking to perform an exorcism here, if you get what I'm saying. We're looking to kill these assholes."

I considered that as Zach tried one of the doors of the closed classrooms. It was locked, but without missing a beat, he swiped out a key card and pressed it against the panel. The door clicked open.

My brows went up. "What is that, an All-Access Pass?"

Zach shrugged a little ruefully. "I've had the run of the place since I got here, pretty much. I've tried to repay the favor to the extent that I can too. These are good guys— women too, for that matter. Though like everything else at Wellington, it's mostly dudes."

I rolled my eyes. "I'll try not to hold it against you all. Enlightenment comes more slowly for some schools."

He snorted, then moved forward quickly in the gloom of the classroom. Several rows of tables stretched out in front of us, with a long whiteboard across one wall filled with Latin and Greek.

"Traditional exorcism commands, the heart and soul of the demonology department," Zach explained. "Judeo-Christian methodology works surprisingly well with demons from any faith system. It's sort of the OG of the exorcism game, and as with most things, it's the innate authority with which those commands are spoken that makes all the difference."

"Interesting." I studied the board as Zach knelt in front of a row of cabinets, pulling one open seemingly at random. He chuckled with satisfaction, though, so it clearly wasn't *that* random.

"Okay, here we go," he said, and I peered over at him. He held what looked like an external hard drive, only equipped with a projector lens.

"We're going to take them out with Death by Power-Point?" I said. "That's what they teach you here?"

"You'll see," he said with a grin. He closed the drawers, and we were out of the room a few seconds later, trotting back down the stairs. We almost made it to the exit when a familiar voice rang out.

"Nina, hey! And oh, Zach, it's nice to...um...wow."

Her glorious auburn hair lashed back into a high pony-tail and her Wellington Academy uniform impeccable from its tailored red polo to her red-and-black-plaid miniskirt and gleaming black boots, Merry Williams strode toward us down the hall. In one hand she held, oddly enough, a red-and-black megaphone that paired perfectly with her miniskirt, but even that distracted me less than the shocked look on her face as her words faltered to a stop. I tried not to appear smug at her reaction to Zach, but it was tough going. "Hi, Zach," she finally managed.

Zach, clueless as ever, smiled at her, completely missing the way Merry's eyes dilated at the force of his leveled-up attention. "Hey there." He nodded. "I would have thought they would have cut the veterinary students loose by now. Shouldn't you guys be getting to your summer co-op jobs?"

"Oh! Oh yes, a lot of the students are, but this is my last year, so I'm taking care of some final paperwork on campus. I have to say, I've never hung around this long after students start to leave. It really is different, isn't it?"

"What do you mean?" I asked, something in her words hitting me the wrong way.

"Oh, you know, the energy and all that." She waved the megaphone. "Everyone seems more *preoccupied* right now, like they don't even see what's in front of them, their heads so full of everything they have to get done, you know? It happens during finals week in the winter, but I guess I've never seen it in the springtime."

"Got it," I said. Exhausted end-of-year students being nervous about their exams wasn't any cause for alarm, and I allowed myself to relax a notch. "How long will you be on campus, again?"

"Through the summer," she said, beaming. "You sure you don't want to take me up on rooming? I *assure* you it'll be tidier at my place than Fowlers Hall."

"Hey, now," Zach protested, but he'd managed to start shepherding us toward the front door. In a few more steps, we were out in the sunshine, and I sensed Zach's urgency kick up a notch, despite his relaxed expression. "Maybe you shouldn't dis a dorm you've never stayed in, okay? Fowlers Hall is very nice."

Merry snorted, rolling her eyes. "Spoken like a true homer. The offer still stands, Nina, if you ever need it."

We parted ways, though I could feel Merry's speculative gaze on us as we hustled across campus. I didn't wonder about what she was thinking for too long, because the guys were waiting for us at the field by the time we reached the monster quad.

Tyler, Liam, even Grim looked excited, even eager to see what Zach had in mind for this particular round of training. I did too, frankly. The demons we'd fought in Bellamy Chapel had felt a lot like regular monsters to me, but the creatures I'd encountered in Zach's mind were far worse, in a way I didn't really understand.

"My *man*," Liam announced as he caught sight of us. "You're breaking my heart telling me we don't need any religious tools. I was all set to create holy water squirt guns."

"Not necessary." Zach laughed as we jogged up to them. Setting aside the tote bag that contained my iron box of mementoes, he pulled out the small external drive, then dropped to one knee.

"Whoa," Liam said, edging forward. "What's this?"

"Frost isn't the only one who's gotten handy with monster simulations," Zach said. "The demonology department also suffers from a critical lack of source material, so I worked this up to give them some ideas on what they may face in the real world. A lot less messy than full-on *Exorcist*-style possessions. Of course, since I knew what would be coming our way eventually, I also made a program with some very particular modifications, complete with AI to keep me on my toes."

He pressed a final set of buttons, then got to his feet,

backing away from the device. As he did, a light flashed from the unit, sweeping the space in front of the box out about fifteen feet. Obligingly, the guys and I fell back, and as we watched, the light flashed back and forth rapidly, eventually coalescing into five distinct figures.

"Five?" Tyler asked quickly, his hands coming up as the creatures began to shuffle and stretch, ranging in size from four to ten feet, but all of them sporting impressive mountain-ram-style curved horns, long snouts, and cruelly taloned hands and feet. They also stood upright, and three of them flicked honest-to-God tails. "There are going to be five of them?"

"Honestly, I have no idea," Zach clarified. "Usually there are two or three that are the main leaders. Sometimes they come with lieutenants, sometimes an entire horde is let loose on the countryside. If you're looking at the horde, though, that's generally the result of an outright attack on the demons versus a sacrifice."

"So in other words, exactly what we're planning on doing," Liam said.

Zach nodded, his eyes on the holograms. "Pretty much."

"*Excellent.*"

"Um, guys?" I asked, as the holographic generation of the demons seemed to complete itself. If I didn't know they were holograms, I'd be pretty freaked out, and even telling myself they were holograms didn't make me all that happy. "What exactly do we do here?" I'd already pulled out my iron-bladed knife from my ankle sheath, but I still felt woefully unprepared.

"To start, we get cocky," Zach said. "The most important aspect to fighting off a demon is your sense of authority. If they know they freak you out, that's more than half the battle for them. It's everything they live for. Make sense?"

"Oh, yeah," Liam said, practically bouncing on his toes. He held a short, serrated blade in each hand, and I glanced over to Tyler, who brandished a single, longer blade, almost a short sword. Grim didn't have anything in his hands, but his meaty paws were clenched into fists. For Grim, I suspected his fists would count as deadly weapons—especially against holograms.

Then the first wave of sulfur brushed over us, and I froze. "Ahh...are they supposed to stink? Is that a part of your program? Because these things *stink* and the last time we had a monster that stank—"

With an unearthly roar, the demons attacked.

It was much less a testament to my sense of ultimate authority than the fact I was scared brain-dead at the surge of real-looking demons that I didn't scream at the top of my lungs. Zach leapt forward first, his arms going out, his face remarkably relaxed despite the urgency in his tone. Was this unexpected to him? Was this part of his program?

"*Desist,*" he shouted, and then followed it up with a long line of Latin I had no hope of deciphering in the midst of the bellowing demons. The demons reacted with impressive animation to his words, though not in the way I expected.

Basically—they got *pissed*.

"*Infant,*" the first one howled, lurching forward as if against some kind of force field, getting farther with each lunge. "You cannot snare us with your traps. We do not care about your souls. We care about your *sacrifice.*"

Zach whipped toward us. "Again!" he shouted, and this time, Tyler and Liam stepped forward, reciting the same line of Latin, Zach had spoken. Grim remained silent, but he'd shaken his hands open, and I noticed one was no longer empty. A pile of something round and silver lay in his palm before he closed his meaty fingers around it. He shifted toward me, but I glanced away as the demons' rage ticked up a notch.

"You will pay for this, you and everybody you love," the largest demon declared, shaking its long, almost equine head, and baring its teeth.

"Okay! That's all the time they'll give us," Zach interjected. "From now on, it's—"

Once again, his words were cut off by a screech of fury. The creatures sprang forward. Unexpected fear rocketed through me, and Grim crossed the short distance remaining between us and grabbed my hand, the jolting fire of that connection immediately dampened by the sense of something smooth and small within my palm. He pulled back his hand, and I saw he'd given me a handful of silver pellets. *What the hell?*

He murmured something I couldn't quite hear, but which jolted me out of my panic. Then he swung away, completing a roundhouse punch as one of the demons raced up to him, talons flailing.

I stared down at the beads in my palm, dumbstruck for another second. These were the same kind of beads like the one I'd seen the squirrel trying to break open over by the park. How had Grim found an entire trove of them—and what had he said as he'd given them to me?

I didn't have time to work it out, as an exceptionally feral, skinny-looking demon, more fang and claw than body, leapt at me. My left hand spasming around the pellets, I slashed at it with my iron blade, but the creature kept coming. It raked its claws across my face, and if it'd been real and not a hologram, I would have been looking at some serious plastic surgery. As it was, the demon stopped its claws midair and reversed direction, and panic suffused me again. Not knowing what else to do, I hurled the tiny pellets at it, cringing back as it exploded in a furious burst of ash and smoke.

Don't be afraid.

Grim's words, finally clear and true, struck me as if they'd been released on a sigh, and I scrambled back, dazed. Liam sent up a cheer.

"She hits, she scores," he chortled, while he and the other guys converged on their targets. It was all a blur of fists and kicks and flashing blades as I picked out the weapons being wielded by the other guys. Though they were able to push the demons back, other than the one I had managed to poof out of existence, the others were not giving up much ground.

"Zach?" Tyler shouted finally, as the creatures pushed forward again. "Are you sure about the crosses?"

"They shouldn't *work*," Zach insisted, but Liam was already bringing his bag around.

"Never look a gift crucifix in the mouth, I always say," he declared, and a second later, metal flashed through the air, catching the light.

Tyler caught the first thrown cross, Zach the second, and I noted the sharpened spikes—these were the same kind of weapons that we'd used in Bellamy Chapel yesterday. Liam shook out a final one, but Grim ignored them—beating down his demon on his own. This time when the guys pushed forward, the demons screamed and fell back, eventually falling beneath the cross pummeling. Within another forty-five seconds, the field was clear.

Zach leaned over, breathing hard, but he didn't look happy.

"That's not the way that should have gone," he insisted.

"These aren't supposed to be typical demons. I didn't program them that way."

"You programmed them to match their environment," Grim countered. "It's a good strategy, choosing to fight them here, but monsters have a long history of adapting to human strategy. An attack that's going to go down on a monster hunting campus requires different tools. Your machine demons figured out how to adjust. Your family's demons might too."

"Fuck," Zach groaned, his disgust plain.

Tools. I frowned. Tools like the silver pellets that Grim had given me, along with the order not to be afraid. Why... why had he said that? And where had he found those beads? I wanted to ask him, but I didn't know how without focusing all the guys' attention on him. I got the feeling he wouldn't appreciate that.

"In any event," Zach said, drawing our attention again, "now we have a plan. Take out the monsters the way you would any creature, but to Grim's point, be ready for a couple of religious nuts in the mix as well." He sounded so exasperated, I couldn't help but laugh.

"We've got this, my man," Liam said, pounding him on the back. "Now we're just better prepared, right? And I'm glad we did this. These demon guys are big, stubborn, and double-jointed, if they're anything like your holograms. We're going to have to make a lot of follow-on strikes to take them down, unless you're Grim and you just want to beat them to death."

Grim grunted, and Tyler turned to me. "Or Nina, with her knockoff blade of destruction," he said. "Great kill shot there."

I blinked at him, realizing he thought I'd taken the demon out with my knife, not Grim's pellets. I opened my mouth, then shut it as my phone buzzed in my pocket. A second later, all the guys' phones buzzed too.

Tyler reacted first, with a quick draw on his phone that would have made any Wild West gunslinger proud.

"It's Frost," he said, peering down at the screen. "Looks like the entire demonology department just showed up at Lowell Library. We've gotta move."

26

We weren't that far from the library, but as we gathered our things and made our way out of the field, we argued about the ramifications of the sudden infestation of demonology students. Frost hadn't indicated why they'd shown up, and didn't respond to Tyler's follow-up text.

"Well, it can't be a demon attack," Liam reasoned. "If it was, he'd have said something."

"Maybe, maybe not," Tyler said. He looked over at Zach. "Are you picking up on anything? Is your demon Spidey sense tingling?"

"I should be, at this point, but I've got nothing," Zach said, shaking his head in irritation. "And I agree with Liam —Frost would have said something if that's what it was."

"Can you, ah, find that out for sure?" I asked. "He's not warded from you, right? So you could read his mind if you wanted?"

"Oh, he's warded," Zach said. "Has been since the day I arrived—before I arrived, actually. Now that I realize he and

Dad were classmates, I bet he got those tats made when Dad was here the first time."

Liam snorted. "Probably. That man doesn't mess around."

As we approached the library, there were more students relaxing in the shared quad spaces than usual—or so it seemed to me. I watched them out of the corner of my eye, though for what, I wasn't exactly sure. It wasn't like they were going to outwardly express their disdain for us, right? Most of the students at Wellington Academy probably didn't know anything about the monster hunter minor other than as a bullet point on an academic list. The whole academy wasn't out to get us. They couldn't be. Right?

Nevertheless, I couldn't help but feel uneasy. The guys were all kibitzing back and forth, acting like everything was normal, their energy up a little because of the training sesh we'd just had. Nothing like killing a few demons to get you amped up, right? But something else was bugging me, and I couldn't quite...

Then it hit me. I was picking up on Zach's emotions—channeling them. This time without any need for holding onto the bracelet. Was this my doing, or simply a result of Zach leveling up? Did we all need to upgrade our bracelets now? Probably, though Zach likely wasn't entirely sure of how he'd leveled up. I narrowed my eyes at him, but he looked ahead at the same time, his expression registering dismay.

"Oh, geez," he muttered, and I followed his sightline to see what had upset him. Wendy Symmes stood loitering in front of Lowell Library, looking woefully out of place. The moment she saw Zach, her face lit up.

"*Zach*," she said, blinking rapidly as she took in his fallen-angel beauty. Even if the guys were oblivious, at least the women of this world weren't. I found myself vindicated once again, but I would have much preferred being vindicated by someone other than a beautiful young coed with huge green eyes. "I was hoping I'd find you here."

I managed not to point out that it was extremely likely she would find him considering how much time we all spent in the library, but I decided to be the bigger person. It pained me.

"Hey, Wendy," Zach said, giving her a smile that made her cheeks heat even more obviously. "What's going on? Is everything okay?"

"Oh, yes," she nodded quickly. "I—well, I told my dad all about what happened yesterday. He's been traveling out of town and just got back. He was super impressed you were able to, in his words, save me from myself." She blushed again prettily. She probably didn't do anything that wasn't pretty. "Anyway, he wanted to invite you to dinner, all of you, he's kind of a big deal with the school, and I don't know, I just thought, you know, it might be a good thing? For your minor and stuff?"

We all got the reference at the same time, and my eyebrows climbed up my forehead.

"Are you sure he wants to see all of us?" Tyler asked, drawing Wendy's gaze. Her eyes widened, indicating a clear willingness to be smitten by any hunky college guy who paid her attention. I couldn't say I blamed her.

"Oh, absolutely," she said. "He was quite specific about that. I don't know if you know this, but my mom, oh God, it sounds sort of ridiculous for me to even say it out loud, but—"

"Your mom is a Lowell," Zach said, as if he'd learned this piece of information somewhere totally ordinary and not by reading her mind.

"*Yes,*" she said, clearly relieved not to have to explain it. Without question, the people on this campus were super weird about family ties. "I don't make a big deal out of it ordinarily, because, you know, who cares, whatever, but she *is* a Lowell, so therefore, we, I mean my family, we're kind of in tight with the academy, right? So I thought maybe this could be a good thing for all of you."

"It's a very good thing," Zach assured her, and there was a strange lilt to his voice that hadn't been there before, one I'm not sure I would've noticed if I wasn't looking for it. That didn't make me feel much better, though, because Zach didn't appear to be doing anything differently than he ordinarily did, making people feel at ease, comfortable, but not expending too much effort to do so. Had he increased his ability to win friends and influence people *beyond* becoming hotter, or was it some kind of new, magic-related skill?

Zach kept going. "We would be totally honored to have dinner with your dad, your whole family. I assume you'll be there too?"

"Oh *God*, no," Wendy said with such emphasis that we all jolted, even Grim. She blushed again, and I wonder if she used a particular type of makeup to emphasize that look. I'd never seen anyone blush as impressively as Wendy Symmes.

"Sorry," she managed with a little laugh. "I know that sounds kind of strange, but my dad isn't really the type to have a casual dinner without an agenda. He wants to meet with you all, like, officially. Sometime soon, but not this week, as he's off again. He wanted me to get your contact information and let you know he'd be calling. I hope that's okay?"

Zach nodded and pulled out his phone as I studied Wendy more carefully. Her relief was obvious. She hadn't been sent here to flirt with Zach, though that was an enjoyable side benefit of the visit. She'd been sent here on a mission from her dad. She was little more than his glorified messenger, which didn't sit well with me, but she seemed to take it all in stride. I got the feeling that such summonses were business as usual for her. What would it be like to have a father that powerful? What would it be like to have a father at all? I'd never missed not having one, though I'd sort of begun fantasizing about it, what with Mom's letters and all.

You know, the letters she'd never sent.

Once the contact information was shared, Wendy wasted no time scampering off, reinforcing my belief that she wasn't actually interested in either Zach or Tyler. Which was handy, because I wasn't sure how I was going to deal with it if she was. I wasn't normally the jealous type, but then again, none of what had happened to me these past two weeks at Wellington Academy could be classified as normal.

Grim had already continued on to the library, and the rest of us hastened to join him. We didn't say anything more until we entered the main chamber...to find a good thirty-odd students waiting for us, Dean Robbins and Commander Frost at their head, along with a man dressed in a black shirt and pants, his pale face world-weary beneath his close-cropped gray hair, but his eyes sharp and focused.

"Bands," Zach said suddenly, and on cue, we all reached over and covered our left wrists. Zach spoke immediately in our minds. *"Don't slow down, but this is wrong, man. This is bad. We've got possessions happening in this group."*

"Who?" Liam asked, as Grim huffed out a sharp, angry breath.

"Can't tell, but roll with it until they break out, because they

are freaking about to burst. Liam, you got salt on you by any chance?"

Beside me, Liam hiked the shoulder carrying his pack. *"By the tube and by the cube, my man."*

"Hit the door and get ready to seal us in. I want to make sure we've got 'em all in here first, but that won't take long."

"Roger that."

Zach signaled to me, sliding my tote bag off his shoulder and making sure I saw him hide it behind the reception desk. Its contents—the iron box I'd carried with me from Asheville—would be safe there, I knew instinctively. Whatever trouble was waiting for us in the library, it wasn't after my mom's letters. Nevertheless, I took the extra second to lean down, checking to see that my ankle sheath was snug, my knife in place. Then we started moving again.

The other students turned as we approached, and we didn't slow our pace until we hit the center of the room. Robbins wasted no time.

"Ah, here we are," he said, his eyes flat and lizard-like, though an affable smile stretched across his face. "Gentlemen. Ms. Cross. I appreciate you coming so quickly. We have an unprecedented cross-departmental collaborative opportunity with demonology that will take up the rest of your day. You'll remain under the direction of Professor Garrison here, and not leave the premises without his permission. I'll notify the instructors of any classes you have today—except for you, Ms. Cross, given your status as an auditing student this semester."

I took the slam in stride as Tyler stopped short. "We're happy to help, but—how?" he asked Garrison, pausing long enough to nod deferentially to Frost and Robbins.

"Actually, Mr. Perkins," the thin man, who I assumed was Professor Garrison, interrupted, "the question is, the question has *always* been, how can we help you? Commander Frost and I have finally had the opportunity to discuss the alerts of demonic activity that have been bubbling up these past several days, but I had no idea how advanced your tracking mechanisms were. While I'm impressed, I think I would have been more impressed if you'd brought us in earlier."

Robbins spread his hands. "I, of course, shared with Professor Garrison the experimental nature of the tracking procedures we've assembled here at Lowell Library."

I noticed the *we*—since when did Robbins want to associate himself with us? Had something happened?

"Very experimental," Frost huffed. "And as I've been trying to explain to you, highly erratic."

Garrison thinned his lips. "Erratic or not, we are the experts in demon management, as you well know. We've brought a few of our own laptops to compare our findings with yours, but I can't help but feel that you've been remiss in not informing us earlier."

As the men argued back and forth, I felt an odd chill lift the hair on the back of my neck. Steps sounded behind me, more students coming in, and I shivered.

"We're close," murmured Zach.

By now, Liam had drifted to the side of the group, his gaze scanning the books stacked high in the shelves. No one paid him any attention, and he moved so casually, it seemed almost ingrained—the well-worn distraction of an academic for books. But he stepped back another foot as I watched, then slipped to the side. Garrison's disapproving voice recalled my attention.

"Again, what you perceive as erratic, academicians with proper training could have advised you was deeply organized and prophetic. The academy could have prepared, shored up its defenses, called in reinforcements against any potential attack. But no."

As Garrison continued, his voice changed—at first subtly, then more obviously, becoming harsh and garbled. "You, in your secretive ivory tower, smug in your misbelief about how special your blighted minor is, chose to remain silent. Dangerous decisions, Commander Frost. Foolish choices. Now you will be held accountable for those choices."

"Uh-oh," Zach warned in our minds. *"Liam."*

"Way ahead of you."

As Liam disappeared into the stacks, I surveyed Garrison's students, not surprised to see many of them beginning to peer at their professor in alarm. I didn't know this professor, but given his manner of dress and personal grooming, he didn't seem given to histrionics. But now he was growing more and more excited, tension snaking out from him into the room. Even Robbins frowned.

"Professor Garrison, I assure you—" Robbins began.

"And *you.*" Garrison turned on him with such vitriol, I flinched. "You have been *exactly* what the festering rot needed to leach deep into the bones of this academy. All of you so smug, so caught up in your petty plays at power. Now you will see *real* power. The power of the horde."

"Eviglio," one of the demonology students murmured beside me, soft and cautious. I didn't know the Latin, but a ripple of awareness spread through the room, many of the students glancing around with growing worry on their faces. Many, but not all.

I noticed something else too. About half the group hadn't come to Lowell Library empty-handed. They carried backpacks similar to Liam's and apparently shared his penchant for the tools of the trade. As the men carped at each other at the front of the room, easily a dozen students pulled their packs around, flashes of silver glinting as they pulled the bags open.

Did Wellington Academy supply these guys with their own set of exorcism tools? And what would those include anyway? Vials of holy water, tubes of salt, crosses? Did they sell starter kits in the campus bookstore?

These idle thoughts crashed together as I noticed that not all of these students were surreptitiously arming themselves. A dozen others stood frozen, transfixed by the drama unfolding at the front of the room. For a second, I thought they were merely impressed with their professor getting fierce, then I realized there was more to it than that. They were too still, too silent, almost as if they were frozen in a thrall.

"I see you," Zach murmured in our minds, and a new swell of awareness flowed through the room, tightening the tension.

"Professor Garrison, I must take exception to your tone," Robbins continued heavily. He looked pissed to be put into the position of defending the monster hunting minor, but he *was* the dean of our program, even if he didn't have a magical bone in his body. Certain protocols had to be observed, and Garrison was totally not playing the usual game of academic respect. "I understand your frustration, but I assure you I've been working closely with Commander Frost to find our best path forward. We're doing everything in our power to find an effective method for collaboration between our two departments. I merely ask that you respect the process as we are evolving it."

"Respect." Garrison curled his lip. "That's all you ever cared about, isn't it, Dean Robbins? The respect of those you secretly feared. The fear of those you could intimidate. Your

time will come, little man." Garrison now sounded like a long stretch of hard road, and Dean Robbins stiffened.

"Professor Garrison," he snapped, but Garrison waved him off.

"Frost saw and didn't share what he knew. You're worse. You can't even see what's right in front of you. How else can you explain having witnessed the arrival of our brothers and not sending up the alarm? Rest assured, there *will* be hell to pay for that."

I blinked, narrowing my eyes on Garrison. Had he said "brothers"?

Zach stepped forward. "You don't have to do this," he began, using his inside demon voice, and Garrison turned his head so sharply, I was surprised it didn't whip off his neck.

"You have grown lax, Zachariah, but no more lax than Commander Frost here," Garrison sneered as both Robbins and Frost took a careful step back, clearly aware that something had gone very wrong with the professor. "Dean Robbins I can almost excuse. He doesn't know any more than what he's told. But you I would have expected more of."

Then he spoke another word, not quite Latin or Akkadian, but it nearly froze my blood. The stacks of books started sparking, and plumes of smoke billowed down the long aisleways. The stench of sulfur filled the air.

"What is the meaning of this?" Robbins blustered, lifting his hands even as Frost squared his shoulders and jutted out his chin, a man clearly on the edge of a brawl. All he needed to do was crack his knuckles. "What's going *on* here?"

Garrison shot Robbins a derisive look. "Our cross-departmental collaboration is a very simple one, Dean Robbins. We'll keep you here and well entertained while our brethren seed the ground of this campus for its harvest of pain. Wellington Academy will pay for Zachariah Williams believing he could defeat us. Starting now, I think."

The library erupted in fire.

27

"Nina!" Turning toward me as I threw up my arms reflexively against the boiling smoke and sparking flames, Zach yanked me to his side.

Chaos reigned around us. Easily a third of the demonology students had turned on their peers, and a vicious hand-to-hand brawl was underway—kicks and punches making do when shouted Latin curses and flailing crosses failed. Frost shoved Robbins to the side and was grappling with Garrison, whose body contorted in horrifying ways, the demon inside him practically bursting through his skin.

Zach shook me back to focus. "Hey, we need to get out of here. The guys can handle this, but Garrison is a good guy, honest. If demons have gotten to him, they're potentially everywhere. And if you've amped me up in some way, I want you by my side until I figure out exactly how. My family demons are mixed up in this, but that's not all that's going on."

He jolted, looking to the front of the room, and I realized he was communicating with one of the other guys—a communication I couldn't hear because I'd removed my hand from my bracelet. Screw that. I yanked off the narrow metal band, and voices filled my head.

"Entryway secured," Liam reported. *"I've got salt everywhere there's a door or window—we're good. You guys need to bolt, though. The board in the war room is lit up like a Christmas tree, and all the hottest locations are here on campus. Something's here, and it's pissed."*

"Agreed," Tyler shouted, and I spun around to see him fighting with a knot of students who were experiencing the same contortions as Professor Garrison—how many demons were we talking about here? *"We'll lock down Lowell and keep this group inside. Go. Get these bastards at their source."*

"But where are they coming through?"

Tyler's response was buried beneath a demon roar, and I jerked my gaze across the room to see Grim pummeling the crap out of a student who had now morphed into a full-on demon. *"Portal sites all over the damned campus,"* Grim gritted out. *"But don't be an idiot. What do they like the most?"*

I snapped my focus back to Zach, who was already nodding. "Unconsecrated ground," he muttered. "Has to be."

Zach and I turned toward the front doors of Lowell Library and took off, pausing only briefly as Liam blocked our path. "Take these," he ordered, shoving two small cloth go-sacks at me, the crest of Wellington Academy visible in the corners. Maybe they did sell these kits in the bookstore.

I didn't have time to explore the goody bags as Liam shoved us through the door, his already uncorked vial of salt ready to repair any damage we did to his protective line. Then we were through the foyer and out the front door of the library.

Hitting the bright, open expanse of campus again was

almost a religious experience, especially given what we'd just left behind. There was no smoke, no sulfur here. The sun shone cheerfully over manicured walkways and lush green space, and while there were still a few students around, it was remarkably quiet—idyllic, really.

We hustled forward, and once we breached the ancient wall to the central campus, things changed. There were more students here, for one, and they eyed us oddly. More oddly than usual? It was so hard to tell.

"They're not possessed, are they?" I asked, as Zach and I forced ourselves to slow down. We didn't want to draw attention to ourselves until we knew exactly what it was that was looking at us.

"I don't think so," he murmured back. "I think we need to focus on what Garrison actually said. The campus is being prepared, like fertile ground. I think the combination of fewer students on campus and the arrival of the horde has set some sort of stage. I've never seen a full-scale attack like this before. It's just not the way demons usually work. They generally prefer to do things quietly, under the radar. This...this just doesn't track with that."

I shot him a nervous glance. "You don't think someone is helping them, do you?"

He shook his head. "No way. It's too disjointed for that. I think it's just a perfect storm of some very strange undercurrents happening at Wellington Academy mashing up against my family demons deciding to make their move. Shitty timing, but it's happening so fast that it doesn't feel strategic, you know what I mean?"

I nodded. I could totally see what he was saying. But that didn't make me any happier. "Well, if this *was* somebody's strategy, we kind of would be screwed. So maybe let's hope nobody's paying too much attention."

"Agreed," Zach said tightly, then glanced ahead again. "Okey doke. Here we go."

I turned forward again to see what had caught his eye, but it didn't take long to figure out. We'd entered campus through the barrier wall from the monster quad, which arguably should mean we were in a more protected location. But the students here were watching us with a malevolence that outstripped anything I'd seen before...and they were glaring from the doorways of classroom and administrative buildings, even the bookstore, ducking in and out like they were getting bitten from unseen mosquitos. Actually—exactly like that. As I squinted, I could see ephemeral clouds of gnats erupting every time a door opened.

"What's this about?" I muttered. "Did something die and no one moved the corpse?"

"You brought them here, didn't you?" a girl shouted from the doorway of one of the buildings. "They're not bothering you, so that means you brought them."

She yelled this at both of us, and Zach and I exchanged a startled glance. So many options, so little time, and I wasn't in the mood to mince my monsters. "Brought what?"

"The *flies*," she moaned, waving her hand again and then darting back inside. I saw them more clearly then, clouds of insects swarming in bunches, scattering the few students who dared to venture out of the classrooms.

"*Scati*," Zach said abruptly, and of course, he was right. My eyes widened as I stared at the tiny flying demons. "Smaller this time, but every bit as obnoxious. They can't alight on anything, at least. They have to stay airborne because the entire campus is consecrated ground other than the demonology department, which has different wards. But you know..."

He frowned, glancing up and down the quad as more plumes of the gnat-like creatures swarmed over the empty sidewalks. "If there's enough of them in a space and nobody takes them out, like if their energy outstrips that of the humans here, they'll eventually tip the balance. At that point...man. The entire campus will become open territory. That's gotta be what they're doing. Crowd all the demonology students into Lowell Library, distract them with a fight, and then seed the campus."

"And they're coming from a portal," I put in. "I mean, you heard Grim. That's got to be Bellamy, right? So we go there, close the opening, and we'll be good to..."

I broke off as we passed the center of campus, heading toward the western sector that was also outside the main wall. New voices sounded ahead of us, coming from the general direction of Bellamy Chapel. There were shouts, chants, roars of approval that only got louder as we moved, and we shifted into a flat-out run. By the time we cleared the wall, the din was deafening. Zach and I skidded to a stop, and I could only gape.

The protestors from the Wellington Academy monster quad had apparently picked up a new cause. They marched in front of the now-opened doors of Bellamy Chapel, waving colorful signs and shouting at the top of their lungs. "Burn it down! Burn it down! Let the demons be unbound!"

"What in the *hell*?" I demanded.

Zach groaned, his gaze darting everywhere. He ran his hands through his dark hair, leaving it standing on end. "You've gotta be fucking kidding me."

"We cannot allow fear to rule us anymore!" an all-too-familiar voice shouted, and I wheeled around, my eyes going wide as I took in Merry Williams standing with the bullhorn that she completely did not need at the front of the crowd. "If we free the demons, let them be our friends, we will free ourselves from fear. Demons deserve rights too!"

"Is she insane?" I whispered. Zach could only shake his head.

"Look behind her." I saw it then. Students entering the chapel in a cheerful line like it was some sort of circus fun house. "That's not good," Zach said. "It's not safe."

As if on cue, an unearthly howl sounded from inside the chapel, loud enough to drown out Merry's bullhorn speech.

"That's just sound effects," she insisted to the cheering crowd. "This entire building is like a movie prop. They're trying to scare you the same way they've scared people throughout millennia. Don't fall for it! Demons deserve their freedom—demons are our friends!"

At that moment, the doors of Bellamy Chapel burst open, and an enormous hand reached out, grabbed Merry around the waist, and pulled her inside.

The crowd went wild.

28

I'd never seen anything like the chaos that prevailed outside Bellamy Chapel. Half the students were overcome with giddy delight at the manifestation of a demon hand as big as a smart car. Half were terrified out of their minds. As Zach and I fought our way through the crowd, however, they mostly seemed like they had absolutely no idea where to run.

"Get out of here," Zach shouted. "Get back to the main campus." But it was no use. The closer we got to the chapel's front doors, the more students seemed to be in our way.

"The church! We have to get to the church."

"*No,*" Zach howled, but his voice was drowned out in the chaos. We were swept along with the tide of students, and as we entered Bellamy Chapel, we pitched forward, suddenly no longer inside the building but dumped out onto an open plain, the grass beaten down and burnt, the trees leafless and cowering beneath an unforgiving wind.

"Portal," Zach gasped as we struggled upright against the gale. We weren't alone. For as many students who shuffled forward, almost zombielike, their faces slack with horror, still others had crumpled to the ground, groaning, their hands to their ears, whimpering beneath the howling wind. At the front of the crowd, the curled-horned demons from Zach's demonstration holograms were dragging students forward, and then sort of jumping on top of them and going poof.

"They're disappearing," I said, squinting hard against the wind as I tried to make sense of what I was seeing. "The demons."

"Not disappearing," Zach countered. "They're infesting them. Trust me, you do not want to be infested this way."

I was pretty sure I didn't want to be infested in any way. "But how do we stop them?"

"We don't. Merry does."

"*Merry?*" In the chaos, I was ashamed to realize I'd forgotten her, but now Zach pointed to the front of the line of demons. There she was, standing with one fist planted on her hip, her other holding the bullhorn to her mouth as she shouted at a demon not three feet in front of her. She was like every person speaking to someone who couldn't understand her language, hoping that if she just spoke *loud* enough, she would get her point across.

"We are your friends," she insisted. "We want to work with you, to live in peace. We don't have to be *enemies.*"

"Um, how tight are you with Merry?" Zach asked as we pushed forward through the shuffling students, stepping over the ones who'd fallen and doing our best to appear hunched over and dazed, evading the watchful eyes of the demon lieutenants.

"Not at all," I had to admit. "I mean, I've spoken to her maybe three or four times in the past several days, and she wanted me to room with her, but it's not like we're friends, you know?"

Zach made a face. "It's gonna have to do. Give me Liam's demon kits. Both of them." I obligingly handed over the small logo'd sacks, and he unzipped the first one. "You know her enough to get her attention? Your link to her has to be stronger than mine—and I can see her through you."

I blinked at him. "Like you did Dean Robbins," I recalled.

"Exactly like that. I'm going to channel through you to reach the demon when it gets inside her."

I glanced from Merry shouting down the demon lieutenant, back to him. "I'm not sure it's going to get inside her. She's pretty deadly with that bullhorn."

"She is. And that's why that guy isn't the problem. Look." Zach nodded to the side, and I turned to see a new creature rising from the thick roiling smoke. It was a demon similar to the one we'd met in Bellamy Chapel yesterday. Large, muscular, with giant horns curling over its ears, its arms and legs too long for its body, it loped across the landscape at a frightening speed.

Merry turned as it reached her, her bullhorn at the ready. "I want to be your friend!" she screeched, and then the creature was on her.

"Now," Zach ordered. We raced forward, my eyes going wide to try to comprehend the horror playing out in front of us. The demon seemed to leap right through the bullhorn and into Merry's mouth, sending her sprawling backward. Zach shoved me in her direction as he shifted to the other demon lieutenants, ripping open the second of Liam's goody bags and shaking free two crosses.

"You don't need to do this," he roared, and in this plane, the words took on a ferocity I'd never heard in his voice. But then I reached Merry, her eyes wide, her body convulsing on the burnt-grass field. I thought of the few conversations we had, and latched on to the only thing we'd ever discussed that had truly seemed to make her happy.

"How are your animals, Merry?" I demanded, drawing her shocked gaze toward me. Her green eyes, suffused with panic, cleared for a moment as she recognized me. She opened her mouth, closed it, and finally spoke.

"What?"

"The animals at the vet clinic. You've been spending so much time there, and they're so lucky to have you. You've helped them a lot, haven't you?"

"I *have* helped them," she agreed, brightening. "Animals are our friends!"

I saw it then, the demon inside her, writhing in confusion at the absolutely manic energy of Merry's mind. Who knew she had such a powerful built-in demon defense?

"There are so many things we can do with them, you know?" she continued. "So many ways we can live in harmony, giving them their best lives and allowing them to inform and enrich our lives as well. They have so much to teach us!"

"They do," I agreed firmly. "And they need somebody like you. Somebody who can be their champion. Somebody who's good."

"I am good," Merry sighed, and her gaze met mine, full of hope and truth. "I'm—"

The demon inside her roared in apoplectic fury, then Zach was there in my mind, speaking words I couldn't understand and didn't need to. He pushed his energy through me and into Merry, and that was all that mattered. I spoke rapidly and intensely, the Latin spilling from me like an avenging fire, making Merry jerk beneath me, her eyes going wide.

"No!" She gasped. "No, you have to stop. Demons are our friends—our *friends.*"

"*Apage,*" Zach ordered, and that one I was pretty sure was the Greek word for *get out.* I yanked Merry to her feet and turned her around as she lifted the bullhorn high.

The voice that came out of her next was not solely her own, but mixed with the infuriated roar of the bound demon inside her, ordering the creatures around it to stop their attack on the students of Wellington Academy. At least that's what I thought it was saying, because in a blink, half the students littering the barren field disappeared. In another three seconds, the line of students in the process of being possessed screeched and spun away, windmilling in terror, then they winked out too, leaving their demon possessors behind. As Merry kept shouting, those demons burst into pyres of flame and ash, until finally, she turned toward me, her bullhorn dropping to the ground, her eyes wide as tears ran down her face.

"Why?" she whispered, sounding truly agonized. "Demons are our friends."

Then she disappeared as well.

Zach and I dropped to our knees on the open landscape, alone. I leaned heavily on my thighs, my lungs burning as I breathed in the sulfurous air. "She's so gonna need therapy after this," I muttered, and Zach snorted.

"She's not the only one. I'm not sure what condition those other students will be in. This is a portal realm, what most would consider a kind of purgatory, a way station between their interpretations of heaven and hell. But it's not a world for humankind. It's the kind of place that best belongs in horror movies and dreams, not memories."

"Will they remember it?"

"Probably not consciously, but I can't say something

won't break through." He shot me a weary smile. "At least we'll have something legit for the demonology students to do once the smoke clears. There's enough data to unravel from this little possession attempt to keep them occupied for years. Not to mention the fact that Bellamy Chapel is a portal. I might be the next person out in front of it to pick up a sign and chant 'burn it down.'"

"Yeah..." I blew out a long breath, squinting out over the landscape. "It still smells like fire, you know? At first, I thought it was sulfur, but it's different now. More...burn-y."

Zach frowned, also peering around. "You know, you're right. I don't know why, though. I would have thought—"

Before he could say anything else, the air snapped tight around us, and then a hole appeared in the smoke-filled sky. A blast of color and energy hurtled into view, crashing to the ground and rolling several feet before sprawling wide.

"I knew it!" Liam howled, scrambling to his feet and whipping around to us. "I knew Grim was talking about Bellamy. I fucking *knew* it."

We stared as he ran up to us, his face alight with excitement. "Did you do that? The flame-throwing shit? Or was that the demons? It sure as hell wasn't the students. The few of them left in the area were practically catatonic."

I blinked from him to the rip in the clouds, finally noticing the flames licking through from the other side. "What are you talking about?" Zach managed.

"Oh, come *on*," Liam protested, waving his arms. "You have to know. Bellamy is on friggin' *fire*." He grabbed Zach's unresisting hand, then turned to me, hauling us both to our feet.

"We've got to get back to the library, though. This is going to be awesome!"

He raced back into the flames.

29

We burst back into the chapel, which was, as Liam had said, ablaze with flames. "What happened?" I gasped.

Liam gestured for us to follow him, bending over nearly double as he scrambled down the center of the chapel, flames licking along the pews. "The few students who were still coherent had no clue. Place just went up like it'd been doused in gasoline, and you can bet your bones it's—whoa!"

He leapt back as a section of the floor gave way, briefly illuminating the chamber below. There were several shelves visible, stacked high with metal boxes, before another blazing crossbeam fell from the ceiling, obscuring our view.

"*Dude,*" Liam dropped to his hands and knees, leaning over the hole without any concern for the heat. "There's shit down there we need to get out. You gotta believe nobody knows anything's down there, and we have to—"

"Liam," Zach ordered, not only with his mouth but with his mind, and Liam spun around, his eyes sparking with new interest as his dark brows climbed high.

"You're right. Out we go first—but this way." He darted

down a charred row of pews, slowing as he approached a side door. "Firefighters are out front. We don't want any part of that."

I blinked. Firefighters? When had they shown up?

"How long have we been gone?" I asked as Liam slowly opened the door. We peeked out into bright sunshine.

"I don't know—a few hours, maybe? Long enough for us to lock down the library, not long enough for us to figure out how to free the demonology students while keeping the demons trapped in there. We're at what you'd call a standoff. And then, you know, came the next round of crazy—be careful. Stay out of sight."

He gestured toward the trucks that had pulled up to the front of the chapel. Men and women in heavy gear and fire-fighter helmets were braced with heavy hoses, spraying huge arcs of water toward the main part of the building. As we watched, Liam reached into his pocket and produced three small metal cylinders, flipping them all on before handing two off to us.

"What are these?" Zach asked, peering down at his with interest.

"Think of them as signal jammers, only the signals are for eyeballs. They cause enough light distortion that—never mind. It's kind of a cloak of invisibility."

"Sweet." Zach grinned.

Slipping out the doorway in a tactical crouch, Liam led the way, practically crab-walking along the side of the church. When we reached the cemetery, he broke in a low run, and we did the same. I practically squeezed the life out of my jammer, but no one challenged us or cried out. In another five minutes, we were deep into the campus of Wellington Academy, keeping to the trees as the smoke billowed up behind us from the burning chapel.

"Eyes forward, boyo," Liam announced when Zach paused to look back. "You've got a date with Lowell Library, fifth floor, where your demonology buddies are now assembled...and, as it turns out, the *scati* as well. Even smaller than before. Serious bugsville. We've got no idea how they got in, but they've driven everyone to the top floor, and someone broke a window, so God only knows what else has flown in there now."

"The *scati*? What are they doing there?" Zach demanded as we started forward again.

"Apparently waiting for their lord and master, who came bursting out of the fiery inferno with Merry Williams in his claws as I was pounding up to the chapel. News flash, I don't think they're going to have a second date."

I jerked my gaze toward Liam, stumbling. "Merry?" I panted. "She's hurt?"

"If she is, she's currently finding comfort in the arms of half a dozen brawny firefighters. They caught her as she fell out of the front door of the chapel, allowing me to skate right by to get to you guys. Fortunately or unfortunately, big bad demon boy managed to bypass the firefighters as well, or they just didn't see it. Which is insane, but seems to be the case." He turned and pinned Zach with his bright, riverstone eyes, and we all slowed to a fast walk as his voice dropped. "That's one of your family demons, right? Ugly guy, curved horns? You got just the one?"

"It changes all the time. I have no idea," Zach said. "But why do you think it's going to Lowell Library?"

Liam grinned. "Other than the fact that most of the demonology students are still stuck in there, including some guys possessed by round-horn's buddies? I don't know. But that's our headquarters, and your stink is all over it. Probably not surprising that the big dude would home in on it."

233

"All those students." Zach winced. "They'll be sacrificed as collateral damage."

"Not if we have anything to say about it," Liam countered. "Turns out those demonology guys don't completely suck after all. They've got all sorts of spikes, mirrors, and these goofy silver beads they swear can take a demon out at twenty paces, though they don't know how to use them yet. Claim they found them in the back closet of the demonology department and haven't had a chance to try them out, no clue where they came from."

I frowned at Liam. Silver beads—was that where Grim had found them? If so, why had one been lying on the sidewalk blocks away from the campus? "Yeah, but if the demonology students have them and they're still trapped in the library, clearly they can't be all that good," Zach pointed out.

"*Au contraire, mon frère,*" Liam chortled. "Frost ordered the students to lie low—not get dead, but not strike out until we could all be there in force. And then, of course, he got pulled away, him and Robbins...after they tied up Garrison and stuffed him into the war room to sleep off his possession."

"What do you mean pulled away?" I asked, all of us still walking quickly. "What could Frost have to do that's more important than getting a demon out of Lowell Library?"

Liam grinned. "As it happens, entertaining his ass off in Cabot Hall for a parade of dignitaries who descended on campus outta nowhere to check out the doings of the monster hunting minor. Or at least that's where he was before Bellamy Chapel went up in flames. Robbins was supposed to go in solo, but he was completely freaked after our little demon throw down and won't let Frost out of his sight, so off they went. Grim and Tyler are holding down the fort at the library, and they sent me to get you. It's been quiet for a while now, but things are starting to heat up again. Something's changed, and it probably has to do with our man Round-Horn the Magnificent, Zach's own personal demon, hitting the scene."

"You know, you really shouldn't be enjoying this so much," Zach muttered, but Liam merely laughed.

"The fifth floor has balconies, right? Like terraces?" I put in. "If any of those students get out and try to make a run for it..."

"Already happened. Grim, because he's a baller, was able to break the guy's fall, but the kid was pretty beat up. Next over the side was some freshman chick. She fared a little better, but finding herself wrapped up in Grim's arms may have given her permanent psychological damage. After that, Tyler was able to put a spell of holding on the building, and its illusion wards are going strong, but that's not going to do us much good if we don't get in there and defuse the problem. The only thing worse than a bunch of dead students..."

"Is a bunch of possessed ones," Zach said.

"Kind of unfortunate for recruiting, not gonna lie."

We took off running again.

30

W e reached Lowell Library five minutes later, and Liam was right. By all outward appearances, the library looked perfect and pristine, late afternoon sunlight streaming off its many leaded windows, hiding away any chaos going on inside. I peered up to the roofline directly above the fifth floor.

"How do we get up there?" I asked.

"We can't go in the front doors. Tyler's spell of holding's doing a good job of deadening the senses of everyone inside, including the demons. But if we breach that barrier, all bets are off. He didn't know if he'd be able to maintain the spell once the energy balance was disrupted. So we climb."

"Excellent," Zach said, while I jolted.

"Climb?" I asked.

They didn't take the time to explain more. Liam led the way to the rear of the building, where thick vines bristled along an ornate trellis that had been affixed into the wall.

"Medieval fire escape, recommended by the Montagues, the Capulets, and forsworn lovers ever since," Liam explained over his shoulder as he started climbing, hand over hand. Below him, Zach turned back to me with a troubled expression. Liam looked down at both of us and nearly fell off the side of the wall.

"Whoa," he gasped, his eyes lighting up as he swayed wildly on the trellis. "My man, what happened to *you*?" His gaze moved immediately to me, and a wide, delighted grin broke out on his face. "But how—when? Like what was that, a purgatory hookup?"

"Can it, Liam," Zach said, his expression hardening. Whatever he was going to say to me could wait, as he turned back to the wall and started up. I had no choice but to follow him. I sure as hell wasn't going to hang out on the ground.

We could hear the screams from the third floor on. Zach shot forward, overtaking Liam and leaving me a distant third. Liam waited for me to catch up, then stopped me as I tried to climb farther.

"Hang on a sec," he murmured. "Seriously. I don't need to know how it happened with Zach, but I know *something* happened. Now that I'm finally looking at him square, Zach's lit up from the inside out. I bet if we studied it, we'd be seeing some pretty major leaps in his mind-meld power, since that's his jam. We can use that."

"Well then, let's—"

"Hold *up*, I said." Liam's expression hardened, his eyes brooking no bullshit. "Frost was able to pull out some of the smarter demonology students from the scrum, and I got a crash course. If this is a personal vendetta against Zach's family, and it is, we've gotta steer clear. Anyone he loves can become weapons against him, and that helps no one."

"I don't think so," I argued. "We're linked to Zach psychically now. And um, based on what we tried in...I guess purgatory, I can even channel some of his ability, sort of borrow it, you know? Because of that connection, I think we can help."

Liam's eyes narrowed as I turned back to the trellis and continued climbing.

"All of us, or just you?" he asked as he started climbing too. "Because we're going to need to test that out. I don't want to be the wimpy little brother here."

I snorted a laugh as he scrambled up beside me. "You're insane. You're the first to throw yourself into the middle of danger and the first to figure your way out of it. You've never been wimpy a day in your life."

The comment must have caught Liam off guard, because he flushed as Zach shouted above us.

"I'm going in," he called down. "Tyler?"

Liam put his hand over his left wrist, activating his psychic link to Zach, while my connection with Zach was already wide open. Tyler's response came through loud and clear.

"Welcome back," he said tersely. *"Grim says the congregation is pretty screwed up. Demons are doing a number on them, getting into their heads. He just tackled another kid to the ground and says he's not in the mood for any more."*

"You can drop whatever wards you've got on the place?"

"Long enough to get you guys in there, yeah. Go."

Zach catapulted over the side of the balcony, disappearing from view. A second later, the flood of Zach's thoughts nearly swept me off the side of the library wall. In an instant, I saw what he saw, in all its horror. A room full of smoke, miniature flying demons, and students pressed against the walls or huddled in heaps together on the floor, and in the center, the tall, powerful demon from beyond the Bellamy Chapel portal, its horns curling back from its elongated face, its burly body braced on heavy legs as its tail lashed furiously around it.

"Make the *sacrifice*," howled the demon, its gaze fixed on Zach as it shifted, becoming first Zach's father and then an older man with a long, sad face and wispy beard, a floppy hat perched on his head and a tattered duster swirling around his body. He looked almost like a hobo, but a prosperous one. The demon shifted again as Liam and I reached the balcony. We slipped over onto the terrace as well, no one paying us any attention. We opened the door to the interior room. "It's time."

"You don't have to do this," Zach said, his voice carrying with its peculiar resonance across the room. "You can let these people go. Your quarrel is with me. Fight me, and let's finish this."

As Zach spoke, he glowed, practically incandescent, causing gasps and shouts from the students. They turned toward him, hope springing up, and the demon flung out its hands.

"These are whom you would impress? These are whom you love?" it demanded, exasperated. "Look at them!"

It gestured sharply, and the students cowered back again, even those gripping their crosses and religious totems. Their belief was being tested to the limit, and I could see their fear crest in their wide eyes, their trembling hands.

Zach stepped forward, and Liam pushed me to the side, waving me away—

But it was too late.

"Ahhhh..." the demon breathed, and the entire room went electric with tension as it turned and focused on me. Liam used the distraction to edge over toward a knot of cowering students, dropping to one knee. I tried not to stare

239

directly at the demon, but it seemed to grow to three times its size in my peripheral vision, looming over the room with quivering glee. "Here she is, at last. Behold, the light of your affection, the female you claim above all others."

"Your fight is with me," Zach insisted again, but the demon lifted its taloned hands, stretching its arms wide as if drawing in all its power.

"Now and ever more, you and your line will pay for the power you *stole* from us," it hissed.

It dropped its hands.

Swooping down from the rafters of the fifth floor, the *scati* descended in a screeching torrent. Over near the students, Liam spun around, instantly overcome by the horde of flying demons. Despite his thrashing, he was beaten to the floor by the swarm. He lurched forward and flung something across the room toward me—the silver pellets. The beads struck several of the *scati* before they reached me, to absolutely no effect. He might as well be hurling marbles at them. I lunged for a handful of the beads anyway, grabbing maybe a dozen, then staggered back upright as the head demon turned to me.

"And your woman still *stinks* of you," it chortled into the chaos, curling its lip. "I suppose congratulations are in order, except that she doesn't know the wedding gift you've given her, does she?"

With that a burst of pint-sized demon lieutenants erupted out of nowhere in plumes of smoke, joining the brawl. Dimly, I was aware of Liam staggering upright, Tyler and Grim racing into the room, but it was Zach who held my attention.

Words flowed from his mouth as his hands slashed and tore, slicing through the wall of *scati*. I closed my left fist around the beads, then leaned down to pull my dagger out of its ankle sheath, while Zach shoved the students back into their own confused rabble. He finally reached the main demon, who erupted into flame as Zach laid his hands around it. I followed right behind, thrusting my blade at everything demonic I could reach, still gripping my magic pellets like my life depended on it.

Zach and his demon disappeared in a spitting convulsion of smoke and fire, but not before I leapt into the middle of that blaze.

31

We crashed onto the open plain with its beaten-down, burnt grass, the roiling clouds overhead still smelling of sulfur and fire. I rolled several feet, my hands going wide, barely able to hold on to my knife as the beads in my left hand went flying. I finally came to a stop, then staggered back, wheeling around toward where Zach and his family demon still battled.

They struggled together in a burst of fire and smoke for another thirty seconds as I watched, helpless, the demon screeching in fury. Then Zach, surprisingly, broke away.

He rolled off the steaming husk of the demon and stood —but the demon didn't. It remained pinned to the ground, and as I stumbled up, I saw its skin was pocked with easily a dozen silver beads. My thrown projectiles had found their target after all and were adhering to the demon's leathery skin like magnets. As I watched, I could pick out a tiny tracery of fire between the beads, as if the demon was caught up in some kind of net. Pretty cool, I had to admit.

The demon clearly didn't think so. "You wield the tools of magic at your peril—it is *forbidden*," it seethed. Its eyes shifted to me, narrowing to slits as it seemed to see me for the first time.

"*Harbinger,*" it spat, glaring back at Zach. "This is whom you would take as your lover? She is a *defilement.*"

"That'd hurt my feelings, coming from anyone other than, I don't know, a *demon,*" I offered, which was about the maximum snark I was capable of, while trying to suck down the infernal air. Zach gestured toward me with the slightest twist of his hand. We weren't quite done with this asshole yet.

"You will not plague my family again, none of you. Your curse is at an end," Zach ground out, drawing the demon's attention back to him. "You will die here."

"You *cannot* kill me," the demon sneered. "That's what you and your father before you, and *his* father as well, failed to understand. No child of God can actually *kill* a demon. The best you can do is send me back home, until one day your son, puffed up with pride and lust, will open the door for me to return. Your curiosity has been your undoing, yours and every generation before yours, since that first preacher wrapped his hand around a trinket he coveted more than anything else in this world. He got his gift, boyo. Tools of the mind, of the spirit—even the strength to face down my brethren. But he got the *curse* that comes with that gift as well. For he could not kill me. And neither can you."

Zach's smile was hard and cruel, his dark blue eyes practically sparking purple flame. "I don't need to kill you, not by myself. Because that was the problem, wasn't it? They all tried to do it by themselves."

"They had to." The demon shrugged, the soul of reason. "No man loves—*truly* loves— someone stronger than they are. Their very souls reject the idea, the core of what makes them human. Even your *harbinger* cannot harm me enough to break the curse. She is only good for chattel."

Something in his voice stuck me as false, though, and Zach heard it too. "You're wrong," he breathed, excitement slipping into his words. "You couldn't be more wrong about that."

"I held you," I said abruptly, pointing at the net. "Those beads—I did that. Zach allowed me to be a part of this battle, but it was my strength that held you, my will that bound you."

The demon sneered at me, though something slithered through its gaze too. Not fear—not yet. But defiance. And perhaps more than that...surprise. "Enjoy your puny victory while you can," it snapped. "My kin are coming even now to break your monstrous spell, while yours are doomed to lose this fight."

"Not anymore," Zach countered. "This time, you die and stay dead."

The demon rolled its eyes at me, clearly unimpressed, but before it could say anything further, Zach continued. "I know I can't kill you myself. No Williams can—that's our curse. That and the pride not to see the truth of it. But I know that pride is bullshit." He nodded my way. "Even better, I've got Nina here to help me. And she is going to kick your ass."

We were right up on the demon by now, who shifted its gaze back to Zach—and froze, transfixed. Zach's voice had shifted yet again, and I felt the power of it ripple through me, like tides before a seaborne storm. "So I say to you, begone," he continued, the words absolute, "and trouble us no more."

"*No.*" The demon gasped, breaking free of its thrall at the last minute with a sharp cry of understanding, but it was too late. Zach and I lifted our hands and plunged our knives into the bound demon's body.

It exploded.

The force of the blast blew Zach and me over onto our backs, the wind rushing over us, screaming across the scorched plain. I blinked, lifting up on my elbows, and Zach watched with equal amazement as the remaining embers of the demon burst upward into the sky—then scattered into the rushing wind.

Another second passed, and even the wind died away. We were blanketed in absolute silence.

Zach groaned and slumped forward. I fell toward him, both of us so exhausted that we simply lay there beneath the angry orange sky a moment longer, staring upward.

"So..." I finally managed, my voice sounding as parched as the ground around us. "I think it's fair to say you've leveled up, yeah?"

He snorted beside me, not taking his gaze from the churning clouds high above. "Are you going to tell me how pretty I am again?"

I sucked in a whiff of hot air, choking on my laugh—when we heard something new. A sharp cry, far in the distance. A shout of pure exultation.

"What is it?" Zach began, then he bolted upright, his head turning sharply. He scrambled to his feet, pulling me up with him. No sooner did we start moving than the air snapped around us, a slice of it sheering away to reveal a swath of blue sky, trees obscured by wispy smoke. I could almost smell the ash and soaked wood in the air—Bellamy Chapel lay through that portal. Had to be.

Zach turned to me as we raced toward it, his eyes wide, his smile broad. "Yeah?" he asked.

I grinned right back at him. "*Definitely!*" I shouted.

We jumped.

Not even a breath later, we landed at the edge of the smoldering ruins of Bellamy Chapel, a bare fifteen feet away from where Liam was emerging from the little church. Somehow, he'd procured a very official-looking jacket, and he waved us forward with all the gravitas of a professional investigator. That's when I realized that we weren't entirely alone. On the other side of the chapel were easily a dozen official vehicles, the swell of activity and shouting finally penetrating my ringing ears.

"Are you seriously kidding me here?" Zach muttered when we reached Liam.

Liam shook his head, the soul of seriousness as he scowled at us. "Do not even start with me, transformation boy," he said. "I needed to be on scene—"

"On scene?" Zach protested. "Really? You're going to go with the lingo and everything?"

Liam continued without skipping a beat. "To make sure there wasn't anything we needed to remove before it was bagged and tagged as official evidence in an arson investigation. Because that's what they're going to call this, make no mistake. And the funny thing is, they're right. I just confirmed it."

"How is that funny?" I asked. "I thought the demon caught it on fire."

"A good thought, but demons wouldn't have needed gasoline as an accelerant."

That caught our attention. "You're serious?"

Liam nodded. "If the powers that be suddenly wanted Bellamy Chapel to be gone, there would have been a fire, all right, but we never would have known what caused it. We don't like to make a big deal of it, but this *is* a magic academy, boys and girls. There are ways of getting such things done. That's not what happened here. This fire was deliberately set and made to look like it was deliberately set, or at least not hidden in any way. The demons passing through were just the frosting on this crazy cake."

"So who the hell do they think set it?" Zach asked.

"One possibility is the administration, hoping no one would notice the gasoline. That they wanted people to believe it was a side effect of the passage of a particular horned demon we've grown to know and love and all his little miniature demonettes yesterday. Another option is our friendly neighborhood anti-monster hunting campaigners, but they would have left a few more signs around claiming responsibility, maybe some glitter paint. You know, the students who aren't still traumatized out of their minds, anyway."

"I don't get it," Zach said. "You think this was done as an act against us? How do we benefit from Bellamy Chapel being destroyed? Before this week, this thing sat here virtually untouched since the last sunrise ceremony a semester ago. And that's a demonology class, which covers multiple majors, not just monster hunting."

"All fair points," Liam said. "And points I fully intend to bring up to Dean Robbins when he asks, and you can bet your ass he's going to ask, just as soon as he gets over his own recent demon trauma. My current theory is that we'll be held accountable for growing unrest on the campus, creating an environment that's not conducive to the effective learning of our students."

He said this last with a pretentious vigor, and I could vividly imagine it. It had the air of university bullshit to it and the ring of truth. A deadly combination.

"Mr. Graham?" somebody shouted, and Liam turned as Zach's eyes bugged out.

"Whoa. Mr. *Graham*?"

Liam made a show of straightening his jacket. "I will have you know I'm a highly respected part of this investigation, young man," he informed us. "So you just run along to class, and try to get cleaned up before dinner tonight."

Zach and I both blinked at him. "Tonight?"

Liam grinned, obviously knowing this was news to us. "As it turns out, we've all been cordially invited to a light supper at the home of Mr. Symmes—Wendy's dad, remember? He's unexpectedly returned to the city, and his schedule has opened up to accommodate us. Lucky us."

"Who all is going to be there?" I asked. "What are we supposed to do? What are we supposed to wear?"

Liam waved us off. "You can bet Frost's putting together a briefing right now. I suggest heading over to the library, I'll be there as soon as I can. I need to get this scene sealed off so that the only one sticking their noses into it is us, later on tonight."

"You're going to be okay here?" Zach asked, eyeing the legitimate cops and crime scene investigators milling around the space.

"O ye of little faith," Liam protested. "I will have you know I'm wearing an energy disruptor that's going to leave everyone's memory of any interaction with me decidedly fragmented. Most of them won't even know I was here. Which is exactly the way I like it."

"You are one dangerous dude," Zach said.

Liam grinned at him, then glanced at me, something inscrutable in his gaze. "And don't you forget it."

32

Commander Frost wasn't at Lowell Library, and he wasn't at Fowlers Hall—though we did recover my iron box, which we safely locked in Frost's office. But regarding the dinner at the Symmes mansion, all we had was an invitation that had been texted to all our telephone numbers telling us where we needed to be in Beacon Hill and when. Attire was listed only as "Academy."

Which was why, a few short hours later, I found myself wearing a plaid skirt and white button-down blouse, knee-high socks, and black boots, while the guys milled around in dark charcoal pants and shirts with Wellington Academy plaid ties. Well, most of the guys, anyway.

"Where's Grim?" I asked.

Tyler shook his head. "Nowhere to be found," he said. "We'll give our apologies to Mr. Symmes, but this kind of meet and greet is a quick way to get Grim expelled, and even Dean Robbins knows it. Grim's been excused."

"Grim in a shirt and tie would upset the flow of the universe," Liam agreed, hiking an elegant leather backpack higher on one shoulder. For Liam, no dress code didn't include a pack.

Even without Grim on scene, there was no denying that the guys cleaned up well. I felt kind of foolish in my miniskirt and boots, but the guys looked like they'd been born to wear these clothes, especially Tyler and Liam, though even Zach looked more comfortable than I felt.

We loitered in front of Fowlers Hall for a few minutes more, then made our way across the campus.

As indicated, there was a car waiting for us when we reached the center quad. Not just any old car either, but a stretch SUV, complete with a man in a suit who looked big enough to give Grim a run for his money, if Grim had been here.

Then, suddenly, Grim *was* there, stalking up to the SUV, looking for all the world like the most feral, untamed academy frat boy that had ever graced a college campus. His cadet blue shirt and rep tie hung perfectly straight, his trousers were pressed and crisp, and his boots were polished. And they were nice boots too, not the usual scuffed footwear he'd worn every other time I'd seen him. These looked like they'd set somebody back quite a bit of money.

"Whoa," Liam said. "Who caught you in a trap?"

Grim curled his lip. "Frost," he said. "Apparently, this invitation means a little bit more than Frost wants to admit. Everyone is watching. Mr. Symmes doesn't want to be embarrassed."

Liam studied him. "Since when do you give a shit about any of that?"

Grim simply regarded him coolly, and Liam's eyes widened. "You brokered a deal, didn't you? You got something from Frost in return for showing up. Something that would convince you to dress up in a monkey suit. What was it?"

"Here we go," Tyler said, and the door of the SUV opened, the beefy chauffeur getting out and opening the back doors.

The man didn't speak, didn't make a move toward any of us, merely stood there, watching impassively as we approached. Tyler took the lead and entered the SUV, Liam following, then Grim.

Zach stood by and handed me into the vehicle, where I tucked in next to Tyler, with Grim sitting opposite us. I glanced over to Grim and found him watching me, his pale-gold eyes glinting as he steadfastly held my gaze. There was something unnaturally stiff about his manner. I realized why a second before Liam did.

"Jesus, you're *bleeding*," Liam announced. Tyler sharpened his glance on Grim as Liam brought his pack around.

"I thought it would stop before now," Grim grunted. Liam yanked out gauze and a narrow bottle that glinted in the cabin lights.

"What did he do to you?" Zach asked. Grim shrugged as Liam rolled up his sleeves, exposing the long, jagged gash.

"I didn't want to come tonight, and he thought he could convince me otherwise. I decided to let him try for a while," Grim said. "It took a spelled tool to make this mark, and after that, he was willing to consider other approaches."

"I knew it." Liam chortled. He didn't ask Grim what the deal had been, though I was totally curious at this point. What did Commander Frost have to offer that he would be willing to give up only after he realized he couldn't beat Grim into submission? I honestly had no idea. Once again, I felt Grim's attention on me, but when I glanced up to meet his gaze, he'd transferred his attention to whatever Liam was using to seal up his arm.

"Definitely a spelled blade," Liam muttered. "You're lucky I come prepared."

"It isn't luck," Grim said simply, and Liam blinked but didn't say anything more. I got the feeling that was probably the highest form of compliment Grim could offer. I liked him better for it. Which wasn't to say that I liked him, I decided, even if he had introduced me to the power of fancy magic pellets. I still needed to follow up with him on that—soon. Not now, but soon.

We arrived at the Symmes house in less than five minutes, a distance we easily could have walked, but I got the impression Mr. Symmes did everything for show. His mansion certainly bore that out. It was an enormous building tucked back onto what had to be incredibly expensive real estate, deep in the Beacon Hill neighborhood. The house itself was elegantly simple, but practically oozed money.

Every light in the place seemed to be ablaze, and as we drove up, Liam let out a short whistle. "This place doesn't suck," he muttered.

We remained quiet otherwise as the vehicle stopped and we exited the SUV. We were ushered into the estate by some sort of majordomo, and quickly found ourselves in the drawing room with a man who had to be Mr. Symmes. Wendy's father was tall and slender, and as monied as his house, with salt and pepper hair swept back from his aristocratic face, a black suit elegantly tailored to fit his narrow form, and glints of platinum at his wrists. Even his shoes gleamed as black as his eyes.

"Welcome, welcome," he said. "Please, let's not stand on ceremony. You know who I am, and my daughter has done me the service of describing you all quite thoroughly. Mr. Graham, I have to assume, given the pack?" He reached out and shook Liam's hand, then turned to Zach. "And Mr. Williams. My sincere thanks for your help in keeping my daughter safe. And you as well, Mr. Perkins."

He turned to Grim, but to my surprise did not extend his hand. Instead, he nodded to Grim in a sign of respect, maybe? Certainly awareness. What did he know about Grim? What had his daughter told him?

"Mr. Lockton. I was given to understand we might not have the pleasure of your company today. I'm glad you saw your way to being with us."

Grim nodded back, and I watched the exchange with interest. These were two fighters, I thought unexpectedly, circling each other in the ring. Yet they couldn't be more different from each other, Grim with his rough-hewn features, his heavy body barely contained by the clothing he wore, while Mr. Symmes looked like he'd never enjoyed anything more strenuous than a rousing game of cricket. What was going on here?

The moment passed, and Symmes turned to regard me. Once again, he afforded me a deferential nod, which took me by surprise.

"Ms. Cross. In the way of twenty-year-old daughters, I'm afraid Wendy did not spend as much time admiring you as she did your compatriots. And when I attempted to secure more information about you, I found my sources woefully inadequate. Mrs. Pendleton's cameras only revealed so much, as you know."

I jolted at the reference to the surveillance, and both Tyler and Zach started to speak at once, but Symmes waved them quiet. "There's much you don't understand about the magical families who make up Wellington Academy, and we don't have time for a history lesson, but I owe you this, at least. Yes, there is a net of watchers around the academy, and yes, Margaret Pendleton is their enthusiastic leader. Hunters are often drawn to Wellington even if their line no longer resides in Boston, and we like to be prepared. We found Zachariah's father that way, though he doesn't know it. He still thinks to this day that his visit to Boston as a young boy with his adoptive father has no link to his eventual enrollment at the academy. We've found other, lesser-skilled hunters as well. But a harbinger—that is something entirely different. You can understand that your arrival has created some excitement."

"You knew what she was from something you saw on those cameras?" Zach asked, but Symmes shook his head as he continued to study me. I shifted uneasily, not used to the scrutiny.

"Not at all. We knew what she was because our cameras shorted out every time she was in the apartment—half the time, the cameras didn't work at all, and when they did, there was so much static, we couldn't see anything of worth. That level of interference shouldn't be possible."

"Baller," Liam muttered, and I pressed my lips together.

"Exactly so," Symmes agreed. He nodded to me again. "I look forward to learning more about you this evening."

I murmured something polite, though I couldn't imagine how much his curiosity was going to be rewarded. But I was already getting the idea I would be wise not to underestimate Mr. Symmes. He had the kind of assurance that came from being certain of getting what he wanted. I suspected that confidence had been well earned over time.

A man appeared in the doorway, providing a discreet signal, and Symmes nodded. "Excellent," he said. "I'm famished. Gentlemen? Ms. Cross?"

He directed us into the room, and though I shouldn't have been surprised, I barely forestalled a gasp at the size of the dining room. It was completely paneled in richly veined wood, and dominated by a massive wooden table that looked like it would be more at home in King Arthur's castle than a Boston mansion.

Over the next twenty minutes, course after course was served, each more mouthwatering than the last—soups, meats and fish, vegetables, and so much bread. I couldn't decide if I was more surprised by the quality of the food or by the fact that the guys were able to put it away without seeming to need to breathe. As we ate, Mr. Symmes quizzed them on all manner of innocuous topics, from the types of courses that they took to their experiences with Dean Robbins and Commander Frost.

It wasn't until small glasses of port were brought out on a silver tray that Mr. Symmes's energy changed. He set down his glass, and studied us. "Gentlemen, Ms. Cross, you have proven to be most gracious guests and I suspect are quite curious as to the real reason why I've brought you here tonight. I do appreciate the general background, though, as it has been some time since I've spoken to a student of the academy pursuing your specific studies. I'd rather thought I wouldn't ever speak to one of you again, in fact."

That brought everybody up short, though Mr. Symmes delivered the line without any overt animosity. Still, Tyler took the lead.

"We're aware not everybody at Wellington is a supporter of the monster hunting minor, despite its historical significance to the school," he began carefully.

"Oh no, no, don't misunderstand," Mr. Symmes replied, waving a lazy hand. "I have no quarrel with your course of study, nor any interest, like so many of my peers, in seeing it eradicated. All things have their time and purpose, including, as it turns out, monster hunters. No. My purpose in calling you here tonight is simply to inform you that our need for you is becoming a matter of some urgency. Commander Frost has kept me well apprised of your development, but the time for caginess is past. We're under siege from within. And we need you to fight."

As usual, Tyler recovered first. "What do you mean under siege?" he asked. "Frost said there was a monster outbreak brewing, but it hasn't hit yet. We'll get on it the moment it does."

"And if I believed your efforts could continue in such a haphazard manner, I would be content to allow you to carry on," Symmes returned. "However, we're not simply dealing with the occasional monster who stumbles upon our portion of the fair city. These attacks are coordinated and not the result of supernatural creatures simply sniffing us out. They're being directed in their attacks. Our defenses are being tested, and frankly, other than your estimable attempts, we're coming up decidedly wanting."

He turned his attention to me. "We haven't been completely lax, of course. Mrs. Pendleton did find you. But if *we* know about you, you can rest assured others do too. Which means, undoubtedly, their timetable has moved up."

"We're ready for them," Tyler said staunchly, "We may not be as prepared as hunters who've completed all four years of training, but we can handle whatever comes. Nina only makes us stronger."

"She does. But the issue of Wellington's past hunters brings me to the next problem," Symmes said. "You are aware, I'm sure, of Commander Frost's attempts to locate and marshal past graduates, the illustrious monster hunters who, in return for their lifetime service to the school, have been given prestige and riches."

Uh-oh. I didn't like where this was going.

"Sure," Tyler allowed. "I know a series of summonses have gone out—"

"None of which have been answered," Mr. Symmes put in, but Tyler shrugged.

"It's early days yet, and some of these hunters are undoubtedly in remote corners of the world. I know I certainly plan to be upon graduation."

Mr. Symmes smiled thinly. "I wish quite sincerely that was the case. But alas, it is not. After careful and thorough review, it appears the reason our illustrious graduates aren't responding is because they're uniformly dead."

"Dead?" Liam blurted, the question as sharp as a pistol shot. "How?"

"It would be poetic to say they died while in the process of dispatching monsters. Once again, we were destined to be disappointed on that score. We estimate the fifteen graduates still alive as of our last census have been systematically eliminated over the course of the past five years. Starting with those who are most remote and the least likely to create any interest, and ending with those who have graduated within the past decade. They're all gone, or they're missing, and I'm frankly not sure which is worse."

"And you just now figured this out?" Liam protested.

"Quite," Mr. Symmes said. "With the general animosity that's been growing against the monster hunter minor, there has been no great interest in bringing past graduates back to the campus or drawing any attention to them at all. They were out doing what they had signed up to do, reports were coming in, all was proceeding as it should with very little verification happening. But when we started looking for them in earnest, we learned the reports were coming from spoofed accounts, and the monster hunters themselves were nowhere to be found. It took another deeper search to identify the first casualties, and while the search remains ongoing, we must proceed with the belief that no more assistance will be forthcoming other than that which is found in this room."

"What about the freshmen?" Zach began, but Mr. Symmes raised a quelling hand.

"They will be informed shortly of the cessation of their course of study at the close of this school year. They are not prepared to face this struggle."

Tyler scowled. "And if we face the challenge, what then? Sure, they won't be part of the fight with us, but the minor will still exist, right?"

"The general consensus is that yes, in the event you succeed, monster hunting studies will resume, but I must tell you..."

"Nobody expects us to succeed," Tyler said.

Mr. Symmes smiled. "This is where it gets interesting."

33

We left the house in a quieter mood than when we'd arrived, mostly because we were now almost certain we were being recorded. By the time we reached the campus, you could cut the tension in the SUV with a knife.

We were unloaded in the center of campus again, unable to shake the mood of impending doom. Students milled around, walking from late classes toward the bar district or just enjoying the night, but the five of us stayed quiet and close together until we reached the archway to the monster quad.

"Where do we go from here?" Tyler asked.

Liam shook his head. "Honestly, we gotta get more information from Frost, even though he's clearly been holding out on us. Dean Robbins is a nonstarter, but if we've got Symmes on our side..."

"We don't know that he is," Grim said. In the short walk from the center of campus, he'd managed to pull off his tie and chuck his dress shirt. His muscles rippled beneath the soft white T-shirt that remained. I was surprised he didn't kick off his fancy boots and walk barefoot. "Symmes has a need in all this we don't know yet. We shouldn't trust him."

"I agree," Zach said. "This doesn't feel right. I should have pushed him. I didn't, but I should have. He's definitely hiding something."

"Even if you'd pushed, you wouldn't have gotten very far," Liam said, hitching his pack higher on his shoulder. "The wards in that place were top-notch. He was not messing around. Which means he does know at least *something* about you and your abilities, Zach. Probably about all of us."

"Or he's careful," Grim countered. "If he knew that much, he wouldn't have invited us into his lair."

His word choice was interesting and, I suspected, deliberately chosen. Symmes was a predator, and I got the feeling we could become his prey. But we hadn't yet. Was that because we could still offer him help? Help he couldn't get elsewhere?"

"What can he gain by making us feel comfortable?" I asked. "We're students at the academy. We pretty much have to do as we're told. Could that be it? He thinks we can be easily manipulated?"

"That's an interesting thought," Zach said. "If somebody hits us up for action and pressures us from a 'do this or you lose your degree' standpoint, that could get ugly really fast."

"Agreed. What's worse, it means Symmes knows something's coming. Which means he knows shit we should probably have already been told," Tyler muttered. "I don't like this at all. I don't know who it is we're supposed to trust."

"You do know," Grim offered. The energy shimmering through him was undeniable at this point. He looked like a caged animal who'd just sniffed the open door of his enclosure. "Each other. Period. Where do you want me to be and when?"

Tyler sighed. "We need to be ready tomorrow for whatever they throw at us. I get the feeling it's not going to be pretty. I need to think."

"Same," Zach agreed.

"Well, I need to find out what the hell is in the basement of Bellamy Chapel." Liam had already half turned to leave and fairly bounced on his toes. "You know that fire uncovered some serious shit. My illusion wards will fool most people, but not if we're dealing with people who shop at the same stores I do. So I'm outtie until tomorrow morning minimum."

"Tomorrow, then," Grim said. The guys all nodded, and he turned away without sparing me a glance.

"Wait," I blurted, and Grim stopped, swiveling back to me with a forbidding expression. I pushed on. "Those beads that, um, the demonology guys brought to the library. Have you ever seen those before? Because they ended up keeping Zach's demon in place long enough for us to take him out." I didn't want to mention the handful of pellets that Grim had given me during our demon-fighting practice, but I couldn't help but think they were important...especially since the other guys didn't seem to know anything about them.

Liam turned to me and Zach. "Really? You cracked the code on how to use them?"

"I've never seen them before," Grim grunted as he glared at me, totally lying to my face. "Ask the demonology idiots." Then he swung around again, setting off into the shadows with a ground-eating stride.

I scowled after him. Hard guy. For every mystery I solved at Wellington, it seemed two more sprang up in its place. Now I needed to figure out the importance of those silver beads *and* get back to reading whatever pages were left of the Apocrypha. There was still too much I didn't know.

Liam took off as well, which left me, Zach, and Tyler standing in the pool of light. As I watched Liam break into a run, my mind still churning, it occurred to me it had suddenly gotten...really quiet. Then I realized why. Zach and me. Tyler and me. Tyler, Zach, and me, alone together for the first time since...

I jerked my attention back to Zach as he blew out a long breath, rubbing the back of his neck. He looked more uncomfortable than I'd ever seen him in his life, and I tried desperately to come up with something to say, but couldn't. "So...um, Tyler..." Zach began.

Tyler folded his arms over his chest and looked back at Zach with stern eyes. "You want to tell me why you been messing with my girl?" he asked in a voice so low and menacing, I swung his way—only to be practically tackled to the ground as Tyler threw out his arms and engulfed both of us in a double-barreled hug.

"Hey!" Zach started, but no matter how much he'd leveled up, he was no match for Tyler's size and strength, and it was all we could do to stay upright as we pushed back at Tyler with all our might. Tyler squeezed us tight, then released us.

"We're bonded," he announced. "Really bonded. I felt something strange in the Force I guess yesterday? But I don't think it really hit me until I felt you fighting in the library, Zach. I didn't want to say anything in front of the others, I know it may be totally different with them—and Nina, for reals, Liam is looking for every loophole out there to make sure you don't feel forced into doing anything you don't want to—"

I opened my mouth to say *too late*...but instead blurted something totally different.

"It's okay. Seriously. I wanted to be with you, Tyler, you know that, and Zach..." I felt myself blush crimson as he turned his beautiful, gothic-angel gaze on me. "The way you and I connect, the way I can borrow your abilities as my own —I mean, it means everything to me. You gave me that."

Zach grimaced. "You can also feel my pain," he said quietly. "When I'm injured, when I bleed. I wouldn't wish that kind of gift on anyone."

"That's so cool, though," Tyler said, only his voice had dropped as well, as if such conversations shouldn't be held where anyone might hear. "Nina, you and I rock the world around us when we're together, but I don't think you pulled anything from me, yeah? But with Zach—his psychic mind-melding work? You can borrow that, you say?"

"Some of it," I said, turning to Zach, who studied me with such unabashed emotion, I felt myself warming from the inside out. Zach had tried out our mind-melding connection when we'd all been getting ready for the Symmes dinner, linking to me when he'd called his dad. So I'd been there when he'd told Reverend Williams that the curse had been broken and their family was safe. His dad's reaction still made me sigh, the preacher's words bubbling over with joy, relief—and, finally, with pride. A pride that was no longer a liability, and which Zach had richly earned. "When we're linked, I can channel his mind-reading ability a little, I guess. I don't know how, but—"

"But it's friggin' *great*," Tyler finished for me as he spread his hands wide. "Maybe because you guys both were natural born hunters, yeah? Like out in the wild, doing your thing. Maybe you just link up more naturally because of that.

Maybe you and I will just take a little longer, have to work harder at it—but either way, it's all amazing."

His phone buzzed, and though Zach and I both visibly tensed, expecting to hear the same summons, ours remained silent. Tyler pulled his up, his brows arching as he read the screen.

"Whoa-ho-ho," he said, then turned it toward us. In the darkness, the brightly lit surface was easy to read—the sender was Frost. The message: *Need you now.*

"Just you?" Zach asked. "We can come—"

"Nope, I think he might spill more if it's just me, though you can bet your next drink I'll be telling you when we all hook up again. White Crane, tomorrow morning, say eight?" He turned to me. "Where are you staying now, with Merry? Back at your apartment?"

I jerked, realizing that neither option appealed to me, but Zach draped his arm over my shoulders.

"I figure we've got so many floors and wings and bedrooms in Fowler Hall we can find somewhere she can feel safe, don't you?" he asked as a grin stretched across Tyler's face.

"I don't know, man," he said teasingly. "What if she needs to feel safe from us?"

"Super funny, standing right here," I pointed out, but both Tyler and Zach were laughing, and at this moment, all I wanted was for them to stay like this: happy, certain, ready for any adventure. Was that why I'd come to Wellington Academy, after all? Was my pursuit of information about my mother's family just a strange trick of the universe to get me here, finding a way to help me succeed?

Life never worked out that neatly for me, but...maybe?

Tyler's phone buzzed again, another solo text, but he had to swipe to read it, so it wasn't Frost.

"It's from Liam," he confirmed. "He's made it inside Bellamy Chapel and..."

He stopped short. His eyes arrowed down to his screen, as if he couldn't make out the words.

"What?" Zach and I asked at once, and Tyler looked up at me, his face drawn tight.

"And the first thing he found was a headstone, down in the undercroft of the church." He turned the phone to me, and Zach's arm tightened around my shoulders as we saw the picture it held.

A small, elegant marble slab, with a boldly cut name etched across the top:

JANET CROSS.

The date on the stone was twenty-four years ago.

"Wait, what? I mean, that's got to be someone else, right?" I heard myself speak as if from far away, as Tyler swiveled the phone back, the three telltale dots springing up as Liam kept typing.

"If there's more, he'll find it," he said quietly. His gaze sharpened again. He swallowed, then glanced up at me. "There's more, he says. You should probably get over there."

Zach's hold firmed on my shoulders. Tyler shoved his phone in his pocket and picked up my hands.

"Hey," Tyler said, and the urgency in his voice made me glance up. His gaze was solid, assured—and it felt, more and more, like coming home. "We're here for you, Nina. No matter what Liam's found, I swear it. Zach and I know a little about having shit for family relationships. There's no way it could be worse than we've gone through, right?"

I smiled and nodded as Zach held me close, the trees shushing around us as the twin effects of Tyler's touch and Zach's mental connection swirled and crackled through the night sky. Then the moment passed, and Tyler squeezed my fingers. "We're your family too, you know. And nothing will get to you without having to go through us, first."

"I know," I whispered, as Zach leaned over to brush a kiss against my temple.

"Breathe," he instructed, and my body responded, my lungs filling with blessed air as Tyler squeezed my hands again, then stepped away. These two guys, already so much a part of my life, had now cemented themselves as allies by my side. I was safe with them. I was strong.

As we turned away from the monster quad to head across campus, however, a long ago cry sounded through the trees, as faint as a blackbird's call.

"Run..." my mother cried.

Her warning was carried away on the whispering wind, and Zach and I turned, making our dark and solitary way to what remained of Bellamy Chapel.

THANK you so much for reading THE HUNTER'S CURSE! I sincerely hope you enjoyed Nina's continuing adventure. If you did and you'd like to help other readers find it, I appreciate you leaving a review for the book. For a sneak peek of Liam's story in THE HUNTER'S SNARE, read on!

THE HUNTER'S SNARE
Monster Hunter Academy, Book 3
Prologue: Liam

WHAT'S A GIRL WANT?

I scowled at the rough stone wall six feet from my face, the blood rushing to my head. Strung up like this two stories below ground, locked in a spike-ridden snare that Houdini wouldn't dare attempt even at the height of his fame, I'd already worked out a half dozen impossible equations in my mind to pass the time. But I always ended up back here.

The life-or-death question I couldn't ignore. The riddle buried in the puzzle locked within the enigma that was Nina Cross.

Harbinger. Monster bait. Cipher.

The answer to all my deepest desires and biggest fears wrapped up into one completely unexpected package. She'd run into our lives not two weeks ago with a monster on her tail and an entire lifetime of mystery surrounding her very existence. A mother who'd lied to her. A father who'd left her to rot. A power so incredible, she would lose her ever-loving mind if she had any idea of who and what she really was.

But I knew.

I'd read the ancient texts, found the forbidden knowledge. I knew everything there was to know about the harbinger...everything Nina had yet to learn.

And oh, what I could teach her, if I could find a way to tempt her into letting me. Lure her into being willing to reach her full potential. But how?

What's a girl want?

I blew out a long breath, glancing at the gleaming LED stopwatch on the floor. Four minutes past the official record set by my late, great-uncle Spencer Graham, the family's most prolific and blindingly rich magician in five generations. He hadn't been able to endure the suspended magical tourniquet for longer than two minutes and forty-four seconds. I'd blown him away three times over today. He was no longer the boss of me.

Not that anyone would ever know that.

My family had written me off a long time ago—too weak to be a spell caster, too mercurial to be an enforcer, too honest to be a ward for the family secrets, too much of an ass to be a negotiator or diplomat. They'd done everything to improve my chances, to help me live up to the powerful magic that was my birthright. They'd even buried tuning rods beneath my skin to pick up any errant supernatural currents that might be floating around in the atmosphere, but nothing had taken.

I'd remained stunted, muted. My magic, a shrunken husk.

So I'd studied. I'd learned. I'd fashioned tools to pull power out of the air, created concoctions, devices, and weapons of intricate and stunning beauty. And I had suffered. Oh, yeah, I'd suffered.

Then a harbinger had hit Wellington Academy and set my world on fire.

I twisted in my vicious tourniquet, feeling the blades cut deep, swinging in a lazy arc as the blood traced familiar trails down my skin.

What's a girl want?

As I turned slowly, the trove of glorious Arcanum slid into view, soaking in its pool of oil. It was time, I knew. I'd studied the stolen pages of the Apocrypha long enough. I knew every inscrutable prognostication, every dire warning, every taboo ritual specifically proscribed...yet included in those hoary old texts with slavering glee. I knew everything there was to know, now.

A little knowledge may be a dangerous thing, but too much?

Magic.

I twisted again. With a flick of my fingers, I tripped the nearly invisible metal trigger trapped in the crease of my palm, causing a spark to flare, then drop to the trail of oil. The fire caught immediately, throwing shadows against the wall that made me look like a slowly swinging slab of meat. Not a bad analogy, really, considering how I'd been carved up over the years.

But this wasn't about me. It was about the tongues of fire that now lanced greedily into the carefully oiled maze. Racing along the snaking lines I'd traced, a complete replica of the Wellington campus map of subterranean byways. I watched with eager eyes to see if this, finally, would reveal the path I needed to take, if this, finally—

But no.

The fire guttered out, dead-ending far short of catching the forbidden pages on fire.

The secrets of the academy would live another day, it seemed. I hadn't solved the riddle. I hadn't earned the right. I would need Nina Cross to walk those dire pathways with me blindly, foolishly, if she was willing. If she dared. If she agreed to finally break me free of the trap of my own life.

I contracted my muscles, straining my joints to the max, and breathed out a long, shuddering breath.

What's a girl want?

I didn't know...but I would do anything to find out.

CONTINUE the adventure with THE HUNTER'S SNARE, and please visit me at facebook.com/authorDDChance to say hello!

Most of all, thanks again for reading THE HUNTER'S CURSE!

ABOUT D.D. CHANCE

D.D. Chance is the pen name of Jenn Stark, an award-winning author of paranormal romance, urban fantasy and contemporary romance. Whether she's writing as Jenn or D.D., she loves writing, magic and unconditional love. Thank you for taking this adventure with her.

www.ddchance.com